THE PAPERCUTS ANTHOLOGY

VOLUME 1

What Happened Here

4
5
6
Here we go for a fast ride.
Here we go with our friends."

Praise for Some of Our Authors

"Christopher Irvin's tone is lightning fast, hard hitting, and leaves the reader breathless and shocked with the sudden and realistic portrayal of violence." —LitReactor

"George Fifield, the bearded curator, scholar, and activist, has been pushing the conceptual ball called contemporary digital and intermedia art up a hill for decades." —The Arts Fuse

"I would follow Abigail Thomas on any journey she ever takes." —Elizabeth Gilbert, author of *Big Magic*

"I love the writing of Jennifer Waddell for its candor, honesty and clarity. She tackles subjects many shy away from, and does so with humor and courage." —Abigail Thomas, author of *What Comes Next and How to Like It*

"Chris Hedges is challenging to people who think change will happen without deep resistance to the current political and economic system, and also an inspiring storyteller." —Chuck Collins, author of *Wealth and Our Commonwealth*

"Jennifer Tseng delivers an elegant exploration of passion and its consequences." —Sara Levine, author of *Treasure Island!!!*

"Stona Fitch is a shining beacon of fucking brilliance." —Scott Pack, The Friday Project, UK

"If Jim Thompson wrote about Boston's mean old days, then you'd have an inkling of the sheer quality of writing and gut-clenching darkness that J. M. TAYLOR provides." —Todd Robinson, author of *The Big Bounce*

"EDAN LEPUCKI is the very best kind of writer: simultaneously generous and precise." —Emma Straub, author of *The Vacationers*

"CAT WARREN writes . . . with the research-forward focus of an academic and the sweat-and-scabs storytelling of someone who has lived in the field." —*Indy Week*

"RANDY SUSAN MEYERS shifts perspective, artfully conveying twisting dynamics and offering no easy answers." —*The Improper Bostonian*

"CATIE DISABATO may be a fresh face in the literary world, but her style and schemes triumph over those of many seasoned scribes." —*PopMatters*

"LYNETTE D'AMICO invents a type of Midwestern Gothic all her own, and a queer Expressionism for the 21st century." —Mary Cappello, author of *Awkward: A Detour*

"ROBIN MCLEAN's fiction is harrowing and wry and compassionate, and always both fiercely rooted in the world and fearlessly willing to take chances. I love her keen sense of our inherent strangeness, and her heartening sense of just how important it is that we never stop trying to close the gap between who we are and who we aspire to be." —Jim Shepard, author of *The Book of Aron*

"Newcomer NADINE DARLING drops an unforgettable stylistic beat." —Lyndsay Faye, author of *Jane Steele*

THE PAPERCUTS ANTHOLOGY

VOLUME 1

What Happened Here

EDITED BY KATIE EELMAN
AND KATE LAYTE

Quill

Published by Quill, an imprint of Inkshares, Inc.,
San Francisco, California
www.inkshares.com

Cover design by Lauren Harms

ISBN: 9781942645009
e-ISBN: 9781942645016
Library of Congress Control Number: 2016931041

First edition

Printed in the United States of America

To the authors and readers who
supported Papercuts in our first year

The only requirements for entry are an open mind, a restless desire to know and an indefinable urge to escape the mundane.

—Azar Nafisi, *The Republic of Imagination*

CONTENTS

Part IV: Fall

FOREWORD

Welcome to Papercuts.

In the fall of 2014, I quit my job working for Little, Brown to open an independent bookstore in my neighborhood of Jamaica Plain in Boston. I am deeply inspired by this neighborhood, especially its literary history. Margaret Fuller—the transcendental thinker, critic, journalist, women's rights activist, and legendary editor of Ralph Waldo Emerson and Henry David Thoreau—lived here, as did Sylvia Plath. Anne Sexton is buried here, and e.e. cummings, too. A few years ago, I got it in my head that I could open a bookstore here. I had experience as a bookseller, and I knew how publishers worked. All I ever did was talk about books.

I got excited and planned for two years—taking free online classes, writing and rewriting a business plan, finding mentors, reading dozens of business books, books about bookstores—and then I took the leap. It was terrifying. I had no money, but I had a solid plan, and I could think or speak of little else. I asked for help and was able to crowdsource my start-up costs. *It was happening.*

Distilled, my goal is to have a physical space to bring great books to my community. But what makes a book great, and how could I articulate that greatness? I had been keeping lists of my favorite books for years, and before opening my store, I reached out to friends and acquaintances with enviable book taste and asked them for lists of their favorite books.

After completing the task of identifying and stocking only the best books (a relentless task), we next had to figure out which authors we would like to host for our event series. There are endless possibilities and complications to consider—many authors are dead, others (most?) probably communicate most effectively in their chosen medium of the written word. Others are feared, revered, or perhaps unknown. We pick the ones we want the most, then my undaunted media and events coordinator, Katie Eelman, works her magic to turn a pipe dream into a legitimate event.

We both read as much as we can, discuss the format, make up questions, and buy wine. The nerves hit. Hope I ordered enough books on time (sorry, Chris). The event is happening! There are people here! Then something profound happens: an author speaks, reads, engages with all of us, answers our difficult questions, leaving us with more to ponder. This is not an ordinary day. *Something's happening.*

I woke up one day last summer with what I thought would be an awful hangover, but instead felt inspired to create something tangible out of these experiences. We knew they were special. We'd been experimenting with a podcast (listen at papercutsjp.com/audio-broadcast), but I wanted something more. Something that lasts longer than a night and sticks around afterward. What if we created a book—a book containing works by the authors who came to our store and made us feel something—and published it as a celebration of surviving our first year? I sketched out the plan for the book, got fired up, and shared the plan with Katie. She took charge and coordinated with the authors. We held a successful preorder campaign with an innovative publisher, and now I'm beyond thrilled to share with you the greatness we've witnessed. You'll discover, or perhaps relive, *what happened here.*

Kate Layte
Owner & Manager
Spring 2016

INTRODUCTION

I can remember, as I'm sure many avid readers can, being a tiny child and sleeping with books under my pillow so that their charms would protect me overnight, stretching on my tiptoes to read spines high on the shelves in the library, learning that a sniff in the center of a new book would bring a unique smell each time. For people who read, there is nothing more magical than what exists between the front and back covers of a book. Except, perhaps, a bookstore.

When Kate told me why she was going to quit her job at the publishing company we both worked for, the one where I had started as her intern, I was immediately elated.

"I'm going to open a bookstore," she told me after a few drinks. She looked nervous saying it, but I wasn't skeptical at all. Rather, I felt entirely prepared—like, finally, all things were beginning to click into place.

"How can I help?"

Kate named me her events coordinator.

The first year at Papercuts was indeed one full of wonder, thanks to the community of readers, the support of the Boston literary scene, and, of course, the authors and artists who visited our store and were kind enough to share their work with us. The goal from the beginning was to create an author event series that wasn't the typical reading and signing. We wanted to fully engage our audience, discuss the meat and bones of the fantastic books that were being published, and use our space to participate in a larger discourse about things that mattered in the world outside our five hundred square feet: issues of the heart and the head, issues of the self and of the other, issues of justice and freedom, issues that are written into literature that leads to change.

With these high ambitions, we started our event series February 28, 2015, with Dr. Emmett G. Price III, author of *The Black Church and Hip Hop Culture,* and Jabari Asim, author of *The N Word.* The two discussed issues of race in America, ranging from the language of racism to the overwhelming disparity of race in the prison industry. We had a full house on a snowy Saturday, and it was stunning to experience the dialogue that took place, with full honesty among strangers. I was more nervous to plan, execute, and speak publicly at this event than anything I can remember, but I was put at ease by the honesty and engagement of a diverse and attentive audience.

I highly recommend a listen to the first-ever episode of the Papercuts J.P. Audio Broadcast to hear the conversation.

In this anthology, we're able to see a brand-new side of Emmett G. Price III, whom I've known as a cultural critic and academic and who now shares some great poetry with us. The poetry in this anthology is sparse, but it is sustenance for the soul. Abigail Thomas, better known for her award-winning memoirs and fiction, joined us with her daughter, Jennifer Waddell (a Jamaica Plain resident, photographer, and incredibly honest and precise writer), for an event on Mother's Day (and Lilac Sunday) 2015. Discussing the dramatic intricacies of family dynamics, love and betrayal, and the ever-mysterious mother-daughter relationship with these two phenomenal women was a dream come true, and it's wonderful to read them both here, Thomas in poetic form and Waddell in a story as intimate as the photos that she takes. Poems were also contributed by Kristen Evans, whose writing is palpable, and Sandee Storey, a legendary JP figure and creator of art with amazing feeling. The poetry in this book punctuates the compilation and provides reflective and rhythmic transitions between the changes of season, which is what this book, and our lives, are shaped around.

Our first winter brought more influential people to the store. George Fifield, founder of the Boston Cyberarts Gallery, introduced himself early and hosted us at his gallery on Green Street for a conversation with David Rose of the MIT Media Lab about the fusion of art and technology. I know nobody that speaks on this subject better than Fifield, and his smart piece in this anthology affirms that.

Winter 2015 was categorically terrible for the city of Boston. As a result of an onslaught of snow (which didn't fully melt until summer), our transit system very nearly expired, people could barely leave their homes, and many businesses suffered intensely. Spring brought a deep liberation from an oppressive season of cold, and as we decorated our door with paper-cut flora and fauna, new customers discovered us on their walks around Centre Street and Jamaica Pond. Spring also brought some killer events. In March we kicked off the Prime Time Crime series with two Jamaica Plain crime writers, Christopher Irvin, for the release of his novella *Burn Cards*, and Zachary Klein for the long-awaited *Ties That Blind*. Irvin's kickoff to this anthology is a piece that teaches us a lesson in tension and innocence on the MBTA; you'll discover why we think he just might be the next big thing in crime fiction. Klein manages to break out of the genre we know him by and speaks, in a completely entertaining and well-researched interview, with dead literary icon Norman Mailer.

Our Prime Time Crime series continued in June with an event featuring Stona Fitch (Rory Flynn), who here shares the incredibly twisted "Mill Burners," and J. M. Taylor, who you will quickly learn is Boston's best-kept secret in crime fiction. In August we hosted two amazingly talented young authors, Catie Disabato and Josh Cook, in a discussion on their mystery-crime novels published by Melville House. Cook writes with a style so uniquely his own, and in a form that makes it impossible for the reader to separate even momentarily from the text.

Another fantastic, truly terrifying book we were enthralled by was *A Head Full of Ghosts*, by author Paul Tremblay. Paul joined us on the first annual Independent Bookstore Day, May 2, 2015, to share some of his favorite stories and talk about the art of writing crime. In this book he shares a chilling story from his 2010 collection *In the Mean Time.* Just hours before Paul's reading on Indie Bookstore Day was a musical set by the legendary Rick Berlin, who deserves your listening attention immediately. Of course, we weren't surprised to learn that he dabbles in the literary arts—his lyrics are narrative in style and always unpredictable and beautiful. It's hard not to smile as I read Berlin's contribution "Sardines" and remember his contagious energy, his top hat, his artfully composed tunes.

One month after Independent Bookstore Day, we sold books at a JP Forum event featuring Chris Hedges, an activist hero and, debatably, the most badass guy alive. Hedges, who mostly writes about the flaws in the political and economic system, here shares with us a eulogy for a close friend from Jamaica Plain. How moving it is to read words of such love, especially with the memory of a speech that left me angry and with my fists up, ready to create change. His piece serves as a necessary reminder that deep compassion and rebellion must coexist.

With summer sun came events nearly every other week, more and more new visitors, and the planning stages of our first anthology. By August it finally felt as though we knew what we were doing—we'd been to our first Book Expo America (BEA) in Manhattan, had hosted countless authors and produced several podcast episodes, and had hosted the first Papercuts Puppy Panel, which involved three authors and a park full of dogs and their humans.

The fiction contributions in this book from authors Jennifer Tseng, Catie Disabato, Lynette D'Amico, Robin McLean, Randy Susan Meyers, and Nadine Darling leave me breathless each time I read them. I'm struck by the characters in Tseng's "The Words *Honey* and *Moon*," and anyone who has read her beautiful and titillating novel *Mayumi and the Sea of Happiness* (Europa Editions) can attest to the originality of this author's voice. Disabato's story reads like a prison break, but not without her incredible dry humor. D'Amico and McLean, who read together at an event in September 2015, are both masters of the craft, and I love that their stories both devastate me and leave me wondering about when it might "all go to hell." How different the narrative is in Nadine Darling's story "Oregon" versus the one in her zany novel *She Came from Beyond*, but just as carefully constructed and mesmerizing.

The nonfiction contributions in this book from Edan Lepucki, author of the postapocalyptic *New York Times* bestseller *California*; Cat Warren, author of the *New York Times* bestselling *What the Dog Knows*; and Nicole Galland, author of *I, Iago* are exquisite. Lepucki and Galland offer sage advice on the art of writing, and Warren allows us to explore with her the life and science of a dog whose job it is to sniff out human remains.

I am proud that we featured these many female voices who represent some of the amazing work being done by women today. It was of the utmost importance to us from the beginning that we provide a venue for all great literature, bearing in mind the voices that have been historically silenced and subjugated.

What Happened Here: The Papercuts Anthology, Volume 1 showcases an array of literature and art that has enriched my life, by authors and artists who have enriched the lives of so many, through their honesty, their narratives, and their stories that allow us to learn, reflect, and engage.

Read this book in whatever fashion suits you—in one long stretch, season by season, or pieces picked at random. Getting to know the authors and the readers in the Papercuts community has completely renewed my sense of wonder about the written word. My hope is that reading our anthology renews in you a magic, as editing it did for me.

Katie Eelman
Media & Events Coordinator
Spring 2016

PART I

WINTER

LEAVING EARLY

First light,
sister of dusk,
whispers of secrets
unearthed in the night.

A man swaddled in yarn carries
a steaming white cup
quickly down the sidewalk,
no place to buy coffee in sight.

Streetlights skim by, still on.
Blurred dawn under dim sky
rides thin air
to settle like dust

on a single sedan
in the back of a parking lot
facing the jagged horizon.
She's leaving it, too, behind.

Bag of clothes on the backseat,
she gets the news fine
with the radio off,
escapes city limits by daybreak.

—Sandra Storey

THE PUSH

Christopher Irvin

Back Bay Station is crammed with bodies. They stir, adjusting sticky shirts, wiping forearms to foreheads while panting from their sprint to escape a summer shower, only to find themselves adding to the gross humidity that has descended on the bowels of the building. Rain, like snow, traffic, and large crowds, is something the city of Boston is not well equipped to handle.

Delaney glances up from the stroller, strawberry-blond curls framing her face, and for the third time asks me if she can have pretzels for a snack. I gently push her toward the yellow rumble strip that lines the edge of the train platform and pull back, apologizing again that she'll have to wait until we're home because Daddy forgot. She knows this, but likes to prod—like her mother.

Yesterday, a woman walked her stroller off the platform onto the tracks at North Station while on her phone. Bystanders dropped their bags and rushed to help pull her and her son to safety, resulting in a happy ending—each pocketing a *remember that one time . . .* story for their efforts. Looking down the tracks toward the darkness of the tunnel, I can't help but picture the security-cam footage of her falling, the lack of surprise on her face. It's like she's not even there.

When the front wheels of the stroller strike the yellow bumps, I wonder which of the bodies pressed close around us would look up from their phone first if I let go. Delaney's had a need to move, a distaste for idle moments, since she was only days old, before she even had a name. I'll rock an empty grocery cart out of habit, muscle memory forever locked in place.

A woman's voice echoes through the speakers overhead announcing the delay on the Orange Line is due to police action at Haymarket, four stops away in the opposite direction of where we're headed. Delaney asks where's the train, Daddy, and I tell her I don't know, maybe the rain is slowing down service. She lets out an audible sigh—copycat of her mother—and pulls a leg up to play with the Velcro strap on her shoe. A pair of college-age bros joke about how one heard police action is code for a jumper—SMACK—emphasizing by slapping a fist into his palm. The stroller's wheels touch yellow. I think about the woman again and wonder if this time she wasn't so lucky, that onlookers were more interested in filming the emergency than taking action. The scene unfolds in my head—the train bearing down as the tense commuter crowd thickens. We're pressed forward, all four wheels on yellow. My fingers tighten around the handles, and I jerk backward, causing a grumbling mass of angry cries whose owners push closer in revenge, leaving the only opening to the front *and down.* Sweat bursts from my forehead, running down to my brow. A student with a backpack bigger than Delaney cuts in front of us and I want to plow into his legs. His toes peek over the ledge, bouncing to the rhythm of whatever tune is bursting from his earbuds. A tap from Delaney might do it. Just one innocent swing and—

A horn blows. The train slowly arrives, without warning or update from the friendly voice above. Electricity arcs along the track in front, and for a half second I see a dark splash across the lead car before shadows shift it away. Its brakes screech to deafening levels on approach. I grind my teeth. Delaney plugs her ears as it comes to a stop, doors opening close enough for us to have a shot at getting in. The crowd on the platform reluctantly parts to let passengers off before cramming on. Two women make room at the sight of Delaney's smile, and we slide inside. I mumble a thank you, but they look away as if I don't exist. Only seven stops to home.

—

It's pouring at Forest Hills. The thunder of excavators pounding into the remnants of the Casey Overpass echoes in the dark sky. Delaney's not interested in trucks. Instead, she wants to walk the rest of the way home, stomping through every puddle, soaking her socks and shoes before we can even cross the street. Between keeping the umbrella out of the wind and the stroller over a shoulder, I don't have the energy to fight her along the four-block walk home. As long as she holds my hand, I let her do what she wants.

She behaves, for the most part—darting out from the umbrella to conquer her enemies. Between the water dripping down the back of my legs from the stroller and the collateral splash damage, I wonder why I even bother attempting to stay dry. I fold up the umbrella, and we run to the end of our street together, Delaney giggling as she kicks out a heel to tag the tiniest of puddles. She freezes when I try to carry our momentum through the turn at the bottom of the hill leading up to our house, her feet glued to the sidewalk.

"Look, Daddy!" she shouts, wide-eyed, small hand pointing across the street at the dilapidated structure haunting the block. I don't see it at first. I'm too focused on the house. The unkempt side yard carrying a century's worth of decaying leaves on which three cars haphazardly park beneath a large oak tree. The house itself, a two-story A-frame, unlike the majority of the triple-deckers in the neighborhood, looks like it should collapse under its own weight. Black plastic garbage bags replace missing shingles, paint peels from every inch. The glass inside the front door is spidered with cracks, and an enclosed porch along the back, full of visible rot, is pulling away from the house. Delaney tugs on my arm and I see the source of her excitement. Trash and debris discarded in front of the house have fallen into the street, diverting the flow of rain water up onto the sidewalk where an inch-deep river flows quickly down the hill. The drainage at the intersection has a handle on the volume for now, but it won't be long before a clog comes along and it floods.

"Come on!" She pulls with all her twenty-five pound body can muster to drag me across the street, but I've had enough. The fun has vanished and I need to get up the hill and inside. She fights every step of the way, until her slick hand slips out of my grip. She stumbles into a sprint, charging down the hill at full speed. I drop the umbrella and take after her, the stroller slamming against my shoulder. It's a game now. I can hear her laughing over the rain-soaked traffic. She knows to stop at the corner, but her mind's on the chase, on splashing into the river and feeling the water rush over her toes.

"Delaney!" She ignores my call for her to stop as she glances for oncoming traffic, her skinny legs careening into a crosswalk she's deemed safe. And it is, but that doesn't stop my blood pressure from skyrocketing. She leaps into the air, both feet landing in the stream, spinning to face me as I catch her—only I'm grabbing at air and she's losing her balance, going down face-first, arms outstretched. I'm too slow, the stroller falling off my shoulder, smacking the water at my side as I scoop her up. She's hysterical, sobbing into my shoulder and then beating at me with clenched fists when she realizes I'm taking her away from her adventure. I push her up over my shoulder, dragging the stroller all the way up the steep hill while the neighborhood listens to her screams.

—

Dinner's over, dirty dishes stacked in the sink. We're getting ready for her bath when I remember I left the umbrella behind. I let out a long sigh. Delaney sits on the tile behind me in her diaper, tugging off her socks.

"Why do you go 'huhhhhhh,' Daddy?" she asks, doing her best impression. I plug the drain, start the water, and tell her it's because I'm tired. She mimics my sigh again, adding "me too," with a cute smile to show off she knows she's doing something she shouldn't. I can't hide a smirk. It's the first thing to take the edge off a rough day. I forget about the umbrella.

—

It's late when Amanda calls, the vibration of my phone waking me from my doze on the couch. She's stepping out to grab a quick bite before heading back into the trenches. She's got her team working overtime to try and finish the audit by tomorrow, but it doesn't look good. She might be stuck in LA for another night. I could grab a red-eye, she offers, but I tell her not to worry. Delaney's fine. She made butter at daycare. Oh yeah? She says, and then there are competing voices in the background and she has to go. I drag myself to the bed, floorboards creaking underfoot.

Amanda's text follows minutes later: *Did you get the deal?*

No, I'm brushing my teeth, I think, but don't text back. Another guy on the sales team is out courting our latest client in my place. The boss even tagged along for a few rounds on the house. I was invited to lead the pitch, but I have my priorities, as the boss likes to remind me. If the man had seen his family in the last ten years I'd take it as a compliment. When I don't respond she follows up with an *xo*. I kill the lights and pretend I'm already asleep.

—

Morning arrives and we're out the door on schedule. The stroller is still wet, but Delaney *needs* to ride in it. We haggle toward a compromise of her riding home after school when she's tired. She wants to have grapes then too, as a snack. I tell her we'll see, which might as well be yes, and we're off.

I get into the office late, but so does the boss. I can smell the booze. The deal went south, but they're giving it another shot tonight. Probably the client is just playing us for another night on the town. He sees the stroller cover drying over a chair beside my desk, but turns away when I look up and make eye contact. He wants to tear into me but can't bring himself to give me the attention. He taps two kids fresh out of college, and they head into his office to strategize. It has disaster written all over it. At least I don't have to disappoint him when I punch the time clock at five. I've got another six months, if I'm optimistic. I'm not as flexible as I used to be.

I leave early to try to beat some of the rush. The sky is still possessed of dark clouds, trapping the humidity, but the rain has held off. There's a stand nearby that sells fruit and knock-off sunglasses. I buy Delaney her grapes with the last of my cash and head across the city to pick her up. I'm greeted with a quick, "Hi, Daddy," before she spots the snack underneath the stroller, and it's all she can focus on, pulling the plastic away to pop the little red juice balls off their stems. Her teacher tells me Delaney's had a rough day. One of the other kids left her with a little half-moon mark on her wrist. The school won't tell me who bit her, but I don't mind. Delaney's done her fair share of damage. After three *Just one more, Daddy*s, I manage to coax her into the stroller.

The train is behind schedule, again. The elevator descends into a mob blocking the entrance. We push our way through to an opening, nudging shins of the inattentive. Six minutes until the next train arrives, *if* the clock is accurate.

"More, please." Delaney finishes her grapes. I tear off another bunch, telling her it's the last she'll get before dinner. When I stand back up, I bump into someone, knocking them aside. It's the kid from yesterday. Like a slow-motion replay, he forces past us to stand in front again, feet on the edge. There's space on either side, and yet he chooses to stand directly in front of us. My knuckles tighten around the stroller, more angry than anxious. I press closer. Delaney pulls her feet up on the seat, legs cradling the grapes. The stroller's wheels stick against the yellow bumps. A little more . . .

I hear the train coming. Delaney's left foot slips off the seat, grazing the back of the kid's calves. His whole body tenses for a split second before he spins around, his backpack nearly sending his neighbor crashing onto the tracks. He looks at Delaney then up at me. There's recognition in his eyes, like he's been waiting for this confrontation.

"What's your fucking problem, man?" He's come off the edge, but only barely.

I lick my lips, feel my face flush. An old man next to me tells the kid to watch his language.

"Fuck you, this guy's trying to push me off."

The train enters the station blowing its horn. I don't hear what anyone says next. There's movement to my right. Someone moving too fast. A scream as the blur leaps from the platform, cutting a path through the headlights of the oncoming train. It sounds like two cars colliding at low speed. The platform explodes in chaos as emergency brakes squeal. I scramble around the stroller and hug Delaney tight against me as people swarm us like a whirlpool, some drawn to the violence, others fleeing. Seconds tick by, the flood of panic dripping to a calm shock. Delaney is scared, her wide eyes darting between concerned adults standing over us. I get her to focus on me, tell her we're going for another ride in the elevator. *The train is broken* is the simplest answer I can come up with to her *why?*

The elevator closes, and we ride up in a bubble, the noise dampened by the thick walls. Transit police rush past us. Emergency sirens echo from blocks away.

"These are good grapes, Daddy." Delaney lifts her chin up to look back at me, arm extended, grape clenched between her fingers. She pops the grape in her mouth before I can ask if it's for me, smiling as she chews, alive in her own little world.

Our first event with Christopher Irvin, in conversation with Zachary Klein, was for the release of his novella, Burn Cards. *We later welcomed Irvin back for an event with Paul Tremblay on Independent Bookstore Day, and for the launch of his newest book, an incredible collection of short stories titled* Safe Inside the Violence.

IN THE GARDEN OF BEBOP

In the Garden of Bebop where the Yardbird rules,
where a monk named Thelonious dances in a sphere while
invoking the musical spirits of the ancestors to serve as
his muse,
there lives the Dizzy one who is well known for eating "Salt
Peanuts" and repeatedly vowing to "never go back to
Georgia."

To most, the Garden of Bebop is a mystical mirage
inhabited by a myriad of masterful maestros and maestras
masquerading incognito.
But to the majestic mass of aficionados, connoisseurs and
epicureans of
zee, bee, dippity-dot
skee, zwee, duppity-do
"Everybody's Boppin'" in the Garden of Bebop,
if you know where to look and what to listen for.

Through the middle of the Garden runs a coal train
that releases so much steam
that some Garden dwellers take refuge at Clark Monroe's

while others hide in the zebra room.
Yet, it is Henry Minton's spot where all
the cool cats, hot chicks, and hound dogs hang.

Along the west side of the tracks strolls a particular
guitar-playing Christian who often chats with the Dizzy
one about the "Cherokee."
Near their favorite walking path grows a bud of Powell
where a roach named Max often settles in for the night.

In the cool of the evening everyone gathers in the center of
the Garden
to surrender to the sweet sounds of sister Sassy.
She always starts her set with sanctified sacred songs of
spiritual sacrilege. Then she satisfies all with sophisticated
salubrious sentiments
that invoke stimulating scents of sweet saffron.

During the day the Dizzy one and the Yardbird
are often found "Pickin' the Cabbage"
until they hear the clamorous cacophony of Klook
dropping bombs while taking giant steps over the train tracks.

Desperate to locate all of Klook's droppings
the Yardbird assembles an exploration team to scout the
Garden.
Today, the quartet of Father Time, the Judge, Bean, and Lady
Day
jook and jive while riffin' across the Garden
until they "Shaw Nuff" find Klook "Groovin' High"
near where Pres, the Count, and the Duke hold high court—
debating the merits of "Anthropology"
and the promise of "Ornithology."

In the Garden of Bebop love abides,
peace is perpetual, and hope
is a daily reality of the articulation of yesterday's melodies and
harmonies.
In the Garden of Bebop justice
is the moon and the sun trading fours, every "Night and Day."

—Emmett G. Price III

Dr. Price participated in an honest and important conversation on contemporary black American issues with author Jabari Asim in our first-ever in-store event in February 2015. Audio of this significant and emotional conversation can be found at papercutsjp.com/audio-broadcast.

COMPUTER SOFTWARE AS A CREATIVE MEDIUM

George Fifield

Code is an interesting word. For such a little word, it has so many meanings. There is genetic code, code as law, secret codes, social codes, and many, many others. The most recent use is software code, that set of instructions one gives to special machines so that they may compute. Computers have been active only since World War II. They had antecedents in previous inventions, like the eighteenth-century Jacquard loom, an ur-computer still used today and programmed to create different patterns in cloth. Also there was Charles Babbage's nineteenth-century Difference Engine, famous for the first descriptions of software code, written by Lord Byron's daughter, Ada Lovelace.

Most of the artists we show at the Boston Cyberarts Gallery use a computer programming language (code) as their expressive medium. Which programming language they use is dictated by what they hope to accomplish. But still today, many people cannot understand how computer code can be a creative medium.

In and around World War II, building on the work of British mathematician Alan Turing, British and American teams built a number of machines that were both digital and programmable. Throughout the 1950s, improvements were made to the hardware and software. Consequently, what began as a military, industrial, and university research collaboration began to attract creative people who wanted to play and then make art. At first, only a few people were tempted, as access to computers was difficult at best.

Even as late as the 1970s, computers were both used and understood very differently from how they are today. They were enormous in scale and, by today's standards, dim-witted machines that could be skillfully coded in obscure languages to perform mathematical and deductive wonders. The military, followed by academic institutions, was the first to adapt, incorporate, and expand the growing technology, changing our relationship to data forever. During this time, a small group of artists from the United States and Europe (many of whose work is included in this exhibition) became fascinated with the power of computer code to perform complex iterations—including an ability to change a shape into multiple interpretations. This was not a simple task. First the artists had to learn code, most commonly the 1950s-era FORTRAN, a computer language developed for scientific and engineering applications that could program a computer to output on a pen plotter. What happened next is best described by computer artist Harold Cohen, who in 1968 started to work on his drawing program, AARON:

> You used card-punch machines to punch your program onto IBM cards, one line to each card, and then you handed your entire deck of cards over the desk to an operator, who would feed them through a card reader

> into the computer along with everybody else's cards. There was little chance you would get any results the same day and when you went back the next day, hoping for a printout that would indicate forward progress, what you got, more often than not in my case, was a cryptic message saying that there was a missing semi-colon on card seventy-three.[1]

In his frustration, Cohen adds, "Computers are supposed to be smart; if the damn thing knew there was a missing semicolon, why didn't it put one in for itself."[2]

And yet, in the 1960s, there was an initial rush of enthusiasm among the artists themselves. There were even a few exhibitions. Freider Nake had a gallery exhibit in 1965 at the Galerie Wendelin Niedlich in Stuttgart, Germany. That same year the Howard Wise Gallery in New York, an early promoter of video art, had exhibitions of computer-generated art by Dr. Michael Noll. Both exhibits were of plotter-pen drawings.

One major exhibition, *Cybernetic Serendipity,* organized by contemporary art curator Jasia Reichhardt, then an assistant director at the Institute of Contemporary Art in London, took place there in 1968. This was more than an art exhibition, as it encompassed a wide variety of media and art forms, including the work of many digital artists. *Cybernetic Serendipity* was an exhibition of three things: computer-generated work; cybernetic devices, including robots and painting machines; and a history of computing. It included electronic music by pioneers such as John Cage and Iannis Xenakis and much early plotter art and robotic sculptures by Nam June Paik, Jean Tinguely,

1 Harold Cohen, "Reconfiguring," in *White Heat, Cold Logic: British Computer Art 1960–1980,* ed. Paul Brown et al. (Cambridge, MA: MIT Press, 2008), 142.

2 Ibid.

and Edward Ihnatowicz. It brought together most of the practitioners of computer art at the time from Europe, the United States, and Japan.

But a backlash was forming. On the one hand, the computer departments where these artists were able to work thought they were dilettantes. On the other, the art world was even harsher. Questions of authenticity were raised—"If the computer did this, who are the artists?" The art world struggled with the idea of computer art. Nick Lambert, on his website Computer Art Thesis, writes:

> A common experience for computer artists is to be sidelined on account of their chosen medium. This suspicion of the computer is, sadly, widespread and long-lived. Writing in PAGE, Paul Brown noted how it had affected Computer Art pioneer Manfred Mohr: "Mohr told us he was no longer going to mention the computer in connection with his work. His reasons were straightforward enough and will not surprise artists working in the medium: all too often people think that the art is created by the machine and this predisposes them to view the work unfavourably." . . .
>
> . . . Because the computer augments the artist's range of possible techniques and realizations, it is therefore assumed to be easier and more tractable than traditional media. Skill is associated with handcraft, and machines are supposed to grant anyone the power to become an "artist."[3]

3 Nick Lambert, "Computer Art Thesis: A Critical Examination of 'Computer Art,'" http://computer-arts-society.com/static/cas/computerartsthesis/index.html%3Fpage_id=132.html.

But the art world also did not understand that these artists were working in a specific discipline—that of code—which had a set of formal questions and responses and was very different from the media used by nondigital artists. Code has certain structures that can be used to explore paths in a very different way from drawing by hand. Iteration, for example, is the repetition of a sequence of instructions that can be adjusted so that each iteration is somewhat different. As Erkki Huhtamo writes:

> The earliest computer artists in the 1960s were all coders. There was no alternative. Each work, whether graphics, animation or music, was necessarily the result of a unique act of writing computer code. As if foreshadowing the recent claims for "software art," some pioneers, like Michael L. Noll and the members of the Japanese Computer Technique Group (CTG), openly stated that the true work of art was the generating program itself rather than the computer-produced output. Most of the early work on computer graphics and music took a formalist path, exploring issues like the possibilities of generative grammars and the relationship between rule-based behavior and randomness.[4]

While art curators and gallery owners were equating computer art with op art, conceptual art, and even minimalism, the artists themselves were exploring the structure of code.

Another hurtle for computer artists to overcome was the basic disdain with which people viewed computer technology.

---

4 Erkki Huhtamo, "Web Stalker Seek AARON: Reflections on Digital Arts, Codes and Coders," in *CODE: The Language of Our Time*, ed. Gerfried Stocker and Christine Schöpf, ARS Electronica 2003 (Hatje Cantz Verlag, 2003).

Manfred Mohr tells the story that in 1971 he "was pelted with tomatoes while holding a lecture at the Sorbonne because he was using a 'capitalist war tool.'"

Like the age of the dinosaurs, the age of the mainframe computer passed on, first to refrigerator-size minicomputers and then to microcomputers. This was accompanied by two other changes: A great deal of software, like Photoshop and PageMaker, became available, which let its users accomplish creative tasks without knowing code. Also, the price of these computers dropped precipitously, making this the great democratization of computing.

This began the "two cultures" of computer art. A large number of people began creating art on the computer using off-the-shelf software like Photoshop and Illustrator. "Throughout the 1990s, the two factions that constituted the Orthodox computer artists and the artists using commercial software remained strong. Orthodox computer artists continued to emphasize originality and integrity through the development of personalized programs, while deriding those who produced what was distained as 'canned' art."[5]

New computer languages were created for these "home" computers. Following the 1984 introduction of the Macintosh by Apple, HyperCard was released in 1987. Since then, numerous programming languages have been written, C++, Perl, Python, and JavaScript, to name a few.

Today there are hundreds of computer programming languages. Software artist Casey Reas writes:

> Some languages are easy to use but obscure the potential of the computer and some languages are very

5 Grant D. Taylor, *When the Machine Made Art: The Troubled History of Computer Art* (New York, Bloomsbury, 2014).

> complicated, but provide total control through providing complete access to the machine. For example, some programming languages are flexible and others are rigid. Flexible languages like Perl and Lingo are good for quickly creating short programs, but they often become difficult to maintain and understand when programs become large. Programming with rigid languages like 68008 Assembly or C requires extreme care and tedious attention to detail, but the results are efficient and robust.[6]

Furthermore, a slew of technologies based on code but with their own purpose and structure, like the World Wide Web (WWW) and virtual reality (VR), have been invented. Artists were some of the first colonizers to these new landscapes. The popular WWW was created by a team at the University of Illinois at Urbana-Champaign. Their hypertext markup language (HTML) browser, called Mosaic, by Marc Andreessen and Eric Bina, was released in January 1993. An HTML web-art site called *the place* was created by Joseph Squier in September 1994. Software art was on the web before pornography, which was not readily available online until 1995.

For those who wish to use a computer programming language as their creative medium—and there are many who do—a slew of new languages invented specifically for artists have been created. Casey Reas and Benn Fry created Processing in 2001. Completely open source and built on top of Java, it runs on Windows, Mac OS X, and Linux. "Processing is geared toward creating visual, interactive media, so the first programs start with drawing. Students new to programming

6 Ars Electronica 2003, *Code: The Language of Our Time*, ed. Gerfried Stocker and Christine Schöpf (Hatje Cantz Verlag, 2003).

find it incredibly satisfying to make something appear on their screen within moments of using the software. This motivating curriculum has proved successful for leading design, art, and architecture students into programming and for engaging the wider student body in general computer science classes."[7]

There is a huge Processing community offering free tutorials and shared libraries and tools. The community encourages you to share your work on the website OpenProcessing.org.

Another open source project, Arduino, is an electronics platform for hardware and software for anyone making interactive projects. Arduino can use sensors to read the environment and can control lights, motors, and numerous other things. "Arduino uses a syntax inspired by that used with Processing, and continues to use a modified version of the Processing programming environment to make it easier for students to learn how to program robots and countless other electronics projects."[8]

SuperCollider is a programming language for real-time audio synthesis and algorithmic composition. Pure Data (aka Pd) is an open source visual programming language that enables musicians, visual artists, and performers to create software graphically, without writing lines of code. And as Processing is built on top of Java, Cinder and openFrameworks are open source languages built on top of C++. Both were designed to facilitate "creative coding" by artists.

In September 2002, Christiane Paul, curator of new media at the Whitney Museum of American Art, organized the first

---

7 Casey Reas, "Programming Media," in *CODE: The Language of Our Time*, ed. Gerfried Stocker and Christine Schöpf, ARS Electronica 2003 (Hatje Cantz Verlag, 2003).

8 Ibid.

exhibition of code as art. CODeDOC invited twelve software artists to each make a short art work.[9]

When the work is clicked on, the first thing the audience sees is the code, written with notations that spell out the functions of the various elements. Only after scrolling down through all the code does the audience see the button that initiates the program. The art was written in Java, Visual Basic, C, Lingo, and Perl. The museum's website explains: "CODeDOC takes a reverse look at 'software art' projects by focusing on and comparing the 'back end' of the code that drives the artwork's 'front end'—the result of the code, be it visuals or a more abstract communication process."[10]

So it is clear that to its long list of meanings, we can add "creative medium" to the word code. And artists who create with code produce the most responsive, miraculous, and visionary art imaginable.

We met George in the winter of 2014 and hosted an event at his gallery at Green Street Station. His space is exhilarating, and his support has been unwavering.

---

9 Whitney Art Portal, "CODeDOC," http://artport.whitney.org/exhibitions/past-exhibitions.shtml.

10 Ibid.

PART II

SPRING

FOLIE À DEUX

In a red sports car
with a French name
whose top they rolled down
together,
a shared delusion of mutual trust
and a trip to the train station,
who's driving not a matter
of who grips the steering wheel.
Sharp parting on the platform,
an illusion of the waiting passengers.
The pair, obsessed—the apparition
they see first thing every morning—
and possessed, as in
to have and to hold
the way of nesting birds
inside.

—Sandra Storey

INTERVIEWS WITH THE DEAD

Zachary Klein

Anyone can interview living people. Just have to fight through their agents, business managers, and publicists. But the dead? They're an entirely different breed and often tough to find. But no less interesting. During the past few days I had the distinct pleasure of interviewing Norman Mailer, though as you'll read, securing the conversation wasn't an easy do.

MR. MAILER SPEAKS

I originally planned an interview with Norman Mailer in Provincetown, but at the last minute he called to reschedule. When I asked why, he simply grumbled angrily. The only word I actually understood was *Capote* and it was said with clear hostility.

Then I realized why he was fucking with me. I had interviewed Truman before him. Damn lucky I haven't already done Gore Vidal, or Norman would have refused my call. Okay, I get it, though I really won't be pleased if he bails on me again. Hell, I have a Dead People Interview series to write.

Since he had originally proposed to meet in Provincetown, I've been scouring every inch of the town with the diminishing hope of finding him. So, as darkness began to shroud the city, I started back to Carpe Diem Guesthouse to pack and finally head home to Boston. About a block away, I heard footsteps approach from behind. I turned and there he was, fists clenched, barrel chest and curly-haired head leading the charge. I wondered if I was going to be punched, but Mr. Mailer just invaded my space standing nose to nose.

MAILER: And where do you propose to conduct this little chat?

I nodded toward the guesthouse, practically grazing his forehead with my own, and led the way inside.

ME: We can use one of their dining rooms.
MAILER: You *would* pick a hotel with rooms named after authors, but none of me.
ME: Must have been an oversight on their part.
MAILER: Poppycock! Provincetown's most famous author an oversight? I don't think so! People have short memories.
ME [*laughing*]: Not at all. You're all over the Internet, your books and essays still in print. Nobody has forgotten you.
MAILER: Then why did you interview that little homo before me? King, I understood. But that pasty-faced, girly man Capote?

Both of us took our seats, and Mailer's fists curled even tighter as he leaned across the wooden table between us.

ME: It was you who said, "Harsh words live in the dungeon of the heart," and that description seems pretty harsh.

MAILER: If you think *that* was harsh, you must be a fag, too.

ME: Have you ever considered that all your misogyny, violence, and homophobia is really about your own love of masculinity? That deep down underneath you're attracted to men—strong men, real boxers, something you weren't or could never become?

MAILER: Do you really expect me to answer your half-assed pop psychology?

ME: I wasn't trying to analyze you, Mr. Mailer. Just looking at facts.

MAILER: And what facts might those be, *Mister* Klein?

ME: Where would you like me to begin, *Norman*? *The Naked and the Dead*? All about the boys who actually fought in the war as opposed to working in the kitchen like you did.

MAILER: You are a cheeky bastard, aren't you? I like that.

ME: You're making my point.

MAILER: I'll use the language the publisher made me use in the book: fug you. I was in the Philippines with the 112th Cavalry.

ME: I know, but by all accounts, you were just in a couple of minor skirmishes before you were assigned to be a cook.

MAILER: Really now? Apparently I fought enough battles for the book to become a *New York Times* bestseller for sixty-two weeks. Oh, and in case you forgot, or didn't *know*, named one of the "one hundred best novels in the English language" by the Modern Library. Not bad for a cook, eh?

ME: A novel about which Gore Vidal wrote, "My first reaction to *The Naked and the Dead* was: it's a fake. A clever, talented, admirably executed fake. I have not changed my opinion of the book since . . . I do recall a fine description of men carrying a dying man down a mountain . . . Yet every time I got going in the narrative I would find myself stopped cold by a set of made-up, predictable characters taken not from life, but from the same novels all of us had read, and informed by a naïveté which was at its worst when Mailer went into his Time-Machine and wrote those passages which resemble nothing so much as smudged carbons of a Dos Passos work."

MAILER [*shaking his head*]: I wondered how long it would take before his name came up. Though you surprise me by not beginning with the Cavett fiasco. There is no greater impotence in all the world than knowing you are right and that the wave of the world is wrong, yet the wave crashes upon you.

ME: If you believe that why do you call it a *fiasco*?

MAILER: I lost the fight, although I still maintain it was just a TKO. I simply couldn't fight my hardest with Janet Flanner present. And, I *have* admitted to being drunk during the show. Handicapped if you will.

I began to speak but Mailer interrupted.

MAILER: Speaking of drink, do you have anything decent here?

ME: I thought you stopped drinking and smoking pot?

MAILER: Actually I stopped because it hurt my writing and health. Don't write anymore, health doesn't matter, and there is little pleasure lying around all day, every day. So, just get us some whiskey.

I was lucky. Bourbon was in one of Carpe Diem's kitchen cabinets. I brought it back with a couple of glasses. Helping himself to a healthy pour, he waved the liquor toward me.

MAILER: Drink up, Klein, it's not every day you get a chance to drink with a literary lion.

ME: Mr. Mailer, you really *were* one of the twentieth century's literary giants, but don't you think all the macho, boxing, misogynistic, bullying, and posturing reduced your stature rather than enhanced it? I mean, head-butting Gore Vidal in the green room of the *Dick Cavett Show*, telling him on air that he ruined Kerouac by sleeping with him?

Nothing ever seemed to be enough for you. Six years later, you threw a drink at Vidal—and punched him—at a Lally Weymouth soirée. And even then Vidal's response made you look small. Still on the floor, he said, "Words fail Norman Mailer yet again."

At first I thought he was going to explode, but he just took a deep swallow and refilled his glass.

MAILER: Time and quiet does give one a chance to reflect, and I've had plenty of both. Still, every moment of existence one is growing into more or retreating into less. One is always living a little more or dying a little bit. I never enjoyed the thought of dying even a little.

I want you and your readers to know that I'm not interested in absolute moral judgments. Just think of what it means to be a good man or a bad one. The good guy may be 65 percent good and 35 percent bad—that's a very good guy. The average decent fellow might be 54 percent good, 46 percent bad—and the average mean spirit is the reverse. So say I'm 60 percent bad and 40 percent good. Should I suffer eternal punishment for *that*?

Also, while Vidal made me look small with his clever retort, he deserved to be on the floor. Would you sit silently by when someone says, "Mailer, Henry Miller, and Charles Manson as brother chauvinists who should be collectively referred to as M3." I may have had many wives, but to be compared to Charles Manson was much too much to tolerate.

ME: You don't seem to be suffering eternal punishment. In fact, there's a strong argument that it was the people around you who were punished. Hell, you nearly murdered Adele Morales, the second of your six wives.

MAILER: I never meant to kill her. It was four a.m. at a party to announce my candidacy to run for mayor of New York, and I walk into a room only to hear her say, "Come on, you little faggot, where's your cojones?" It's public record that I spent time in Bellevue for that farce, which, while I won't discuss, I do regret.

ME: Not at the time. Numerous people say you stood over her while she was hemorrhaging on the floor and said, "Let the bitch die."

MAILER: Adele has written a book about our life together. She can have the final words on the subject. But here we are talking gossip and public behavior when you yourself say, and I'll quote, "Mr. Mailer, you really were one of the twentieth century's literary *giants*." Yet all of our book talk amounts to Vidal's insult of *The Naked and the Dead*. Have you really spent this much time pursuing me to talk about my public persona, or are we going to talk about my *work*?

ME: We're there now, Mr. Mailer.

Mailer was right, so we sat in Carpe Diem's breakfast room the entire night and more—much to the chagrin of the other guests who came down for coffee and omelets and had to be rerouted to another area.

ME: You won the Pulitzer Prize for general nonfiction and the National Book Award for *Armies of the Night. Miami and the Siege of Chicago: An Informal History of the Republican and Democratic Conventions of 1968* was brilliant, and *Of a Fire on the Moon* might be the definitive work about the beginning days of NASA. Yet you once said, "If a person is not talented enough to be a novelist, not smart enough to be a lawyer, and his hands are too shaky to perform operations, he becomes a journalist." Why did you do so much of what you didn't value?

MAILER: You disappoint me, Klein. If you had done your homework, in *The Armies of the Night*, I describe my conversation with Robert . . .

My macho flared and I interrupted him.

ME: . . . Lowell. I think I remember the words exactly, "You know, Norman," said Lowell in his fondest voice, "Elizabeth and I really think you're the finest journalist in America."

MAILER: Good jab, but you forgot the counterpunch . . . my response to him. "Well, Cal, there are days when I think of myself as being the best writer in America."

ME: When was a hierarchy of writing established?

MAILER: Since people used stones on cave walls. Actually, long before. Storytelling.

ME: Aren't you creating a false distinction? Storytelling was as much about history as make-believe, and the same could be said about cave paintings.

MAILER: The difficulty I have is not with journalism per se—despite what I said. The problem has been—*was*, now that I'm dead—the attempt to define the books you mentioned as *simply* journalism when so much more creativity went into them. Every one of my books killed me a little more, yet too many people made them sound as if readers were reading a digest of newspaper accounts. As I believe you well know, that is *not* what they found.

ME: Yes, those works were written in a highly subjectivized style and used techniques that were thought to be the sole domain of fiction at that time, but you were, in fact, reporting.

MAILER: I think it's impossible to tease out reporting from what you termed "highly subjectivized." [*Mr. Mailer grinned mischievously.*] Did you just make up that word?

ME: Nah, I ran across it preparing for our interview.

MAILER: I always found it more fun to write about something I didn't completely know but would discover on route. A friend once told me that "The only time I know anything is when it comes to me at the point of my pen." I hope our interview manages to replicate that.

A stuffy answer, I thought, and smiled at his ever-present ego.

ME: So do I, but I'm still stuck on the journalism issue. I'll never understand why *The Executioner's Song* [Mailer's book about the life and death of murderer Gary Gilmore] won the Pulitzer for *fiction.*

MAILER [*pouring both of us another drink despite the morning hour*]: Perhaps we're both too concerned about categories. It's true I much prefer, *preferred,* to be thought of as a novelist, but that might have been shortsighted on my part.

Mr. Mailer broke into laughter.

MAILER: I probably should have touted myself more as the best living *writer* than argue about being a novelist rather than a journalist. Truth was, I sifted through thousands of documents before writing Gilmore's story.

ME: I'll be honest with *you*, I thought the first two-thirds were genius. Each paragraph seemed to be in the voice of the person you were writing about . . ."

MAILER: You have a good ear, Klein.

ME: But the last third, when your attention turned to the press and, frankly, yourself, well, it just wasn't as compelling.

MAILER: Reporters' voices *shouldn't* grab you the way main characters do; it's the nature of their craft. But I'll take "two-thirds genius." It goes well with bourbon.

ME: One last question about *Song*. You've been quoted as saying, "The mark of mediocrity is to look for precedent." Doesn't *The Executioner's Song* follow in the steps of *In Cold Blood*?

MAILER [*shaking his head*]: I'm dead and *still* being asked that question. Yes, there are similarities, but remember an entire movement called *New Journalism* was rearing its head. Capote, Tom Wolfe, later Hunter Thompson. And me, of course, right up there in the vanguard. Hell, we created the *Village Voice* to encourage a meld of fiction and nonfiction. So while I understand the question, I believe the notion that Capote set a "precedent" is a stretch.

Mailer raised his bushy eyebrows.

MAILER: And you certainly wouldn't call *The Executioner's Song* mediocre, would you?

ME: Something else jumped out while preparing for our talk . . .

MAILER: Pretty confident that I'd talk to you, eh?

ME: I figured if I pounded on your gravesite shouting "GORE VIDAL" long and loud enough you wouldn't be able to help yourself.

Mailer chuckled in a surprisingly wholehearted way.

MAILER: Funny, but that's not why I'm here. I've read your books, and you too are trying to redefine a category. Hardboiled detective fiction where, instead of just plot, plot, plot and shoot, shoot, shoot, the focus is on the inner life of your main character and interpersonal relationships.

ME: Well, thank you. That's a hell of a compliment coming from you.

MAILER: I said "trying." I didn't say succeeding.

ME: You took "two-thirds genius," I'll take "trying."

MAILER: Just stay at it. Perhaps you'll actually succeed where I didn't in *Tough Guys Don't Dance.*

Mailer refreshed our glasses.

ME: Here you are encouraging another author, but during your lifetime it seemed as though you were always at war with other writers. I'm not just talking about Vidal. But even your friends like James Baldwin, who liked you and wrote "you strode through the soft Paris nights like a gladiator." But in *Advertisements for Myself,* you wrote that he was incapable of saying fuck you to the reader.

MAILER [*shrugging*]: Is it an insult if it's true—at least at the time? Anyway, he eventually got his punch in with, and I quote, "The Negro jazz musicians among whom we sometimes found ourselves, who really liked Norman, did not for an instant consider him as being even remotely 'hip.'" Now *that* was an insult.

ME: And *I* quote, "Is it an insult if it's true—at least at the time?" But it wasn't just Baldwin. According to you, Styron had "compromised himself"; Bellow wrote "in a style I find self-willed . . . I cannot take him seriously"; Kerouac lacked "discipline, intelligence, honesty." "There were no talented women writers at all." You can't really believe that about women, can you?

MAILER: Again, one needs to look at the context of the times. I was savaged by virtually every notable woman, writer or not, after I published *Prisoner of Sex*.

ME: Excuse me, Norman, I quoted you from 1959, and you didn't publish *Prisoner* until 1971. What *context* are you talking about? Please! You called your cock "The Retaliator" in *Prisoner*.

MAILER: I was pretty angry when I wrote *Prisoner*.

ME: You think? Whatever year we're talking about, you have an across-the-board reputation of being "psychologically, creatively, empathetically tone-deaf when it came to women, his female characters a creamy mélange of angel-whores whose lipstick was ripe for smearing . . ." Perhaps that's why your novels don't receive the acclaim your other writing does. In fact, your last wife [Norris Church Mailer] wrote that she begged you to eliminate the meanderings that made *Harlot's Ghosts*, *The Gospel According to the Son*, and *The Castle in the Forest* critical failures.

MAILER: She might have been right, but no writer can afford to pay much attention to criticism. Then who the hell are you? And those fucking literary critics; I hate, excuse me, hated them most of all. They *still* don't understand the importance of *Oswald's Tale: An American Mystery.*

ME: Let's take a break and stretch our legs. When we return, I'd like to begin with *Oswald's Tale.* It's a perfect segue into your political activism and other writings.

—

MAILER: That walk was delightful—don't get around much anymore. Ha!

ME: So, in its own way this interview has been a relief?

MAILER: In some ways, yes. It's good to get out once in a while. But in other ways not at all. I'm terribly angry about this country's direction.

ME: Not the first time is it?

MAILER: You're talking about John Kennedy, aren't you?

ME: Impossible not to. At first you loved the guy. I remember what you wrote about the 1960 Democratic convention: "Yes, this candidate for all his record; his good, sound, conventional liberal record has a patina of that other life, the second American life, the long electric night with the fires of neon leading down the highway to the murmur of jazz." In fact, you called him "an existential hero."

MAILER: Well, in looking back I was wrong about many things. That was one of them. His secret war on Cuba, the Vietnam War. His snarky little brother Bobby. So I did what was called for. Joined organizations and protests about their policies and leadership. Now I look around and see virtually the same thing. A black president. A man who seemed as a flame to moths and had the potential of becoming a transformational figure for real change. But nothing is different. America continues its horrific downward slide. Even after he seemingly rediscovered his progressive voice.

ME: I don't disagree, but which slide are *you* talking about?

MAILER: Where should I start? *Any* war that requires the suspension of reason as a necessity for support is a bad war. Right now, we're in several. And I include the one on our liberty in the name of security. Talk about the suspension of reason! Also, one only has to look at the stranglehold the corporate world and their media has on the American people. My God, they bought themselves a Supreme Court that allows the ruling class to own any candidate they choose. And finally, we have an ideological schism that is tearing the nation apart.

ME: On the last page of *Miami and the Siege of Chicago,* you predicted the cultural divide: "We will be fighting for forty years . . ." And we have been, only longer.

MAILER: A fight we have apparently lost. As well as losing any semblance of a middle class. It's quickly becoming a society of those who have and those who don't.

ME: In *Oswald's Tale,* you wrote, "If a figure as large as Kennedy is cheated abruptly of his life, we feel better, inexplicably better, if his killer is also not without size. Then, to some degree, we can also mourn the loss of possibility in the man who did the deed. Tragedy is vastly preferable to absurdity." So you believe we are living in the absurd?

Mailer shook his head and rubbed his eyes. He was growing tired.

MAILER: It's much worse. *That* quotation was about individuals and their lives. Now we're talking about an entire empire disintegrating, and I have no faith that we won't take the rest of the world with us. Throughout my entire career people always talked about "Mailer's ego." But if the world perishes, it will occur because of *America's* ego. Rather than absurdity, we're mired in tragedy.

ME: I'm surprised that you're as pessimistic as this. You spent much of your life "boxing" for causes that you believed in. Was it your death that changed your attitude?

MAILER [*reaching for the bottle and pouring the remains into his glass*]: Abbot. Jack Abbot. The letters that flew between us while he was in jail convinced me he was rehabilitated. I had it in my power to help him by getting *In the Belly of the Beast* published. I think something changed in me after he stabbed that waiter to death six weeks after parole. I never realized how deeply I was affected until after my own death. Now I understand my role in that, and it will haunt me for eternity.

ME: Well, your political outlook was much more upbeat in 1969 when you ran for mayor of New York City.

MAILER: Whose wasn't? Of course I was hopeful. It was also fifteen years before Abbot.

ME: Hopeful or on an ego trip?

MAILER: That's certainly how they portrayed it at the time. But tell me New York City wouldn't be better off as its own state? In 1969, citizens of New York City paid approximately $22 billion in income taxes to the federal government, and New Yorkers received only about $6 billion from federal coffers. If the city kept that $22 billion in their own hands, every neighborhood would get a lot more bang for its buck.

ME: Perhaps, but your slogan, "Throw the Rascals In," made the campaign kind of a joke, don't you think? Isn't that why it was called an ego trip?

MAILER: I liked the slogan they *wouldn't* print: "No More Bullshit!" And where is it written that campaigns have to be dull and serious? Certainly not at that moment in time. Even though the press focused on my succession plan, I took positions on a wide range of issues. I opposed compulsory fluoridation of the water supply. I advocated for the release of Black Panther party leader Huey Newton. I saw the city, its independence secured, splintering into townships and neighborhoods, each with its own school systems, police departments, housing programs, and governing philosophies.

And no one seems to recall that I was endorsed by libertarian economist Murray Rothbard, who said, "smashing the urban government apparatus and fragmenting it into a myriad of constituent fragments offered the only answer to the ills plaguing American cities." And finally, no less a political journalist and historian than Theodore White called it "one of the most serious campaigns run in the United States in the last five years . . . [H]is campaign was considered and thoughtful, the beginning of an attempt to apply ideas to a political situation." Not entirely an ego trip was it?

ME: You do remember that you came in fourth out of five candidates?

MAILER [*yawning*]: I was ahead of my time. Always have been. You didn't pound on my grave site because I was a know-nothing.

ME: I pounded on your grave because I think you are one of the most important and creative writers this country has ever produced.

MAILER [*rising somewhat wobbly to his feet*]: Well, we certainly agree about that. But right now I'm a bit tired. Not as alive as I once was. And, as for my giant ego, would you mind helping me home?

"I don't think life is absurd. I think we are all here for a huge purpose. I think we shrink from the immensity of the purpose we are here for."

—Norman Mailer

A PARTIAL BIBLIOGRAPHY OF NORMAN MAILER'S WORK

Novels

The Naked and the Dead. New York: Rinehart, 1948.
Barbary Shore. New York: Rinehart, 1951.
The Deer Park. New York: Putnam's, 1955.
An American Dream. New York: Dial, 1965.
Why Are We in Vietnam? New York: Putnam's, 1967.
The Executioner's Song. Boston: Little, Brown, 1979.
Of Women and Their Elegance. New York, Simon and Schuster, 1980.
Ancient Evenings. Boston: Little, Brown, 1983.
Tough Guys Don't Dance. New York: Random House, 1984.
Harlot's Ghost. New York: Random House, 1991.
The Gospel According to the Son. New York: Random House, 1997.
The Castle in the Forest. New York: Random House, 2007.

Plays

The Deer Park: A Play. New York: Dial, 1967.

Short Stories

The Short Fiction of Norman Mailer. New York: Dell, 1967.

General Nonfiction

The Armies of the Night. New York: New American Library, 1968.

Miami and the Siege of Chicago: An Informal History of the Republican and Democratic Conventions of 1968. New York: New American Library, 1968.

Of a Fire on the Moon. Boston: Little, Brown, 1970.

The Prisoner of Sex. Boston: Little, Brown, 1971.

St. George and The Godfather. New York: Signet Classics, 1972.

The Faith of Graffiti. New York: Praeger, 1974.

The Fight. Boston: Little, Brown, 1975.

Of a Small and Modest Malignancy, Wicked and Bristling with Dots. Northridge, CA: Lord John Press, 1980.

Why Are We at War? New York: Random House, 2003.

The Spooky Art: Some Thoughts on Writing. New York: Random House, 2003.

The Big Empty: Dialogues on Politics, Sex, God, Boxing, Morality, Myth, Poker and Bad Conscience in America. New York: Nation Books, 2006

On God: An Uncommon Conversation. New York: Random House, 2007

Essay Collections

Advertisements for Myself. New York: Putnam's, 1959.
The Presidential Papers. New York: Putnam, 1963.
Cannibals and Christians. New York: Dial, 1966.
Pieces and Pontifications. Boston: Little, Brown, 1982.

Biographies

Marilyn: A Biography. New York: Grosset & Dunlap, 1973.
Portrait of Picasso as a Young Man: An Interpretive Biography. Atlantic Monthly Press, 1995.
Oswald's Tale: An American Mystery. New York: Random House, 1996

Famous Essays and Articles

"The White Negro." San Francisco: City Lights, 1957.

Decorations and Awards

1969: Pulitzer Prize and National Book Award for *The Armies of the Night*
1980: Pulitzer Prize for *The Executioner's Song*
2002: Austrian Cross of Honour for Science and Art, 1st class
2005: National Book Award for Lifetime Achievement
2006: Knight of the Legion of Honour (France)
Commander of the Ordre des Arts et des Lettres (France)

Zachary Klein came to Papercuts for an event with Christopher Irvin to launch our Prime Time Crime series. He read from Ties That Blind, *his first novel in over twenty years and a continuation of his acclaimed Matt Jacob Series.*

SARDINES

Rick Berlin

I don't get to fly much, at least not in the last twenty years. I liked airplanes as a kid. The undulating porpoise backs of those four-prop TWAs obsessed my little-boy brain. The Ipana stewardesses patting my head, fluffing pillows, pouring Coke over ice cubes gave me the shivers. The scale of the plane when you bounded up silver stairs from the tarmac seemed like storybook magic. In the 1950s, flying from San Francisco to Connecticut with my sisters and my mom, I realized something was wrong: "Hey! Ma! There's smoke coming out of the engine! There's flames!" We swooped down into O'Hare like a wounded gull. I wasn't afraid; after all, I'd saved us by spotting the smoke. Now all that's changed, all that little-boy turn-on. I loathe planes. They pack you in like sheep to the slaughter; the seats can barely fit our bloated butts. The neck cramps, insidious farting, and used-up air is enough to make you want to murder someone. Meanwhile, there's no free anything to drink or eat. OK, I admit that I like the takeoffs and landings. I like watching streets, cars, and houses recede into monopoly pieces. I like the new stewardesses and (gay) stewards who aren't Hollywood hot anymore and have saggy old-bra breasts, age lines, thinning hair, and bad makeup. But that all goes awry when I imagine crashing into shark water, or skyscrapers, when I'd be forced to make friends with the idiots on board just to survive. I wonder if I'd have what it takes, or if they would. Or will it be war? All this amuses me quietly. I feel my brain-dead bimbo Mona Lisa smile smiling above it all, smiling at myself smiling at them. Ah, the guru witness, what a joke! Soon enough it all unravels and it's torture time. The tin-can trap becomes a nightmare. I try not to touch the fatty on my left or work up a conversation with the good-looking kid who by chance takes the seat next to mine, baseball hat backward, earbuds fending off inquiry. I try to sleep. I read until my eyes ache. I hold off a piss. After a century of fetal cramps and window squinting, the squawk box announces descent. Down, down, down as cotton wisps slither across the wings and tiny house dots enlarge. The sun sparkles off man-made lakes. The shadow jet hurtles across the relief map below like a jackrabbit. The flaps rise, the wheels lower, and we're down, landed, safe, nudging up through the uncircumcised cock tube as we hurry through, like sperm to the airport egg. That's when it happens. That's when all hell breaks loose as we wait for the sheep to yank out their bags from the overhead and get the fuck off the fucking plane. When I stand up, the curved ceiling crooks my neck like a hanged man. It's then that I hear it, the scream, the silent Edvard Munch scream that sucks up the stale space in the cabin like a cyclone. We all hear it, seething silently. The level of impatience is at code red. Sweaty necks, clenched jaws, and beady eyes turn us into cattle just prior to execution. That's when we're all alike. That's when we cumulatively despise the out-to-sea asshole who can't locate his carry-on, staring up at the stowaway like a stoner, oblivious to the rage of the angry rats behind him who would strangle him given half a chance. Now I understand how frightening the group impulse of a

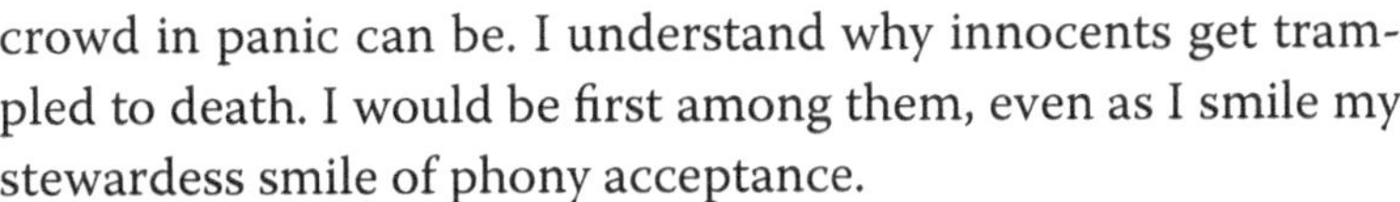

crowd in panic can be. I understand why innocents get trampled to death. I would be first among them, even as I smile my stewardess smile of phony acceptance.

Rick Berlin, a Boston musical icon, was kind enough to play a set in the store on Independent Bookstore Day. He drew a huge crowd, and there were people gathered on the sidewalk to hear the music coming from inside the store.

GROWING THINGS

Paul Tremblay

1.

Their father stayed in his bedroom, door locked, for almost two full days. Now he paces in the mudroom, and he pauses only to pick at the splintering doorjamb with a black fingernail. Muttering to himself, he shares his secrets with the weather-beaten door.

Their father has always been distant and serious to the point of being sullen, but they do love him for reasons more than him being their sole lifeline. Recently, he stopped eating and gave his share of the rations to his daughters, Marjorie and Merry. However, the lack of food has made him squirrely, a word their mother—who ran away more than four years ago—used liberally when describing their father. Spooked by his current erratic behavior, and feeling guilty, as if they were the cause of his suffering, the daughters agreed to keep quiet and keep away, huddled in a living-room corner, sitting in a nest of blankets and pillows, playing cards between the couch and the silent TV with its dust-covered screen. Yesterday, Merry drew a happy face in the dust, but Marjorie quickly erased it, turning her palm black. There is no running water with which to wash her hands.

Marjorie is fourteen years old but only a shade taller than her eight-year-old sister. She says, "Story time." Marjorie has repeatedly told Merry that their mother used to tell stories, and that some of her stories were funny while others were sad or scary. Those stories, the ones Merry doesn't remember hearing, were about everyone and everything.

Merry says, "I don't want to listen to a story right now." She wants to watch her father. Merry imagines him with a bushy tail and a twitchy face full of acorns. Seeing him act squirrely reinforces one of the few memories she has of her mother.

"It's a short one, I promise." Marjorie is dressed in the same cutoff shorts and football shirt she's been wearing for a week. Her brown hair is black with grease, and her fair skin is a map of freckles and acne. Marjorie has the book in her lap. *Oh, the Places You'll Go!*

"All right," Merry says, but she won't really listen. She'll continue to watch her father, who digs through the winter closet, throwing out jackets and itchy sweaters, snow pants. As far as she knows, it is still summer.

The gregarious colors of Marjorie's book cover are muted in the darkened living room. Candles on the fireplace mantle flicker and dutifully melt away. Still, it is enough light for the sisters. They are used to it. Marjorie closes her eyes and opens the book randomly. She flips to a page with a cartoon New York City. The buildings are brick red and sea blue, and they crowd the page, elbowing and wrestling each other for the precious space. Merry has colored the streets green with a crayon worn down to a nub smaller than the tip of her thumb.

They are so used to trying not to disturb their father, Marjorie whispers: "New York City is the biggest city in the world, right? When it started growing there, it meant it could grow anywhere. It took over Central Park. The stuff just came shooting up, crowding out the grass and trees, the flowerbeds. The stuff grew a foot an hour, just like everywhere else."

Yesterday's story was about all the farms in the Midwest, and how the corn, wheat, and soy crops were overrun. They couldn't stop the growing things and that was why there wasn't any more food. Merry had heard her tell that one before.

Marjorie continues, "The stuff poked through the cement paths, soaked up Central Park's ponds and fountains, and started filling the streets next." Marjorie talks like the preacher used to, back when they went, back when Mom would force them all to make the trip down the mountain, into town, and to the church. Merry is a confusing combination of sad and mad that she remembers details of that old, wrinkly preacher, particularly his odd smell of baby powder mixed with something earthy, yet she has almost no memory of her mother.

Marjorie says, "They couldn't stop it in the city. When they cut it down, it grew back faster. People didn't know how or why it grew. There's no soil under the streets, you know, in the sewers, but it still grew. The shoots and tubers broke through windows and buildings, and some people climbed the growing things to steal food, money, and televisions, but it quickly got too crowded for people, for everything, and the giant buildings crumbled and fell. It grew fast there, faster than anywhere else, and there was nothing anyone could do."

Merry, half listening, takes the green crayon nub out of her pajama pocket. She changes her pajamas every morning, unlike her sister, who doesn't change her clothes at all. She draws green lines on the hardwood floor, wanting their father to come over and catch her and yell at her. Maybe it'll stop him from putting on all the winter clothes, stop him from being squirrely.

Their father waddles into the living room, breathing heavy, used air falling out of his mouth, his face suddenly hard, old, and gray and covered in sweat. He says, "We're running low. I have to go out to look for food and water." He doesn't hug or kiss his daughters but pats their heads. Merry drops the crayon nub at his feet, and it rolls away. He turns and they know he means to leave without any promise of returning. He stops at the door, cups his mittened and gloved hands around his mouth, and shouts toward his direct left, into the kitchen, as if he hadn't left his two daughters on their pile of blankets in the living room.

"Don't answer the door for anyone! Don't answer it! Knocking means the world is over!" He opens the door, but only enough for his body to squeeze out. The daughters see nothing of the world outside but a flash of bright sunlight. A breeze bullies into their home, along with a buzz-saw sound of wavering leaves.

2.

Merry sits, legs crossed, a foot away from the front door. Marjorie is back in the blanket nest, sleeping. Merry draws green lines on the front door. The lines are long and thick, and she draws small leaves on the ends. She's never seen the growing things, but it's what she imagines.

The shades are pulled low, drooping over the sills like limp sails, and the curtains are drawn tight. They stopped looking outside after their father begged them not to, and they won't look out the windows now that he's not here. When it first started happening, when their father came home with the pickup truck full of food and other supplies, he stammered through complex and contradictory answers to his daughters' many questions. His knotty hands moved more than his lips, removing and replacing his soot-stained baseball cap. Merry mainly remembers that he said something about the growing things being like a combination of bamboo and kudzu. Merry tugged on his flannel shirtsleeve and asked what bamboo and kudzu were. Their father smiled but also looked away quickly, like he'd said something he shouldn't have.

Outside the wind gusts and whistles around the creaky old cabin. The mudroom and living-room windows are dark rectangles outlined in a yellow light, and their glass rattles in the frames. Merry stares at the wooden door listening for a sound she's never heard before: a knock on her front door. She sits and listens until she can't stand it any longer. She runs upstairs to her bedroom, picks out a pair of new pajamas, changes again in the dark, and carefully folds the dirty set and places it back in her bureau. Merry then returns to the nest and wakes her older sister.

"Is he coming back? Is he running away too?"

Marjorie comes to and rises slowly. She lifts the book from her lap and hugs it to her chest. Her fingers crinkle edges of the pages and worry the cardboard corners of the cover. Despite the acne, she looks younger than her fourteen years.

Marjorie shakes her head, answering a different question, one that wasn't spoken, and says, "Story time."

Merry used to enjoy the stories before they were always about the growing things. Now she wishes that Marjorie would stop with the stories, wishes that Marjorie could just be her big sister and quit trying to be like their mother.

"No more stories. Please. Just answer my questions."

Marjorie says, "Story first."

Merry balls her hands into fists and fights back tears. She's as angry now as she was when Marjorie told all the kids at the playground in town that Merry liked to catch spiders and rip off each leg with tweezers, and that she kept a jar of their fat legless bodies in her bureau.

"I don't want to hear a story!"

"I don't care. Story first."

Marjorie always gets her way, even now, even as she continues to withdraw and fade. She only leaves the nest to go to the bathroom, and she walks like an older woman, the joints and muscles in her legs stiff with disuse.

Merry asks, "You promise to answer my questions if I listen to a story?"

All Marjorie says is, "Story first. Story first."

Merry isn't sure if this is a yes or a maybe.

Marjorie tells of the areas around the big cities, places called the suburbs. How the stuff ruined everyone's pretty lawns and amateur gardens and then started taking root in the cracks of sidewalks and driveways. People poured and sprayed millions of gallons of weed killer, liquid plumber, lye, and bleach. None of it worked on the stuff, and all the chemicals leeched into the groundwater. Water supplies were poisoned.

As with most of Marjorie's stories, Merry doesn't understand everything, like what groundwater is. But she still understands the story. It makes a screaming noise inside her head, and it is all that she can do to keep it from coming out.

She says, "I listened to your story, now you have to answer my question, okay?" Merry takes the book away from Marjorie, who surprisingly does not resist.

"I'm tired." Marjorie licks her dry and cracked lips.

"You promised. When is he coming back?"

"I don't know, Merry. I really don't." With the blankets curled and twisted round her legs and arms, it's as if she's been pulled apart and her pieces sprinkled about their nest.

Merry wants to shrink and crawl inside one of her sister's pockets. She asks in her smallest voice, "Was this how it happened last time?"

"What last time? What are you talking about?"

"When Mommy ran away? Was this how it happened when she ran away?"

"No. She wasn't happy so she left. He's going to get food and water."

"Is he happy? He didn't look happy when he left."

"He's happy. He's fine. He isn't leaving us."

"He's coming back though, right?"

"Yes. He'll come back."

"Do you promise?"

"I promise."

"Good."

Merry believes in her big sister, the one who once punched a third grader named Elizabeth in the nose for putting a daddy longlegs down the back of Merry's shirt.

Merry leaves the nest and resumes her post, sitting cross-legged in the mudroom, in the shadow of the front door. The wind continues to increase in velocity. The house stretches, settles, and groans, the sounds eager for their chance to fill the void. Then, on the other side of the front door, brushing against the wood, there's a light rapping, a knocking, but if it is a knocking, it's being done by doll-sized hands with doll-sized fingertips small enough to find the cracks in the door that nobody can see, small enough to get inside the door and come through on the other side. The inside.

Merry stays seated but twists and yells, "Marjorie! I think someone is knocking on the door!" Merry covers her mouth, horrified that whoever is knocking must've heard her. Even in her terror, she realizes that the gentle sounds are so slight, small, quiet that maybe she's making up the knocking, making up her very own story.

Marjorie says, "I don't hear anything."

"Someone is knocking lightly. I can hear them." Merry presses her ear against the wood, closes her eyes, and tries to finish this knocking story. Single knocks become a flurry issued by thousands of miniature doll hands, those faceless toys—maybe they crawled all the way here from New York City—and they scramble and climb over each other for a chance to knock the door down. Merry wraps her arms around her chest, terrified that the door will collapse on top of her. The knocking builds to a crescendo, and then ebbs along with the dying wind.

Merry rests her forehead on the door and says, "It stopped."

Marjorie says, "No one's there. Don't open the door."

3.

Marjorie hasn't eaten anything in days. They are down to a handful of beef jerky and half a box of Cheerios. In the basement, there are only two one-gallon bottles of water left, and they rest in a corner next to the staircase landing. Flashlight in hand, Merry sits on the damp wood of the landing, plastic water jugs pressing against her thigh. It's cooler down here, but her feet sweat inside her rubber rain boots. The boots are protection in case she decides to walk toward the far wall and hunt for jars of pickles or preserves her father may have stashed.

Merry has been sitting with her flashlight pointed at the earthen floor for more than two hours. When she first came down here, the tips of the growing things were subtle protrusions, hints of green and brown peeking through the sun-starved dirt. Now, the tallest spear-like stalks stretch for more than a foot above the ground. The leafy ends of the plants would tickle her knees were she to take the trip across the basement. She wonders if the leaves would feel rough against her skin. She wonders if the leaves are somehow poisonous, despite never having heard her sister describe them that way.

Earlier that morning, Merry decided she had to do something other than stare at the front door and listen for the knocking. She put herself to work and rearranged the candles around the fireplace mantle, and she lit new ones even though, according to her father, she wasn't old enough to use matches. She singed the tips of her thumb and pointing finger watching that first blue flame curl up the matchstick. After the candles, she prepared a change of clothes for Marjorie and left the small bundle, folded tightly, on the couch. She picked out a green dress that Marjorie never wore but Merry not so secretly coveted. Then she swept the living-room and kitchen floors. The scratch of the broom's straws on the hardwood made her uneasy.

Marjorie slept most of the day, waking only to tell a quick story of the growing things cracking mountains open like eggs, drowning the canyons and valleys in green and brown and drinking up all the ponds, lakes, and rivers.

Merry runs the beam of her flashlight over the stone and mortar foundation walls but sees no cracks, and scoffs at the most recent tale of the growing things. Marjorie's stories had always mixed truth with exaggeration. For example, it was true that Merry used to hunt and kill spiders, and it was true that all those twitchy legs were why she killed them. Simply watching a spider crawling impossibly on the walls or ceiling and seeing all that choreographed movement set off earthquake-sized tremors somewhere deep in her brain. But she was never so cruel as to pull off their legs with tweezers, and she certainly never collected their button-sized bodies. Merry never understood why Marjorie would say those horrible, made-up things about her.

Still, Merry initially believed Marjorie's growing-things stories, believed the growing things were even worse than what Marjorie portrayed, which is what frightened Merry the most. Now, however, seeing the sprouts and stalks living in the basement makes it all seem so much less scary. Yes, they are real, but they are not city-dissolving, mountain-destroying monsters.

Merry thinks of an experiment, a test, and shuts off the flashlight. She hears only her own breathing, a pounding base drum, so big and loud it fills her head, and in the absolute dark, her head is everything. Recognizing her body as the source of all that terrible noise is too much and she starts to panic, but she calms herself down by imagining the sounds of the tubular wooden stalks growing, stretching, reaching out and upward. She turns the flashlight on again, surveys the earthen basement floor, and she's certain there has been more growth and new sprouts emerging from the soil. The sharp and elongated tips of the tallest stalks sport clusters of shockingly green leaves the size of playing cards, the ends of which are also tapered and pointed. The stalks grow in tidy, orderly rows, although the rows grow more crowded and the formations more complex as the minutes pass. Merry repeats turning off the flashlight, sitting alone in the dark, breathing, listening, and then, with the light back on, she laughs and quietly claps a free hand against her leg in recognition of the growing things' progress.

Merry indulges in a fantasy where her father returns home unharmed, arms loaded with supplies, a large happily-ever-after smile on his sallow face, and he's not squirrelly anymore.

The daydream ends abruptly. In a matter of days her father has become unknowable, unreachable, a single tree in a vast forest or a story she once heard but has long forgotten. Was this how it happened with Marjorie and her mother? Her sister was around the same age as Merry is now when their mother ran away. To Merry, their mother is a concept, not a person. Will the same dissociation happen with their father if he doesn't come back? Merry fears that memories of him, even the small ones, will recede too far to ever be reached again. Already she greedily clutches stored scenes of the weekly errands she ran with her father this past spring and summer while Marjorie was at a friend's house, how at each stop he walked his hand across the truck's bench seat and gave her knee a monkey bite—that is, unless she slapped his dry, gruff hand away first—and then the rides home, how he let both daughters unbuckle their belts for the windy drive home up the mountain, Merry sandwiched in the middle, so they could seesaw-slide on the bench seat along with the turns. Did he only tolerate their wild laughter and mock screams as they slid into each other and him, hiding a simmering disapproval, or did he join the game, leaning left and right along with the truck, adding to the chorus of his daughters' screams? She already doesn't remember. Merry cannot verbalize this, but the idea of a world where people disappear like days on a calendar is what truly terrifies her, and she wants nothing more than for her and her loved ones to remain rooted to a particular spot and to never move again.

Merry considers asking Marjorie all these questions about her parents and more, but she's worried about her sister. Marjorie is getting squirrely. Marjorie didn't even open the book for this morning's story. And when Merry left the living room to go to the basement, Marjorie was sleeping again, her eyelids as purple as plumbs. What if Marjorie runs away too and leaves her all alone?

Merry puts the flashlight down on the landing, leaving it on and centering its yellow beam in an attempt to illuminate as much of the basement floor as possible. She lifts a one-gallon water bottle, peels away the plastic ring around the cap, and then steps off the landing and walks toward the middle of the floor, unable to see anything below her ankles, which is as low as the focused beam of light hits. Under her feet, the disturbed and clotted earth feels lumpy and even hard in places, a message in Braille she cannot decipher. She hopes she is not stepping on any of the new shoots.

She pries off the cap, jarring the balance of the bottle in her arms, spilling water onto her hand and her pajama shorts. Her forearms tremble with the bulky jug set in the crooks of her pointy elbows. Water continues to spill out spastically and gathers on the leaves. She knows they can't spare much, so she pours out only a little, then a little more, hoping the water reaches the roots.

Merry puts the cap on the bottle and walks back to the landing. She'll bring the water upstairs, pour two cups, and give one to her sister, force her to drink. Then she'll curl up in the nest with Marjorie and sleep, thinking about her plants in the basement. She will do all that and more, but only after she sits on the landing, shuts off the flashlight, listens in the dark to the song of the growing things, listens some more, and then, eventually, turns the flashlight back on.

4.

She did not blow out the candles before collapsing and falling asleep on their nest of blankets. All but three candles have burned out or melted away. Wax stalactites hang from the fireplace mantle. Merry wakes on her left side and is nose to nose with her sister. Having gone many days without being able to bathe or wash, Marjorie's acne has intensified, ravaging her face. Whiteheads and hard, painful-looking red bumps mottle her skin, creating the appearance of fissures, as if her grease-slicked face is a mask on the verge of breaking up and falling away. Merry wonders if the same will happen to her.

Marjorie opens her eyes; her pupils and deep-brown irises are almost indistinguishable from each other. She says, "The growing things will continue to grow until there aren't any more stories." Her voice is scratchy, obsolete, packed away somewhere inside her chest like a holiday sweater that was a gift from some forgotten relative.

Merry says, "Please don't say that. There will be more stories and you have to tell them." She reaches out to hug her sister, but Marjorie buries her face in a blanket and tightens into a ball.

Merry asks, "How are you feeling today, Marjorie? Did you drink your water?" On the end table between them and the couch is the answer to her question: the glass of water that she poured last night is full. "What are you doing, Marjorie? You have to drink something!" A sudden, all-consuming anger wells up in Merry, and she alternates hitting her sister and tearing the layers of blankets and sheets away from the nest. It comes apart easily. She throws *Oh, the Places You'll Go!* over her head. It thuds somewhere behind her. Marjorie doesn't move and remains curled in her ball, even after Merry dumps the water on her head.

Merry kneels beside her prone sister and covers her face in her hands, hiding what she's done from herself. Eventually she musters the courage to look again, and she says, "Tell me a story about our father, Marjorie. About him coming back. Please?"

"There are no more stories."

Merry pats Marjorie's damp shoulder and says, "No. It's okay. I'm sorry. I'll clean this up, Marjorie. I can fix this." She'll gather their nest blankets and sheets, and she'll dry her sister and the rest of the water spill, force her to change out of the wet clothes and into the green dress, and then they'll really talk about what to do, where they should go if their father isn't coming back.

Merry stands and turns around. The nest blankets Merry threw into the middle of the living room have become three knee-high tents, each sporting sharp, abrupt poles raising their cloth above the floor. The poles don't waver and appear to be supremely sturdy, as if they would stand and continue standing regardless if the world fell apart around them.

Merry puts her fingers in her mouth. Everything in the living room is quiet. She whispers Marjorie's name at the tents, as if that is their name. She bends down slowly, grabs the plush corners of the blankets, and pulls them away quickly, the flourish to a magician's act. Three stalks and their tubular wooden trunks have penetrated the living-room floor, along with smaller tips of other stalks just beginning to poke through. The hardwood floor is the melted wax of the candles. The hardwood floor is the poor blighted skin of Marjorie's face. Warped and cracked, curling and bubbling up, the floor is a landscape Merry no longer recognizes.

She believes with a child's unwavering certainty that this is all her fault because she watered the growing things in the basement. Merry tries to pull Marjorie up off the floor but can't. She says, "We can't stay down here. You have to go upstairs. To our room. Go upstairs, Marjorie! I'll get the rest of the water." She wants to confess to having poured almost half the one-gallon jug on the growing things, but instead she says, "We'll need the water upstairs, Marjorie. We'll be very, very thirsty."

Merry maps out a set of precise steps. The newly malformed floorboards squawk and complain under her careful feet. Green leaves and shoots on the tips of the exposed stalks whisper against her skin as she makes her too-slow progress across the living room. She imagines going so slow that the stalks continue to grow beneath her, pick her up like an unwanted hitchhiker and carry her through the ceiling, the second-floor bedrooms, and then the roof of the house and into the clouds, then farther, past the moon and the sun, to wherever it is they're going.

Merry pauses at the edge of the living room and kitchen, near the mudroom, and there is someone rapping on the front door again. The knocking is light, breezy, but insistent, frantic. She's not supposed to open the door, and despite her absolute terror, she wants to, almost needs to open the door, to see who or what is on the other side. Instead, Merry turns and yells back to Marjorie, who hasn't moved from her spot. Merry urges her to wake, to go upstairs where they'll be safe. There are shoots and stalk tips breaking through the floor in the area of the nest now.

Merry runs into the kitchen, and while there are the beginnings of stalk tips in the linoleum, the damage doesn't appear as severe as it is in the living room. She takes the flashlight off the counter and opens the door to the basement stairwell. She expects a lush, impenetrable forest in the doorway, but the stairs are still there, and very much passable; her own path into the basement, to her garden, is preserved. She ducks under one thick, wooden stalk that acts as a beam, outlining the length of ceiling, and she descends to the landing, where the bottles of water remain intact.

Once on the landing, which is pushed up like a tongue trying to catch a raindrop or a snowflake, Merry adjusts for balance and gropes for the water bottles. She tries picking up both, but she's strong enough only to take the one full bottle and hold the flashlight at the same time. She contemplates making a second trip but doesn't want to come back down here. The half-full second bottle will have to be a sacrifice.

Before going up the stairs, she points her flashlight into the heart of the basement, starting at the floor, which is green with countless new shoots. She aims the flashlight up next and counts twelve stalks making contact with the ceiling, then traces their lengths downward. The tallest stalks have large clumps of dirt randomly stuck and impaled upon their wooden shafts. There are six clumps; she counts them three times. One clump is as big as a soccer ball but is more oval shaped. Four of the other dirt clods are elongated, skinny, curled and hang from the stalks like odd, over-ripened, and blackened vegetables. Three stalks in the middle of the basement share and hold up the largest of the dirt formations; rectangular and almost the size of Merry herself, it's pressed against the ceiling.

Merry rests the flashlight beam on this last and largest dirt clod. Something else is hanging from it, almost dripping or leaking out of the packed dirt. After staring for as long as she can stare, and as her house breaks into pieces above her, Merry realizes what she is looking at is a swatch of cloth, perhaps the hem of a dress. She can almost make out its color. Green maybe.

Although the previous night was more about the rush of her discovery, of the growing things, and of her flashlight game, looking at the basement now and seeing what she sees, specifically the cloth, Merry remembers walking the basement floor in her rubber boots, walking on what she couldn't see, the unexpectedly hard and lumpy soil, and she now knows she was walking upon the bones of the one who disappeared, of the runaway.

Merry shuts off the flashlight and throws it into the basement. Leaves rustle and there's a soft thud. She climbs the stairs in the dark, thinking of all the bones beneath her feet. Merry is furious with herself for not recognizing those bones last night, but how could she be blamed? She never really knew her mother.

Merry runs up the basement steps into the kitchen and stumbles over and past the continued growth. The knocking on the front door is no longer subtle, no more a mysterious collection of dolls' hands. The sound of the knocking is itself a force. It's a pounding by a singular and determined fist, as big as her shrinking old world, maybe as big as the growing new one. The door rattles in the frame, and Merry screams out with each pounding.

She shuffles away from the mudroom and into the living room. Marjorie is still there, but is up and out of the nest. She's kneeled between the stalks that have erupted through the floor. She pinches the shoots and leaves between her fingers, plucks them away, and puts them in her mouth.

The pounding on the front door intensifies. Her father said if there was a knocking on the door, then the world was over. A voice now accompanies the unrelenting hammering on the door. "Let me in!" The voice is as ragged and splintered as the living-room floor.

Merry shouts, "We need to go upstairs, Marjorie! Now now now!"

More pounding. More screaming. "Let me in!"

Merry imagines the growing things gathered outside her door, weaved into a fist as big as their house. The leaves shake in unison and in rhythm, their collected rustling forming their one true voice.

Merry imagines her father outside the door, the one she never knew, eyes wide, white froth and foam around his mouth, spitting his demand to be allowed entry into his home, the place he built, the place he forged out of rock, wood, and dirt—all dead things. His three-word command is what heralds the end of everything. She imagines her father breaking the door down, seeing his oldest daughter eating the leaves that won't stop growing, and seeing what his youngest daughter knows is written on her face as plain as any storybook.

Marjorie doesn't look at her sister as she gorges on the leaves and shoots. Then Marjorie stops eating abruptly, her head tilts back, her eyelids flutter, and she falls to the floor.

Merry drops the water jug, covers her ears, and goes to Marjorie, even if Marjorie was wrong about there being no more stories.

Merry tells Marjorie another story. Merry will get her up and bring her upstairs to their bedroom. She'll let Marjorie choose what she wants to wear instead of trying to force the green dress on her. They'll always ignore the pounding on the door, and when they're safe and when everything is okay, Merry will ask Marjorie two questions: What if it isn't him outside the door? What if it is?

A Head Full of Ghosts *was an early favorite of the staff at Papercuts. Before its publication, Paul Tremblay joined Christopher Irvin for an in-store conversation on Independent Bookstore Day in May 2015.*

WHILE CLEANING THE OUTSIDE OF MY TUB BEFORE MY 40TH BIRTHDAY PARTY NYC 1981

When I am old and fat and white
all shoulder, rump, and ribcage
unable to move any more than this tub
can, I trust someone will hunch
over me with a blue sponge
and attend to my surface as I
am attending to the streaky outside
of this tub, this substantial, curvaceous
unerotic old mother of a tub
and not fuss at me, or ask me
what my memories are, not expect me
to smile or sigh, because I will be
beyond all that, I will have earned
the right to keep still; not murmur

endearments unless they are part
of the job, part of the rhythm
of the work (good old girl,
you are a good old girl)
and if this sprucing up is ritual
so much the better, since I
have always been just surface
everything I know I have always known
first with my skin. And when
company is coming and you want
to look your best, battered is noble
and worn out and beat up
and still able to hold water is honorable.

—Abigail Thomas

On Mother's Day 2015, Abigail Thomas discussed her just-published book, What Comes Next and How to Like It, *with her daughter, Bostonian photographer and writer Jennifer Waddell. Audio of this dynamic conversation can be found at papercutsjp.com/audio-broadcast.*

THE MOUSE

Jennifer Waddell

It startled you when you went to the kitchen and you screamed. It was still, but breathing, sitting quietly on the floor. A soft plump mouse.

You had put down poison, and this one is dying in front of you. You put the nearest thing—a chipped glass storage container, long and thin like a coffin—over it and go about your business. Your daughter insists on giving it cheese and you reluctantly let her, worrying all the while about germs as she touches the floor it has been walking on. You call your brother, who lives downstairs, for assistance, but he's busy helping a neighbor. You call your sister, who tells you to pick it up with a napkin and put it in a box with soft bedding and some food so it can live out its final hours in comfort with a snack. You fill a box with crumpled junk mail flyers, half a strawberry, and yesterday's uneaten cheese. You get it ready but leave the mouse, who has shifted position ever so slightly under the glass. You know you won't use anything napkin-like to make the transition, but you don't tell your sister.

You take your dog out for a walk in the warm rain. Her ram's fur mats down slightly. You go to the churchyard she knows as her own. It's usually dark, but tonight the lights are on and the windows open. You see the sandwich board announcing the contra dance. You watch couples, young and old, dance to the music played by a fiddler, their heads visible, then hidden, as they move around the floor. Even the foot stomping sounds quiet. You notice the man you've seen with his dog, the one going through a divorce, through the glass doors on the first floor of their house, the kitchen ablaze with light. He and his wife are contemplating a silicon spatula. Who will keep it when he moves out?

The rain is falling and the ground is soft despite the hard freeze earlier this week. You should plant the tulip and hyacinth bulbs you bought last fall in the morning, but your soil is filled with the roots of a tall pine tree and is hard to work without a pickax. You no longer see the man who would have gladly chopped the ground open for you.

As you walk home, your dog lagging one step behind, the gray-black snow is slowly melting, and the salt dumped in piles after last week's storm has disappeared. A few Christmas trees ignored by the trash collectors have been blowing from position to position all week. You see three of them on your walk.

You get your kids to sleep and put on the bathrobe your mother gave you for Christmas, the one your children fight over. It's soft and warm and brown like the mouse. You finally place the mouse in the box and take it outside. In the morning you will bury it amidst the tulip bulbs. The shovel is waiting.

Jennifer Waddell joined her mother, author Abigail Thomas, for an event on Mother's Day 2015. The two discussed family dynamics, the tender mother-daughter relationship, and writing. Listen to the dialogue at papercutsjp.com/audio-broadcast.

EULOGY FOR A FRIEND

Chris Hedges

The night Terry died it was raining. Lightning streaks rent the sky. I walked after I left the hospital in the downpour to Harvard Divinity School on Francis Avenue. I did not go there because of nostalgia for the divinity school. Terry and I had more than enough of Harvard's elitism—which he had already got a good taste of as a Harvard undergraduate—and the university's propensity to turn the poor and the oppressed into airy abstractions. Most divinity students and nearly all divinity-school professors stayed clear from the inner city of Roxbury (a poor, primarily African American neighborhood in Boston), where Terry and I lived and worked. Being an intellectual, Harvard showed us, is morally neutral.

But I wanted to look at the darkened Gothic stone face of Andover Hall because it was where Terry and I were young. It is where we studied to be pastors. It was where we built a lifelong friendship. It was where we tried to fathom what it meant to live a life of faith. It was where we understood that if truth was to be heard, as Theodor Adorno wrote, suffering must be allowed to speak. It was where our ministry began.

Terry knew early on, as Montaigne wrote in "That to Philosophize Is to Learn How to Die," that we must constantly examine and slay the old self to create a better self. This is the act ritualized in the Eucharist. A constant death. A constant rebirth. And it is why the Eucharist meant so much to him. The ancient church rituals, icons and saints, the liturgical music, the formality of High Mass buttressed this death and rebirth. These props, symbols, and rituals offer guidance and support that many Protestant denominations, stripped down to a dangerous intellectualism and rationalism, often fail to provide.

In the Dark or Middle Ages, Terry would have been an abbot, singing Gregorian chants in a long black robe before sunrise, leading High Mass with rows of candles and incense no doubt wafting upward from a swinging thurible. He would, much as he did in this church, have provided refuge to pilgrims, nurtured the sick, fed the poor, educated the children, comforted the bereaved, denounced the oppressor, and copied out Aristotle, Cicero, Virgil, and Catullus so it would not be lost to human civilization.

I loved Terry for his brilliance, his deep intellectual curiosity, his humility, and his incredible compassion and gentleness. He hated emails. He sent handwritten notes, often on cards he had taken the time to pick out, to say thank you or express condolences or tell you he was thinking of you. I expect that nearly everyone in this church today received such notes, along with books he thought you should read or small gifts he wanted you to have. There was something very human about this practice in an age of instant electronic communication. I will miss his handwritten messages. I will miss the books he sent. One of his last gifts to me was the three volumes of *The Gulag Archipelago.* And when I came to Boston this past year to visit, we would talk about Solzhenitsyn's insight into human nature, oppression, resistance, and faith.

Solzhenitsyn writes of a Serb, a teacher in forced exile in the Soviet Union named Georgi Stepanovich Mitrovich. He had been recently freed from the camps. Mitrovich would not give up his dogged battle with local authorities for justice for his students. The description of Mitrovich is a description of Terry.

"His battle was utterly hopeless, and he knew it," Solzhenitsyn wrote. "No one could unravel that tangled skein. And if he had won hands down, it would have done nothing to improve the social order, the system. It would have been no more than a brief, vague gleam of hope in one narrow little spot, quickly swallowed by the clouds. Nothing that victory might bring could balance the risk of rearrest—which was the price he might pay (only the Khrushchev era saved Mitrovich). Yes, his battle was hopeless, but it was human to be outraged by injustice, even to the point of courting destruction! His struggle could only end in defeat—but no one could possibly call it useless. If we had not all been so sensible, not all been forever whining to each other: 'It won't help! It can't do any good!' our land would have been quite different. Mitrovich was not even a citizen—he was only an exile—but the district authorities feared the flash of his spectacles."

Terry, who came from a working-class family in Flint, Michigan, and whose fierce loyalty to workingmen and -women and the destitute never waivered, chose sides. He stood with the oppressed. Life was about making the world a more humane place. It was about treating everyone with dignity.

He knew the dark side of human nature and the tragedy of human history. He knew the propensity of human beings to do what we should not do. He wanted to save souls, which meant saving people from squandering their lives chasing wealth, power, or fame. And this was only possible, he knew, if we placed the sacred at the center of existence, if we realized that in the end it is not about us but about our neighbor, about the stranger, about the outcast, and about this precious planet that we must protect.

If you stand with the oppressed, you get treated like the oppressed. You have enemies. You evoke hatred. You can be killed. Terry, when he visited with me in El Salvador during the war, was profoundly moved by the mortal danger church workers, who documented and denounced the savagery of the death squads, faced daily. Many paid for this witness with their lives. This is what it means to lift up the cross. It is the fundamental call of the Christian gospel. It was why Christ accepted suffering, why Christ was abandoned, beaten, and left to die alone on a cross. There is no justice without self-sacrifice. Loving deeply hurts. And Terry bore this hurt.

Confronting evil has a price. And we must be willing to pay this price. And this is why Terry was willing to go to jail in acts of civil disobedience for workers who had lost their jobs and to defy fossil fuel corporations that are destroying the Earth.

Flannery O'Connor, in a passage Terry loved, recognized that a life of faith entailed a life of confrontation. "St. Cyril of Jerusalem, in instructing catechumens, wrote: 'The dragon sits by the side of the road, watching those who pass. Beware lest he devour you. We go to the Father of Souls, but it is necessary to pass by the dragon.' No matter what form the dragon may take, it is of this mysterious passage past him, or into his jaws, that stories of any depth will always be concerned to tell, and this being the case, it requires considerable courage at any time, in any country, not to turn away from the storyteller."

For Terry, simple human kindness, divorced from creeds or freed from ideology or religious doctrine, kindness that does not ask if the recipient deserves this kindness, is, as Vasily Grossman wrote, "what is most truly human in a human being."

And this kindness, as Grossman wrote, "is powerful only while it is powerless. If Man [or Woman] tries to give it power, it dims, fades away, loses itself, vanishes." The highest morality is the morality of kindness. It is higher than a morality based on principles, doctrines, or creeds. It is one person reaching out because another is alone, in despair, or in distress. Nothing is nobler than a life dedicated to caring for others. And kindness, as Rousseau wrote, is the single quality that makes possible all other "social virtues." Terry lived by this. And because of that, his life was magnificent.

Willow, Amelia, and Lucy [Terry's children] were raised, as I was raised, in the embrace of a church community whose beating heart was their mother and father. And, years from now, you will run into someone who will tell you how your mother or your father helped them to endure tremendous suffering or showed them kindness when no one else would. These are the invisible acts that go into a ministry. They are tiny miracles. And there are many, many people in this church whose lives, if not made whole, were made endurable because your parents cared. And this is what we are called to do.

We face today the mystery of life, death, and love. In the great, inconceivable span of time that is the universe, all of us are ephemerons, creatures whose lights momentarily sparkle and then vanish. How to use this brief gift of light. This is what Terry showed us. When you use your light to sustain and nurture others, that light is eternal. It passes from soul to soul. It is with you. It is with me. It is with everyone in this congregation. It is Terry.

Chris Hedges gave a riling and inspirational speech to a huge crowd at the First Church of JP at an event organized by the JP Forum in the spring of 2015. Hedges was kind enough to stop in to Papercuts, and gave a lovely shout-out to the store: "You have a beautiful independent bookstore here which is a cultural treasure." We agree. This piece, "Eulogy for a Friend," was originally delivered at the funeral of the Reverend Terry Burke, who spent thirty-one years as the pastor of the First Church of Jamaica Plain. The two were close friends and former classmates at the Harvard Divinity School.

THE WORDS *HONEY* AND *MOON*

Jennifer Tseng

Woo honked the horn lightly, unconvinced by his wife's urgings that it was an American custom. He was embarrassed as it was by the eight tin cans she had tied to the fender with string. Camille laughed at his timorous tapping and called it a "Chinese honk." Finally, when it was clear that he would not soon Americanize its duration or intensity, Camille leaned over, put both her hands on the car's black apple, and pushed with all her willowy might. The street filled with the music of their German car's horn, and someone nearby honked back. Though by this time, they were miles away from the church. The few who had stayed on the front steps to wave and to whistle their support were out of earshot and the newlyweds were on their way west.

They drove, according to Woo's plan, directly from the church to Kenosha, Wisconsin, and arrived in plenty of time to visit the Kenosha County Zoo, first on their list of dazzling destinations. The Kenosha County Zoo was no petting zoo. It was the largest zoo in the state of Wisconsin and contained an endless array of exotic animals. There were, among other mammalian and ornithological treasures, a pair of giraffes from the African veldt, a snow leopard from the mountains of Central Asia, a Kivu highlands gorilla, a flock of Palmetto flamingos, an Arabian cheetah cub (though no adult cheetahs), three black Louisianan swans, a few new-world monkeys, and a small family of zebras on loan from William Randolph Hearst's California ranch.

This multifarious collection met with Camille's instant approval and garnered for Woo a generous supply of bonus points in their slit eyes versus green eyes game. Her only grievance was that they did not have even one giant panda, the animal she most closely associated with China and therefore with Woo. He quickly appeased her with an optimistic allusion to an upcoming (petting) zoo in Nebraska. In his eagerness to please her, he too became excited and could almost see the dressy, oversized bears in his mind's eye, munching on crisp branches of young bamboo, next to their horse and cow neighbors.

For dinner they ate in a pleasant lakefront restaurant whose only distinguishing feature seemed to be its inclusion of a separate menu for children twelve and under, no doubt the feature that had captivated his colleague Mac's darling Isabelle and earned the restaurant its place on their list. To Woo's delight, Camille confessed she had never tasted shellfish or steak. In the spirit of education, he recklessly ordered one of each for her, along with a prime rib for himself. She was more easily charmed by the shrimp, those C-shaped curls of coral flesh, than she was by the steak, which she greeted with confusion as a bloody, cabbage-less version of her mother's corned beef. Where were the peppercorns, she wanted to know. Didn't he agree that peppercorns and beef were perfect complements?

"Ah ha, you are so gourmet for someone who never try gourmet before," he teased.

"I am?" she asked, and her eyes went greener and rounder than he had ever seen them.

Woo found dinner on the whole banal. He took solemn note of the frozen vegetables and canned fruits and thought wistfully of the day he would pick fresh corn and carrots from his own backyard, plump oranges from his own Valencia tree. He declined dessert but watched Camille suck on a series of spoonfuls of "orange" sherbet. The carnival color of those soft, sugary moons chilled him. He accepted a spoonful fed to him by her gemmed, ecstatic hand only to surprise her with the hope that she might open her eyes in response, which she did. To his palate, the taste was cloyingly sweet and artificial. He patiently kept this knowledge to himself, the way a parent might suppress the falsehood of Santa Claus for the sake of a child, though he made plans to introduce her to something finer as soon as the opportunity presented itself. Belgian chocolate, he thought, or macaroons. Surely there would be no mung-bean pastries or shaved ice with coconut milk en route to the western coast of the United States, and so he called to mind a list of all the superior European and American sweets he had tasted since his arrival in his wife's country.

"I'm still hungry," Camille said excitedly.

"That can't be," Woo laughed, while simultaneously calculating the bill so far. "Two appetizer, two entree, one dessert! Holy Toledo!"

"It's true," she smiled. "I get really hungry when I'm happy. Does that happen to you?"

"No such a thing. I'm hungry when I don't have food. Work hard, eat more. Exercise, eat more. Happy no happy, this is irrelevant."

"Well, I'm still hungry."

"Then you must be very happy," he said, looking at her directly.

"Mmmmhmmm," she hummed, her fingernail tapping the various dessert options in a jaunty dance on the laminated menu. "What do you think? A slice of apple pie with cheddar cheese or raspberry cheesecake?"

Woo brooded silently for a moment over Americans' preoccupation with cheese. It was his own pet theory that cheese was the culprit responsible for America's obesity problem. He entertained the thought of his leggy, slit-eyed child bride turned happy and voluptuous. He could get used to there being more of her, but if it meant eating out more often, whether or not his wallet could adjust was another story. Then he felt a pang of confusion. Had she ordered so much food because she was happy or was she happy because she had ordered so much?

"Tell me which one to get," she said. "You choose and we'll share."

"No, no, no. I don't want. Your favorite you pick."

"Are you sure? Is it okay? Am I eating too much?"

"My poor growing girl," he said. "You eat! You eat!"

She ordered the cheesecake with a scoop of sherbet.

"Mother says I don't eat enough. But at home I'm never that hungry. It's not that I'm unhappy, just not happy enough to eat. Not like now with you. I'm so happy. Why do you think that is?"

Camille chattered away while Woo listened and interjected the occasional peppercorn of wisdom to please her conversational palate.

"In China we have a saying, the best appetizer is hunger. Eating is like getting married. When you wait, when you are patient, it tastes good. When you are hungry, everything tastes like the best."

Later, when the waiter came to bring their dessert, he found the table was so cluttered by the many dishes Camille had sampled that there was no place to slip the bill except next to her right elbow. Woo reached awkwardly over the dirty plates to take the ticket.

It dawned on him that she did not have any money, probably not even a few coins in her small beaded purse. What sort of girlish things did she store in there? Lipsticks and tissues, perfumes and picture postcards of places she had never been? Now and in the future he must pay for her. He pulled two blue twenty-dollar traveler's checks from his wallet and signed them carefully. A Chicago bank had issued them to him; he knew they were valid, but the blue, almost purple color of the notes was so different from the green of American currency. It looked to him more like play money extracted from a children's game.

—

The Milky Way Motel was situated like a mole on Kenosha's high eastern cheekbone. Contrary to its illuminated sign, which promised a buxom, braided blond girl pouring a pitcher of glowing, milk-colored stars into the night sky, its small lobby contained a gaunt, spidery man with bruised eyes seated at a metal desk. Woo surmised that the girl from the billboard sign must have been born of this man's imagination, a girl from the world that existed behind the lids of his bruised eyes while he slept. It was dusk, and the man looked as if he might doze off momentarily. He was wearing square, plastic reading glasses that magnified the shadows on his face as he scanned the classified section of a newspaper and sipped from a small tumbler of milk. There was a poster of the solar system on the wall behind him and a Swiss-cheese block paperweight on the desk. The green glass lamp by which he read was the only light in the room other than the moon. Had either newlywed known of such a thing, they might have thought the office looked like that of a California fortune-teller's.

When Woo stepped into the dim, milk-scented lobby, the man held up a room key and continued scanning the classifieds.

"Good evening," Woo said, stepping up to the desk. "Pardon me, please. I am Joseph Woo. I have tonight reservations. Two people. Husband and wife."

The man continued reading and took a sip of milk. Woo wondered if he was to reach out and take the key from the man's hand. He didn't think it a wise idea.

"You're supposed to take the key," Camille whispered in his ear. "He's busy."

Something was wrong, Woo thought. He was sure this was not the custom. The man was supposed to take their names, signatures, identity verification. What kind of establishment was this?

He pulled out his wallet and found the three-by-three card that he had cut from a three-by-five to fit. There in his own Royal typescript were the words:

The Milky Way Motel
725 Lake Dr.
Kenosha, WI 53141

There were no Motel 6s in Wisconsin. Woo had hesitated each time he had booked a non-6 reservation. It was likely that independent motel keepers were not regulated to the extent that chain-motel keepers were. There was no systematic quality control, no centralized power to enforce high standards. The man at the Milky Way Motel was precisely the type Woo had feared: a lazy, unregulated clerk with no consideration for the customer.

He longed to be in Iowa—their next destination—where a Motel 6 clerk named Candy had given him clear directions not only to the motel but to the state fair as well. She'd recommended the apple fritters and told him to have a safe trip.

He thought that if they stood in front of the reading man long enough, he would have to look up, that shame or self-consciousness or both would force him, but the man continued reading and sipping like a machine. In fact, he seemed so undisturbed that had he not been holding out the key, Woo would have thought he hadn't noticed them. Had he not been reading, Woo might have thought he was blind. Finally the man finished his milk. As he tilted his head back toward the solar system to allow the last drops to fall on his tongue, Woo snatched the key angrily out of his hand. Woo was defeated. His fantasy of driving through the night to Iowa had been brief. Their day had seemed as long as his stay in America, a small lifetime. His new wife was tired, and he noted with affection that her green eyes were sleepy, verging on accidental slits. Such pale skin, such thin arms, such a long and fragile neck. So tired. They could not go back and they could not proceed. They must stay.

Woo carried both the suitcases upstairs to their room. Camille followed him like a sleepwalker. He fumbled with the key in the dark (surely Motel 6 would have lights burning near the doors at night), checked once more to see that it was Room 8, and then opened the door. The sight of the double bed filled his startled, exhausted body with a jolt of electricity.

"Woo Tai Tai," he said brightly, trying to maintain his composure. "Welcome to your bridal room."

"Woo Xiansheng," she said, climbing into the bed. "Your wife is very happy."

Woo turned the bedside lamp on and switched off the overhead light. Perhaps she would fall asleep immediately and he would not be faced with the frightening prospect of seducing her. Which was stronger? His desire to touch her or his desire to avoid touching her? He didn't know. She seemed to have fallen deeply, prophetically asleep.

He leaned his face close to hers the way he had seen her do with the names of the smallest towns on the maps. Her orange-blond hair smelled of green apples and of the German wood of his father's rolltop desk. He had thought it would smell of persimmons. This is not to say he was disappointed, no, not even mildly. He was fond of the unexpected fragrance, but it was yet another indicator of his lack of ability to calculate and predict in matters of Camille and/or in matters of the body. He continued to look at her face without touching it. He tried to understand its many parts, which moved even in sleep. The happy slits of her eyes quivered as she slept, and he could see the strange marbles of her eyeballs beneath the lids, crossing back and forth as if reading a hidden book.

There was a light dusting of freckles on either side of her elfin nose, so few in each sprinkle that the marks seemed like a mistake or an afterthought on the part of her maker. Between her nose and her lips was a slight valley dotted with fine downy hair, so pale in color that it was visible to him now for the first time. Her lower lip was larger than the upper; it looked almost swollen, and he wondered if she was feverish. But her face was not flushed, and he could feel without touching it that its temperature was cooler than that of his own. Her ears, which also surprised him by not detecting his approach, had lobes that were attached to the side of her face, so that the outline of the ear was one long continuous curve, unlike his own, whose curves were interrupted by the separation of the lobe from the rest of the ear. He thought hers a less formed and simplified version of his own. His discovery of this recessive trait pleased him in some way and emboldened him to touch her.

Of all her many girlish and alien traits, he found her eyebrows to be the most exquisite. Made of the same persimmon color as her hair, the brows were orderly, as if their maker had measured and cut and counted each feathery piece by hand, assembled the arcs, and then trimmed and combed them with a mechanical device. Woo touched each brow once with the tip of his middle finger as if painting them on. *Ruan de*, he thought. How soft. Softer than he could have predicted. Their softness made him all the more curious about the down valley above her lips. The fine pale hairs must be softer there in that ethereal slope, that tiny shadow. He thought to drag his tongue across the delicious ditch, but then Camille sighed heavily as if to warn him away. Better to let her sleep.

He took off his shoes and began to pad around the carpeted room in his socks. Through the picture window he could see the dark shine of Lake Michigan. There were several boats in the dock, and each one had a small light at its helm. The sight of the boats waiting to sail, the black water, filled him with sad thoughts, and so he walked away from the window and set to unpacking their things.

He would leave the curtains open so that his wife might see the water when she woke up. All through dinner she had looked at it and pleaded with him to take her to the beach the next day. She wanted to see everything in daylight. She wanted to lie on the sand. Was it like the ocean? She'd wanted to know. Though he'd planned to take her to a penny arcade, he deferred to please her and to defray costs.

He opened her suitcase without thinking for a moment that she might see it as an invasion of privacy. He had nothing to hide. Why should she? He hung up her dresses and brought her yellow-and-white toiletry bag to the bathroom. He unzipped the bag and began routing through its contents for her toothbrush, which he thought ought to be allowed to air dry to protect it and the bag from mildew. Camille had the good habit of brushing her teeth after meals, but he suspected that she seldom remembered to shake the brush after rinsing, and when she did it was not with much vigor. Of course, he had never witnessed her in the act of brushing, but he had made subtle inquiries.

He found her white plastic brush and its wet bristles without difficulty, though not before leafing past several other items, including a tube of lipstick, two paper packages each marked "slender regular tampon," a pair of tweezers, a beige compact, and a box of prophylactics still wrapped in cellophane, all of which electrified him. Though it was the sinister cellophaned box that delivered the deepest bolt to his body's core. This was very bold of her. She had been thinking something about him. The most maddening currents of fear and electricity crept through his fingers as he studied the box. It contained twelve prophylactics, and among the many words printed on its modest back were "pleasure," "contact," and "sexual intercourse." Woo threw the box back in the bag, zipped the bag, and pulled his hands away in haste, as if the items might electrocute him.

He stepped back into the bedroom carefully, afraid now more than ever to wake her. He hung his own clothes up next to hers, pulled out a few more necessary items (a fresh bar of Dove soap, a wash cloth, a jar of peanuts, an orange, a Chinese-English dictionary, the latest issue of *Reader's Digest,* and a pair of gray pajamas), and then stowed the suitcases in the closet. Then, as quietly as he could, he arranged the peanuts, reading materials, and orange on his nightstand and sat on the side of the bed that was farthest from Camille. Perhaps he should double-check the lock on the door, he thought. This he did swiftly. And the window. Was there one in the bathroom? He couldn't remember. He brought his personal belongings into the bathroom and closed the door. Locked it. Leaned into the shower to look for a window and found nothing but a minty expanse of tile.

Woo ran the faucet until the water was hot and then began turning the bar of soap over and over in his hands in order to produce a generous lather. He carried a bar of Dove with him wherever he went—to the university, to the library, to the movie house. Whenever he felt anxious, he excused himself from the anxious-making situation and went to the nearest restroom to wash his face. The strong smell of the soap calmed him, and the emollients left his skin feeling clean and elastic. Now he massaged the bubbles into his cheeks, breathed deeply, and waited for the familiar sensation to relieve him. What was wrong with him? The Dove trick had failed. He checked the bathroom lock and then changed into his gray pajamas. The light cotton trousers that were usually so comfortable made him feel exposed. The fabric was quite thin, almost sheer! Could she possibly see through it? No such a thing. Ridiculous. Time for bed. You'll feel more relaxed tomorrow if you sleep.

Woo slipped into the bedroom. He turned off the lamp and climbed as stealthily as he could into the bed. He closed his eyes and tried to quiet his breathing. The sheets were cold and slick, though his bride's body emanated warmth from its brief distance. When he opened his eyes, the room was filled with light and he was overcome by dread, thinking that morning had come. But only two minutes had passed. A large boat that he could now see was docking, its lights flooding their room. He closed his eyes again, and when it was dark again, he opened them.

Without moving his body, he turned his head to look at Camille. Her head was turned away from him, her hair a silky, messy flame on the white pillow. Slowly, slowly he lifted the covers up so that he might look at her. It was then that he was reminded she had climbed into bed fully clothed. This fact relaxed him somewhat, for now he was comfortably occupied with how wrinkled her clothes were becoming. Without a hint of irony, he said to himself that he should remove her clothing immediately and hang it up at once. There was the removal of clothing for the purpose of hanging it up, and there was the removal of clothing for other purposes. Each form of clothing removal was, in Woo's mind, easily compartmentalized, neither threatening to undermine the other, until, however, he reached out to unbutton the top button of his wife's blouse. He paused and boldly pulled the covers down to the foot of the bed so that he might see everything, only then beginning to understand his own truest motives.

To his utter fright and delight, there were only four buttons on her blouse, so that once he had unbuttoned two, he was already halfway to ecstasy or dread, he didn't know which. He unbuttoned the third and fourth quickly, afraid again of waking her, and then realized that the real terror would be in pulling the blouse open to expose her. This he did and almost choked on the air that was racing to reach his lungs. By a much-needed brand of newlywed's luck, he transformed the beginning of the choke into a subtle, even elegant throat clearing. He was determined not to wake her—not for fear that she would unwrap her sinister cellophane box, for that was swiftly seeming less and less sinister, but for fear that he might not complete his heavenly task of saving her wardrobe from wrinkles.

The skirt went next, side zipper, hook, eye, and then her red leather sandals with their crossed straps each fastened by a single sharp tooth of steel and a red tongue of leather, easy to release. As he arranged her sandals next to his own black shoes, his restless child bride pedaled her bare feet twice, as if on a dream-manufactured bicycle, and made a gurgling, little dove noise. Was she cold, he suddenly wondered? To him the room seemed warm, it was summer after all, but he could not presume to know how she felt then. Should he leave her underclothes intact and cover her? The wrinkles, unfortunately, were no longer an issue. He scanned the room for a thermostat and was overcome with gratitude to the motel staff, to even the blind reader downstairs, for furnishing such a luxury, when he spotted a compact silver box mounted next to the bathroom door. He raised the thermostat to eighty degrees and turned to his love.

She was in what is called by sleep experts, the "runner's position." Though Woo was no Freudian, he interpreted this change simply as an opportunity to unlatch and remove the elastic contraption that persisted in keeping her upper half secret from him. Her arms were languid and soft as he pulled them this way and that through the straps. His poor girl was being so good. Whether it was his accurate assessment of the depth of her sleep or his raving desire's rationale, Woo became convinced that Camille would never wake. He moved quickly to her lower half and unrolled her lemon-yellow underpants slowly out and down over her plump curve. He fumbled during the final moments of untangling the yellow bonds from her ankles and feet. When the bonds were free from her body and her body free from its bonds, he turned her from the runner's position so that she was on her back.

He looked at her. He watched her grow cold and stiff and then warm and soft again. He watched her return to the runner's position and pedal her feet and turn her head. He grew self-conscious and tried to read his magazine in the near dark. This cycle lasted throughout most of the night. He would watch her sleep and then grow self-conscious. He would read his magazine and then grow impatient with its drab articles and idiotic cartoons. He would curse the insufficient light, and then as if to punish himself, he would read on until he thought he would hurl the magazine at the picture window, and then he would set it quietly down on the night stand and resume looking at his nubile wife.

During these intervals he was ravenous and ate both the entire jar of peanuts and the orange, along with a roll of different-colored hard candies that he had found in Camille's toiletry bag. Any chance he may have had of falling asleep was quickly reversed by this massive intake of protein and sugar. The room was hot and smelled of peanuts. In Woo's opinion, a pleasant smell, a comfy cocoon. His pajamas were damp with sweat, but he did not dare remove them. Between his lovely bride and his tasty snacks, his jangled nerves and his exhaustion, the night provided him with a seemingly endless supply of tortured insomniacal bliss. It was not until the sun began to rise over the lake and Camille began to stir that Woo's eyes closed at last. As he fought and then failed to stay awake, he pored over the maps in his head, revised his budget, and thought of the strangeness of the words *honey* and *moon*. Were they two words or one? He reviewed the many words he had recently learned—*snow leopard, zebra, flamingo, raspberry, sherbet, Milky Way, prophylactic, Maidenform*—and thought it unlikely that he could possibly remember them all.

—

He woke at eleven a.m., and his first thought was of Pang and the terrible morning he'd slept past eight a.m., a story he'd never told Camille. And then, corroborating his fear that laziness leads to disaster, he heard the sound of his child bride vomiting in the bathroom. Eat too much, he thought. Maybe learn her lesson.

"Camilla," he knocked softly on the bathroom door. "You need some help? Can I get you anything?"

"No," she said whispering. "Please go away. I don't want you to see me. I'm sick."

"Silly girl talking nonsense. Daddy doesn't mind. His poor girl is sick, maybe need something, eh?"

"No, thanks, please go away!"

Woo dressed quickly and went out to buy her some ginger ale, which he found for sale by the can in a vending machine behind the building. He returned to find her in an orange sundress on the floor, tracing the strawberry-red line of the map with her finger. She looked as ripe and as healthy as she had the night before.

"I'm better now," she said, springing up and kissing his cheek. "I just ate too much. I think that's all it was."

"Drink anyway." He opened the can, wiped its aluminum lip, inserted a straw (one of ten he had taken from the restaurant), and handed her the ginger drink.

She sucked on the straw obediently, collapsing her cheeks and puckering her mouth until her sucking noise resonated as air and droplets in the empty can. She was cured.

They spent the day at the beach, on Milky Way Motel towels. Camille lay in her white two-piece bathing suit watching the water, while Woo, hatted and in slacks, sat reading the last of his Chinese newspapers. He refrained from looking at her sun-lotioned body and concentrated instead on conjuring images of her he had on file from the previous night.

The kiss on the cheek this morning had been a puzzle to him. They were not in the habit of touching each other. He thought with pleasure of the possibility that Camille had been awake for part or even all of his late-night roamings and that the kiss had been a clue to him, an affirmative peck. Now he longed for Iowa, if not for Candy the clerk, then for the day to end and the night to arrive so that he might have a second chance.

"Joseph," Camille pulled her hair back with a silver barrette. "Thank you for hanging my clothes up last night. I was so tired."

"Sure, sure. Sleep in your clothes no good. Not comfortable. Too many wrinkles."

"I really like that you did that."

"You did?" He was alarmed at the possible meanings she intended. "Were you able to sleep?"

"Mmm, like a baby." She tilted her face up to the sky and closed her eyes. "I thought you might be upset with me," she said with her eyes still closed.

"Why upset?"

"Well, you know, it being our honeymoon and all. I sort of slept through it."

"Sleepy girls need their rest, no problem."

"Can I ask you a personal question?"

"You talk nonsense. Anytime ask questions."

"Did I like it?" she asked, sounding intrigued.

"Shenma 'like it'? What's the meaning of this question?"

"Do I have to say it? I just mean, you know, did I like IT?"

"Shenma 'it'? What is IT?"

"What you did to me while I was sleeping."

"Oh, my golly, you're some kind of crazy girl! Number one, while you're sleeping I'm reading magazine, have some snacks. No such a thing do to you anything. Number two, you like something you tell me, I'm not telling you! Huh!" he grunted, mildly offended.

"You mean you really just hung my clothes up?" Camille started to laugh.

"What's funny?" Woo demanded. "Of course I'm hanging your clothes up for you. What do you expect?" He sounded shocked, as if the reckless thought of making love to her while she slept had never crossed his ancient, puritanical mind.

—

There are women who can articulate their wants quite clearly, so that for even the most inexperienced of husbands, supplying those wants becomes easier. And there are men who can, without their wives' lucid articulations, intuit their wants and expertly supply them. Neither Camille nor Woo were quite so fortunate. If just one or the other had been one of these types, the matter of their lovemaking would have been greatly simplified. But as it was, Camille had never been counted on to articulate anything before, much less something as embarrassingly intimate as her own physical wants, and Woo, a bachelor in the truest, deepest sense of the word, had never before supplied anyone's wants but his own.

This they quickly learned during the series of long nights that unfolded in variously sized Motel 6s across the country. Each was patient with the other afterward. Their nights were tender even as they failed to satisfy. But the continuous lack of known demands, coupled with the continuous lack of successful supply, led to a relational revolt that took a toll on their waking hours. Each injured party responded in a different way to the crisis.

Woo lost interest in their evening ritual entirely. That is, he began by feigning a loss of interest that then conveniently turned genuine. Certainly at first the electrical sensation he'd been experiencing in Camille's presence threatened to derail his celibatic mission, but eventually he found that the longer he ignored his own electricity, the less frequently the voltage flared up. He'd never felt quite so manly and utterly in control before and was relieved to be rid of that dangerous tangle of wires—so many variable bolts and sparks and invisible force fields exploding and firing without his permission. Better to maintain control of the charge, to ignite it and snuff it out for his own benefit only.

Camille, on the other hand, became insatiable. Her eyes were fierce slits more often than not, and the many attractions that had delighted Mac's easy Isabelle did not satisfy Woo's impossible bride. No roller coaster was fast enough, no carousel horse the right color. He won carnival game after carnival game, but none of the fun prizes caught her eye. The cotton candy was too sweet, the popcorn too salty, the petting zoo full of nothing but farm animals. "Where are the pandas?" she cried. "Why can't we go dancing?"

She began demanding more and more—she wanted dinners out and movies, museum tickets and dancing—a number of items that were not on their itinerary nor part of their detailed budget. She wanted Iowa City instead of Des Moines, Badger Creek instead of Lake Anita, Kansas instead of Nebraska. All of it arbitrary, Woo was convinced. All of it designed to madden him. The more she asked for, the more he refused. This he did not out of spite but on principle. There were times when he adored her fierceness and longed to turn the car in any direction she wanted to go, but his principles outweighed his adoration for her and he drove on.

When they arrived at the Motel 6 in Des Moines, she refused to get out of the car. "Why do we always have to stay at Motel 6? I don't want to stay at another one." She had her sandaled feet on the dash to spite him and was looking at the map through the slits of her eyes as if plotting an alternate route.

"Motel 6, what's the problem? We have reservations." Woo didn't understand. What a nice clean motel! The night before had been particularly tender and unsatisfying, and their daytime personalities were revolting.

"I don't mind staying in a few here and there, but every single time? What will people think?"

"What people?!" Woo shouted, incredulous.

And then, for the first time since their journey west had begun, Camille understood that she was stranded. There were no other people. No heartland, no mother, no father, no movie dates or trinkets, white rabbits or dried plums—just a husband. She began to cry.

There was nothing, aside from sex and communism, that frightened Woo more than tears, and so while Camille wept over the road atlas, he went into the Motel 6 office and canceled their reservations. He got on Interstate 80 going west and began searching for signs to Lake Anita.

It was at Lake Anita (for which he had silently sacrificed the highly touted Badger Creek) that Woo and Camille encountered a handful of those "people" whom Camille had unwittingly referred to, just thirty miles earlier, as if her naming of them had made them exist. The incident, which Woo was loathe to recall in detail, involved a group of four ten-year-old boys who suddenly and in symphony threw wet stones at Woo's sweatered back while he was at the edge of what he thought was a desolate thicket, relieving himself. He was in midstream when the first stone struck, though his sweater cushioned the stone's impact and distracted him from seriously considering its source. Ping! Ping! The second and third struck in quick succession, and then a shower of smaller stones, also wet, hit him like rain. The usual racial epithets were hurled as well, and then as quickly as they had ambushed their man, the boys vanished into the thicket. *Ha ha, ha*, he could hear them, *heh, heh, heh.*

Woo did not let the incident disrupt him. He finished out the stream, shook and tucked himself in; button, then zipper, then belt.

Camille, who had watched through the car windshield, sprang up out of the car when he returned. She rushed up to him and kissed him on the cheek. It was a kiss of the same variety as the kiss in the motel room, the sort she spontaneously doled out on rare occasions.

"Why didn't you yell at those lousy jerks?" she asked.

"This is minor incident. Too much trouble for nothing," he said, alluding to a wider spectrum of incidents she knew nothing about.

"Why didn't you at least tell them you aren't Japanese?"

"Why didn't you?" he asked.

She bit her thumbnail and looked down at his sweater, which he had taken off and folded.

"Why were you wearing that sweater? It's so hot! If I was a man, I'd take my shirt off."

"No such a thing. It is unsafe to expose oneself in an isolated location. Hot, cold, doesn't matter."

"Gosh, that's so paranoid," she said. He had looked so funny in that sweater, standing in the August sun.

After the two of them were in the car again, she watched his black eyes scan not just the unknown road in front of them but both mirrors and the shoulders, too. From time to time he looked briefly at her face. She saw that he too was stranded. No Chinatown, no bachelors, no newspaper, no plums. In the cities and towns to come, who would understand him? Who, if not she, would keep him safe?

—

So it was that the newlyweds, each marooned in their own way, made of the time remaining a temporary life. He drove the car he had given her that she was incapable of driving, and she held in her small lap the many maps he had purchased for his own private pleasure. They ate fresh fruit and dry cereal for breakfast, according to his taste, and they stopped at McDonald's for lunch according to hers. They adhered to Mac Celan's list of restaurants for dinner, less because their tastes correlated with his or Isabelle's but more to prevent disagreement between them. Woo misplaced Celan's list of favorite destinations, and it was just as well.

In Nebraska, he bought her a set of checkers, and it became their habit to play in the motel room after dinner. Sometimes while they played, they sipped ginger ale poured from cans into complimentary tumblers filled with complimentary ice. The ring-shaped pieces of ice, which Camille loved to slide on her fingers, Woo retrieved from a metal machine every evening. It was Camille's duty to take as many complimentary postcards from the Motel 6 lobby as was appropriate, according to the number available and the clerk's disposition. When she was bored, which was seldom, she shined his shoes, for he loved his shoes to be shiny but disliked blackening his hands. And when he was feeling tender (also seldom), he ran her a bath.

Their German engine rumbled and coughed and dust flew through the open windows. They were always in the car unless it was evening, and because of this, Woo felt dirty at the end of each day. She learned that his sweat, like water, had almost no discernible odor; he learned that she hummed while she ate. He sensed at times that she was homesick; she began to suspect that he dyed his hair. Both grew accustomed to the sound of traffic roaring past them, the sounds of "people" motoring swiftly and mysteriously past them, even as they slept. The bright red-orange 6 became a beacon to both, though it meant something different to each of them. They exhausted their supply of prophylactics and did not buy more. It was difficult to connect that which they did in the dark with their nomadic, sunlit selves.

Their conversations quieted and then ceased, and that was for both of them an unexpected comfort. And then one morning they crossed the California state line and Woo said,

"Tonight we will be home." And Camille said, not without a sadness, that she had lost track of the days and in so doing had almost forgotten where it was they were going.

Jennifer Tseng spoke candidly about her experiences as a librarian on Martha's Vineyard during an event highlighting Mayumi and the Sea of Happiness *(Europa Editions), a Papercuts favorite and Tseng's first novel. Hear the audio at papercutsjp.com/audio-broadcast.*

PART III

Summer

'TIL DEATH

He can't get her to leave.
She glares at him in the mirrors
growls each time he smiles.
The judge declared them
split, irreconcilable
but he didn't check the walls.
He tries changing addresses,
but she moves with him,
dangling from his DNA.
He sips green tea
to cure her headache,
though he once drank espresso.
Careful to turn out the porch light
before he goes to bed,
he still hears her barking orders in the dark.
He tries to escape with Leo Bloom
but she cuts his fingers with the pages;
he gets nowhere, just closer to the end.
Another woman briefly took him
everywhere she could.
But it was not away.
Before he got the wife
he thought his worst nightmare
would be living alone.

—Sandra Storey

MILL BURNERS

Stona Fitch

They clawed at the thick door with rusted hammers and fire axes. The loud boys wanted to see what was inside the top floor of Crown Woolen; the quiet ones were ready to give up and leave it locked forever.

"I know there's something good in this one. Got a feeling. They locked this place up for a reason." Whit stared at the door as if he could dissolve it with his eyes. "Let's get at it."

They took turns smashing at the door until their pale faces glistened with sweat and their breath steamed in the cold air. When the hasp broke and the heavy lock fell, then they stepped back to make way for Whit.

"Now we'll see what they were hiding." He pushed the door open to reveal a vast workroom. Their flashlights washed over rows of peeling wooden beams and an emptiness that seemed to stretch on without end. Dust swirled in their flashlight beams and soured their mouths.

Silence settled over the boys as they gazed at their latest disappointment. Some of their friends broke into abandoned factories and mills and posted their videos on ruin porn sites. But these boys weren't here to explore.

"Motherfuckers!" Whit threw the lock and it skittered across the floorboards into darkness.

The boys said nothing. Only Whit imagined buckets full of gold coins waiting behind every locked door. At best, they found broken looms like the sprung works of a giant's piano. Whit said he could come back with a truck and sell the machines to museums in Boston for thousands of dollars, but he never did.

The boys huddled near the doorway as if waiting for someone to invite them into the silent, lunar room.

Kevin pointed his flashlight deep into the gloom and the dim light fell on a slump of bodies scattered on the floor. "What the hell is that?"

Whit walked slowly toward the shapes, hand on his knife.

"Let's get the fuck out of here," whispered Kevin, always the first to doubt.

Luc shoved Kevin toward the Doyle twins, John and Paul, red-haired and feral.

"Fuck off," Paul said, shoving him back. "I want to see."

Whit pulled his hunting knife from his belt and knelt on the floor next to the bodies. He slit one open and reached in.

"*Yes sir, yes sir, three bags full.*" He tossed handfuls of wool in the air to float down in gray clumps.

The boys walked closer to kick the bags.

"I don't know about you," Whit said, "but the moon's making me crazy tonight. I'm feeling . . . vivid." He knelt and unbuckled his studded belt. Straddling a bag, he cut a slit with the tip of his knife. "Who's gonna get some?"

"Not me. No way," Kevin said. "I'm ain't fucking an old bag of wool."

Whit mounted and pushed inside. "Whatever. All I know is this feels mighty good. Almost like the real thing."

The Doyles dropped their flashlights and claimed their mates, pushing deep into the wool, soft and slick, warmed by their heat.

"*Gross*." Kevin gave a quick shiver. "Hey, what about rats?" he shouted. "Did you think of that? You guys feel any rats in there? Nibbling or anything?" But nothing could interrupt their ancient rhythm.

Kevin held up his cell phone. "Smile for Reddit."

"Shut the fuck up," Whit shouted. "At least we're getting some." Sheathed in his black leather jacket, Whit's narrow back rose and fell, and the chains on his boots rattled on the floorboards.

"Some *what*?" Kevin rolled his eyes. "It's too cold to be whipping it out," he said to Luc. "Know what I mean, dude?"

"Right." Coupling with bags of wool was just the latest of Whit's stunts. *People who have to prove they're crazy,* Luc thought, *probably aren't.* Then an urgent stirring made him almost join the others on the floor.

"The first time I do it, it's not going to be with a sheep in any form." Kevin waved his cell phone in a slow arc across the ruined workroom, so much like all the others. Socantum Thread. Boxford Wire. The Jenckes loom factory. These and many more had been pillaged, but none raped—until tonight.

The dyer's apprentice stepped from behind a distant wooden post, thumbs hooked in the pockets of his pleated wool trousers, gray shirtsleeves rolled to his elbows. He watched the boys hunching on the ground. *Comme des chiens,* he whispered, lips blistered from drinking the lye that had looked so much like milk.

But little dogs, eh? Imogène whispered to the handless girl, forearms severed by a loose transmission belt.

One by one the Youngest Workers stepped out of the shadows like a catalog of mother-fears. A fallen pallet of Scotch woolen claimed the crushed girl. Imogène, once at the end of every loom fixer's gaze, hummed to herself, her long white dress glistening with amniotic hemorrhage. Blackened faces marked a regiment of the burned.

Their hard stares followed Luc and the others, so inappreciative of being alive. A living boy's days charted a clean trajectory, like water arcing up and over a mill wheel, while their nascent souls stalled below in the murk of eddying leaves. Luc would grow older and stronger. He would fall in love, work, make money, see the world beyond the valley, grow older, falter, die. But they could only hover in the mills, revenants caught in amber.

The groans turned louder, sending the Youngest Workers retreating to the dim corners. Whit let out a howl, followed moments later by low grunts from the twins. They stood and wiped themselves with flannel shirttails.

Whit fastened his belt and walked over to Luc. "Don't know what you're missing."

Luc raised his eyebrows, tucked his hair behind one ear. The stark moonlight turned him black and white, dark hair on pale skin. "You're disgusting," he said. The others gave nervous laughs.

Whit's smile fell, and he pulled his arm back to slap Luc, but just stared him down. His hand floated down to Luc's shoulder, and he smiled at the new boy, the smartass, his favorite. "I like that, Luc. Fucking brutal. No respect at all."

"Respect leaves no room for honesty," Luc said flatly.

"You guys hear that? *Respect leaves no room for honesty.* Lofty, ain't it? You're like a poet, Luc. A fucking poet. I tell you what. You keep being honest. I mean that. I do." Whit was breathing hard. They all were—a handful of Kevin's Ritalin amped up the night. "We're destroying the temple. We're stamping out the vineyard!" Whit's hair flailed in wild strands like an inky mop.

"That's good, yes?"

"That's real good, Luc. Now, let's get to work, boys. You, Mister Robert Frosty the Fucking Snowman, keep a lookout."

Luc sat next to the window and watched the others grab Whit's narrow legs and raise him up to scratch a black pipe, looking for copper. Whit squinted at the pipe. "Probably lead. They didn't give a shit if their workers got poisoned."

Luc shrugged, unmoved by the plight of long-dead strangers when his own was much more urgent. So far tonight, he had already spent ten dollars for food and gas at the QuikMart, and there was no sign of a windfall coming his way. A coin glinted in the dust, and Luc knelt down to pick it up, but it was just a shiny penny that had fallen from one of their pockets. He tossed it toward the corner of the workroom. He needed more than pennies.

Luc first saw Whit working behind the counter at Vinyl Solution in Smithville. With his wild hair and leather jacket, he looked like he might be a roadie for a metal band. But he drove a wrecker for his father's junkyard during the week, worked at the retro record store on weekends.

"Do you like to burn things?" he had asked Luc at the checkout counter. On that day, Luc quit complaining about the valley and started destroying it.

A section of tin ceiling fell with a crash, and Luc remembered he was supposed to be watching the road. He scanned the dark woods, the abandoned lot behind the mill. In the distance, headlights crossed a bridge.

Whit glanced at him. "Everything okay, poet boy?"

Luc gave him a fast smile. "Yeah, okay. Really fine."

Whit stabbed at a pipe while Kevin and the Doyle twins swayed beneath his weight. "Get with the program, morons."

They tumbled to the floor, raising squalls of dust and stirring the Youngest Workers in the corners.

The boys stood, picked up their flashlights and cell phones. Whit reached down to retrieve his knife, stuck deep in the splintered floor. "That's it," he said. "Next time we bring a fucking ladder."

Whit pulled a can of lighter fluid from his leather jacket and sprayed a long line across the floor toward the bags of wool. He struck a match.

Kevin backed away. "Shouldn't we be downstairs before we burn this sucker?"

"Lift high the cross!" Whit held the can high. The stream passed close to the flame and dripped fiery clots on the crusted floor. The wavering blue flames shot across the workroom.

The boys ran toward the door. Whit backed out, admiring the rising flames, then joined the others stomping down the stairs.

After the last footsteps faded, the Youngest Workers stepped out of the shadows. Flames spiraled up to blacken the dry beams and raced along frayed wires. The Youngest Workers walked toward the cleansing fire, which couldn't hurt them anymore, could only set them free.

"Was that another job well done by the Bomb Squad or what?"

"What?" Luc sat in the front of the van, where Whit liked him to ride.

"You know. B–O–M–B Squad. Burners of Mill Buildings. Came up with it last week, remember? I think it's a pretty good name for us, if you ask me."

"Yeah, okay." The name hadn't really taken off with the boys, who thought of themselves as something less than a squad. In the back of the van, they struggled with silent guilt. Kevin imagined burning timbers falling on some honest firefighter, father of four, the kind of tragedy that brought out the plastic donation jug at the QuikMart. Paul Doyle worried somehow that the wool bags wouldn't burn, that investigators would find his clotted seed and identify him like they did on *CSI*. The cops would storm into homeroom and reveal him as a mill burner, a wool humper.

"When I go away to the vo-tech next fall, there's going to be a real chance for you to step to the plate, Luc."

"What does this mean, 'step to the plate'?" Americans seemed to have a secret dictionary of confusing phrases that his mother laughed about. *A head above the rest. In it to win it.*

"It means you've got a real opportunity to take charge of the squad," Whit said.

"Yeah, okay."

"I know what you're thinking."

"No, you don't." Luc was thinking that there had to be better ways of scraping up enough money to get back to his real friends in the Marais.

"You're thinking you might not be up for this gig, ready to take the reins and truly wail on the mills," Whit smiled. "But it's a land of opportunity."

"So what?"

"In America, any little boy can grow up to shoot the president." Whit looked over to watch Luc's reaction, but he just stared out the window.

"What I mean is, we've all got unalienable rights here in America. We can make our beliefs known to the world through freedom of expression, as guaranteed by the Bill of Rights. Burning mills is my way of saying *Forget the past. History is shit.* Others may take up arms. But all I need is a dollar seventy-nine can of lighter fluid and a pack of matches, which stores give you for free, generally."

Luc nodded. They drove through the outskirts of Hartwell, past the blinking bank clock, a martial-arts studio, a parking lot mounded with leftover Christmas trees blanketed with snow.

"I mean, you could get some real attention for the squad, a fast kid like you. You could take our work to a new level. I mean, people around here are really starting to see a difference."

Luc shrugged. There were hundreds of mills in the valley. Their work, as far as Luc could tell, had gone unnoticed. Sometimes weeks passed before anyone found burnt timbers and exploded bricks deep in the woods. The blazes earned only a couple of lines in the *Mill Valley Call* at best.

He cleared the foggy window with his sleeve and the snow-glazed playing fields of Friendship Park appeared. "Let me off here."

Whit slowed the van and the others lurched forward. "Catch you later."

Luc opened the van door and looked back. Whit's wild hair looked no more menacing than a clown's wig. His dark eyes gleamed in the moonlight, and he seemed to be waiting for Luc to thank him. For what? For wasting another long night? For not finding anything valuable in the mills, again? The others were asleep in the back, piled like dogs. Luc jumped down and slammed the door, walking away without looking back. The van sped off toward Farnumsburg, tires skidding.

Luc's boots marked the new snow on Harmony Street. A religious sect founded Hartwell, planning to farm the crops of Bethlehem and build a glass temple. But in the end nothing paid like millwork. The true believers took jobs tending looms. Only the uplifting street names remained.

Ahead waited the dark hulk of the L'Evangile mill. Snow-covered stairs led to entryways locked with rusted chains. Plywood covered the tall banks of windows. The enormous looms once set Hartwell thrumming. Now a carnival scent of machine oil and rot floated from the rows of shattered windows. Luc shivered as if a cold creature brushed by him on the street, seeking warmth. He passed the dark mill and turned down Joy Street, walking toward what he called home, for now.

For the release of his novel Third Rail, *Fitch brought strong cocktails to his spring event with novelist J. M. Taylor at Papercuts. "Mill Burners," is a chapter from* White Spirits, *a novel in progress.*

FORest-9176

J. M. Taylor

Driven from his house in the middle of the night, driven by that . . . *harpie,* Ed desperately needed a place to stay. Alone at the diner counter, he opened a newspaper. He knew he couldn't afford his own apartment. Not if he needed to ante up first month, last month, and security. Not after she'd emptied their joint account. Reluctantly he flipped through the listings past one-bedrooms, past studios, until he came to Rooms to Rent.

Has it really come to this? After all that I built over the years, she turns on me for one wrong step? Couldn't she remember all the good he'd done in their lives? Couldn't she remember just one good thing? The blunt nub of a pencil rested in the crook of his fingers like the cigarette he wished he could be smoking.

"Those days are long gone, my friend," the waitress, a tough old bird like himself, said. She sloshed more coffee into his cup. "You know they got better listings on Craigslist," she said. "My daughter found a place that even had a yard for a kiddie pool."

Ed shook his head. "The best places still advertise in the paper." He circled one, then another. "See? The old ways are the best ways."

She put her finger over another, and he circled that, too. "Three right off the bat," he said.

—

The first place was taken. At the second, he found a pair of cackling gnome-like brothers watching four mismatched TVs in a Dickensian shell of a mansion with bare, dusty floors and plaster walls crumbling with mold. He left before he even saw the room.

He found the third house, the one the waitress pointed out, on the edge of the city, not far from where he'd grown up. Small houses, neat yards. Madonnas on the half shell.

Put on a show of confidence, he told himself, stepping onto a weathered porch. He knocked and someone moved inside. He heard the lock shoot back.

The woman who peeked from behind the door was no elderly shut-in. Ed's breath hitched in his throat. She looked to be in her thirties, with brown hair to her shoulders and small oval glasses. A smile as neat as the lawn.

"Um, hi." He held up the folded newspaper. "I'm here about the room? Or did you beat me to it?"

The woman laughed lightly. "No, I'm renting it out." She looked him up and down. "Are you willing to make yourself useful?"

"Sure am," he answered through his smile.

She opened the door wider and put out her hand. "I'm Belle. Come in and have a look."

"Ed," he answered. Her hand was delicate, like a butterfly's wing. He followed her inside. Everything plain and clean. "The room's in the back," Belle said over her shoulder. "I'm afraid it's a little dated, but it was my Gram's. She wouldn't 'hold with newfangled ideas.' You know, like color television."

"Sounds like my kind of gal," Ed chuckled, immediately regretting his stupidity. But she laughed, and he watched Belle's figure, in tight jeans and loose blouse, sway to the bedroom. Her small feet padded along in plain canvas shoes.

A short hall off the kitchen led to a bathroom, then the back room. Belle opened the door and waved him in. He got a whiff of her perfume before it died in the mustiness of Gram's den.

"You weren't kidding," he said, stepping into the room. A twin bed with ornate posts and knobby bedspread filled the far dark-paneled wall. A threadbare love seat sectioned off part of the room. Next to it, a yellow rotary phone crouched on a little table. The chair faced an old console radio and turntable unit as big as a counter. "No TV," she said. "But if you're interested, Gram kept some old records in the cabinet."

By the green-shaded window there was a small breakfast table and a single wooden chair. It still had a hot plate, sugar bowl, and heavy ashtray made of yellow glass. "The rent was pretty low, even with being useful," he said. "I'm surprised no one else has taken it."

"The last boarder just moved on," she said. "And I'm careful about who comes in. There's a lot of creepy people, you know. But you seem pretty safe." She smiled and he grinned back. *Yes, things were definitely looking up*. He turned quickly, pretending to examine the room more closely, and then said, "I'll take it."

She handed him the key. "You can use this bathroom, and there's a shelf in the fridge for you. I only ask that you don't go through the rest of my house. That's private, ok?"

"More than ok. Thanks."

"And about the phone. Keep the long distance at a minimum, all right?" They both laughed.

Then he added quickly, "Don't worry. I can cover the rent. I'm getting unemployment right now, but I'll get something any day now." *Thank God they let me have that, after what they threatened to do.*

"Oh, I could always find a way for you to work off what you owed if it came to that." Something in her voice disoriented him, but then she winked and his heart started again. "The thing is, you have to pull your weight in this world. Either with money or . . . some other way."

That night, after he moved his meager bundles in, Belle came in to invite Ed to dinner. He jumped when he realized she was right beside him. He'd been setting up a mirror on his bureau, but it must have been angled away from the door, or he would have seen her coming. "It's just meatloaf and roast potatoes," she said. "I don't know how to make much else, but Gram liked them. So did my last boarder."

He ate seconds, then thirds, while she watched. When he finished eating, Ed said, "Reminds me of my mother's. You're gonna fatten me up."

Belle grinned and Ed felt that strange stirring again, but he reminded himself she was both his landlady and too young for him. He asked her how it was she was at home herself in the middle of the week. "Gram left me a lot of properties scattered around the city."

"With single men staying in each of them?"

She raised a mischievous eyebrow. "A husband on every porch, you mean? You never know." It seemed like an offer, but before he could say anything, she stood up and started cleaning the table. She shook off his offer to help. "You've got your own little world to arrange." She jerked her head toward his room, and he read it as a dismissal.

The sunset lingered in the sky. It would take no time to put the rest of his things away. "Time for Ol' Blue Eyes," he said to himself. He sifted through the pile of records and found *In the Wee Small Hours*.

It reminded him of his parents, how they'd play it on a Saturday night after he went to bed, still laughing at whatever trouble Jackie Gleason had got himself into. He'd hear the tinkle of ice in glasses, their quiet murmuring, a little shuffle to the music. Nothing like the hell he'd just gone through. The record finished, and he put on another, and another. Before he knew it, it was near midnight. In the dark, he smoked a cigarette and examined his room. *It's coming along,* he thought. *They wanted to punish me, but look where I landed.* A few minutes later, he was dreaming fitfully. He woke up with a feeling that someone had spoken to him in the night, a familiar voice, but it was gone, leaving him with a vague uneasiness.

He spent most of the following week delivering job applications and eating cheap lunches in the park. This week, the beginning of October, Belle was on a business trip, so he came home to a dark house. She traveled a lot, but she never complained. He even thought she looked more rested when she came back. "Where do you go?" he asked her once.

"Just checking the properties," she said. "You know, all those husbands on porches."

That night he ate from a tray on his lap in front of the stereo. He wasn't in the mood for Sinatra, so he turned on the radio. He spun the knob up and down the AM dial. Nothing but static.

Sighing, he stood by the window. The paper said there'd be a meteor shower tonight. He pushed up the sash, leaning out into the chilly night. Clear skies. It should have been good for the radio but . . . *hey, there's one!* Jiminy Cricket warbled in his head. What should he wish for? Probably to go back, back before all the horror of the past year. Harassment? Embezzling? The monsters decided to believe the worst about him. Didn't they remember all the good he'd done for them?

On a whim, he picked up the phone again and tried his childhood number, turning the rotary dial more to listen to the familiar clicking than anything. He remembered it by the old exchange word, FORest-9176. As each number slid through the dial, he felt the vibrations as a gentle caress on his ear.

To his surprise, it rang. Of course, the number had been reassigned. It hadn't been his in over fifty years. He was about to hang up, too guilty to go through with a prank call, but then it was too late: someone picked up.

"Hello?" said a little boy no more than eight.

"Hi." Should he hang up? No, follow through. "Can I talk to your mommy or daddy?" he asked.

"They're not here." *What kind of parents left a kid alone that young these days?*

"What's your name, young man? Isn't it a school night?"

"School's out. My name's Eddie."

He laughed. What were the odds? "That's my name too."

"Oh," said the little boy. "What do you want?"

"Just to talk to your parents. When will they be back?"

"I don't know." He seemed to drop his worry, and said quickly, "Do you like to watch TV? I sure do."

"Sure," said Ed. "What are your favorite shows?"

He talked to the little boy for over an hour. Somehow it was no surprise that little Eddie watched the old black-and-white comedies Ed remembered. And all of his friends had the same names as Ed's. Where were they all now? Then Eddie abruptly said, "I have to go now. Bye."

"Wait! Eddie, can I call you again tomorrow? Would your mother mind?"

"I shouldn't, but she won't be here. You can call. Bye."

Ed once heard that radio waves and old TV broadcasts went on forever into space. That somewhere out in the universe, some beings might be watching *I Love Lucy*. Did the same thing happen to phone calls? He tried calling his old friends. Harry, Bill, old Johnny MacIntosh! The numbers leaped out of some forgotten vault in his mind. But one after the other, he got the jarring tones signaling an out-of-service number.

—

The unemployment checks ran out in the middle of January. When he told Belle, she just smiled. "Well," she said. "You could paint the bathroom and wallpaper the front hall. I'll get you the supplies." He also cleaned out decades of junk from the basement, left behind by other boarders, she told him. Panting with the effort, he felt like one of those gnome-like men from the second room he'd gone to see.

One snowy morning, while Belle was on another trip, he was shoveling the driveway. Before he knew what happened, he'd slipped, dislocating his shoulder. The pain shot through him like a snake bite. He couldn't drive with one arm, and would never be able to pay for an ambulance and hospital visit. Fighting tears, he found a doctor in the phone book who he could walk to. The physician put his shoulder back in place, hung a sling around his neck, and gave him a packet of Percocet.

Before he left, Ed asked the receptionist if he could use the phone. He tried calling Belle, but she still wasn't home. He left a message anyhow. Then, his shoes soaked through with snow, he made his way back home, the burning pain in his shoulder keeping him warm. When he got back, the house was silent and cold.

For the first time, he felt truly alone. His shoulder throbbed, and he couldn't find a way to lie down without aggravating it.

Hours later, he finally slipped into a troubled, sobbing haze of Percocet and pain.

A squeezing hand on his bad shoulder jerked him awake. Belle. "I got your message," she said. The corner of her mouth twitched like a cat's, and her eyebrows nearly touched over her nose. "I can't take care of an invalid. You need to leave."

"By Friday?"

"By tomorrow," she said. "Or sooner."

Before he'd focused his eyes, she was gone. He heard the front door slam.

He lay back in bed, his shoulder screaming. Where would he go? He couldn't afford a motel. He couldn't even drive. Would the harpie take him back, just for the night? Who was he kidding? He remembered her last words to him: "Only a monster would steal from a children's Last Wish charity, then screw the intern on the break-room counter."

Desperate, he dialed his only friend.

"Eddie," he said, breaking into sobs. "I've made so many mistakes."

"Ask her to let you stay," Eddie told him, as simply as any child.

"I owe her too much as it is."

"If you don't ask her, we can't talk any more."

He tried to sound cheerful. "I'll call you, Eddie, wherever I am."

"No," the boy insisted. "You can't."

"What will happen to you, then?"

"Just go ask her. Please."

Ed sighed a long, jagged breath. "She's not even home."

"Yes, she is," Eddie told him. "She's upstairs. I have to go. Please." He hung up.

Ed staggered through the dull scent of new paint that hung in the kitchen, past the newly papered front hall. As Belle had demanded, he'd never gone upstairs. Without hesitation, he went up now.

How did he let himself become the stupid wife in the Blackbeard story? His mind reeled through a thousand images from movies, from *The Twilight Zone*. What would he find? He imagined Belle as some giant black widow, her bedroom an intricate web.

He reached the second floor and pounded down the hall. He noticed that everything up here seemed new, fresh, not like the old crap downstairs. The closer he got to her door, the cleaner it got. Her room was right above his own. Did she listen to him crying himself to sleep every night?

The throbbing in his shoulder gave him strength. In two steps he covered the short hallway. His chest was heaving with the strain, but he needed one more burst of strength to take down the stout door. He braced himself and tilted his good shoulder toward the wood.

But before he made contact, Belle had swung the door open, and he just managed to keep his balance.

"I told you not to come up here."

Ed stood dumbly, his eye skating across the room. He was mildly disappointed. No webs, no torture devices. Belle was in a simple pair of pink pajamas, her hair unkempt. The only threatening thing about her were her eyes, which blazed with fury.

"What are you doing?" she demanded.

"I . . . well . . ." Had he fallen so low? All he'd ever wanted was a little attention, a little love. He wondered if he'd lost his mind. He must have. How else to explain how he'd spoken to his boyhood self? A twisted sob escaped from his throat.

"Ed?" Her voice wavered. Not a monster's hiss.

She leaned against the doorjamb. A movie seductress pose. She'd taken off her glasses and rubbed her eyes tiredly. He felt the stirrings of hope deep in his belly, and a bit lower. But then he saw her skin ripple, and, just for a moment, he saw her unearthly form. "Ed. I'm sorry. Here, sit down." She waved him into her room, pointing at a stool by the window. She patted him on his good shoulder as he passed. He could still feel the gesture even as he sat down.

"What are we going to do?" she asked. He didn't like that patronizing tone.

"I just need a job. But something's going to come through, I know it."

"No, Ed, it won't." She sounded sad but sure.

"If I just . . ."

She put up her hand. "No," she said. "You've missed too many calls. Some of them sounded quite promising. But they weren't . . . useful to me. And you know, I can only keep my pets so long as they're useful to me."

"I got calls and you didn't tell me? Why?"

She put her glasses on again and smiled. It didn't make her look any better. "Call it your pound of flesh. But Ed, what about all those late-night phone calls? Long distance is expensive, you know. And that's mighty long distance."

Ed's fingers went numb, and the tingly feeling crept past his wrists, toward his shoulders. He wanted to stand but found he couldn't feel his feet, either. He blinked. "Wait. Pets? What are you, some kind of monster?"

"You were an easy catch, Ed. Gram spotted you at the diner right off. But if you can't be a worker drone, your usefulness is pretty much at an end. I'll need a new boarder."

"You're going to kill me." His arms, his legs were fully numb. He could feel it reaching greedily toward his heart.

"No, Ed," she laughed. "Too late for that. No, I think I can find a place for you in one of the pens. Remember that run-down wreck of a house with the two brothers? Milch cows, so to speak. Very good when I'm feeling run down. You'll be new blood." She smiled. He noticed she had too many teeth, and they were needle sharp.

"The phone calls? Eddie?"

"Oh, that poor kid. This is probably a good thing for him."

He could barely breathe. "What do you mean?"

She loomed over him. "Do you know what happens after death, Ed? Not heaven, not fire. Just memory. The lucky ones get remembered happily. Most are just forgotten and go into oblivion, like little Eddie. But you, Ed, you're going to be remembered. By your ex-wife, your coworkers, everyone who read about your miserable, petty office escapades. That's hell, Ed. And you've been in it since the day you knocked on my door."

The cold hand touched his heart.

J. M. Taylor was an avid supporter of Papercuts from the start. We feel like we unearthed a treasure when we learned he had written the dark and twisted novel, Night of the Furies. *We had a great event with him and author Stona Fitch (Rory Flynn) at Papercuts for some boozy and brutal Prime Time Crime.*

SHUTTING THE DRAWER:

WHAT HAPPENS WHEN A BOOK DOESN'T SELL

Edan Lepucki

In August of 2011, I published the following essay on the books and culture website The Millions. At the time, I had a two-month-old son and no offers on my first novel, *The Book of Deeds,* which had taken four years to complete. Writing about the pain of rejection, and the hope I still nurtured for future literary success, was enormously cathartic for me, and I was grateful to receive so much support from readers of the site. Many people who commented on the essay urged me to self-publish, which led me to write two subsequent pieces for The Millions: one about successful self-published authors, and one about why I didn't want to go that route. At the time I was hard at work on my next novel, and my agent was eager to submit it to traditional publishers. She did so a year later, and the dejected writer who wrote the following essay would be thrilled to know that, this time, we triumphed. *California* sold to Little, Brown in the fall of 2012 and came out in the summer of 2014. After an impossible-to-predict turn of events, which included a dispute between my publisher and Amazon, and an unlikely champion named Stephen Colbert, *California* debuted at #3 on the *New York Times* bestseller list and got more attention than I could have ever dreamed of. I found readers! (People, this was not how I expected my first publishing experience to go.)

Rereading this essay makes me feel a little sad for my first novel, which was ferocious in interesting ways, but also deeply flawed. Mostly, though, I am happy my career took the path that it did. *California* is a better novel than *The Book of Deeds*, and I'm proud to call it my debut. I'm a stronger writer and person because of the rejection I struggled through, and the enormous luck that *California* enjoyed—well, I am still thankful every day for it. Such luck led me to Papercuts J.P. on my paperback tour, after all.

—Edan Lepucki

P.S. The fake bio mentioned at the beginning of the essay has led to Wikipedia believing I was born in Poland. Stupid Internet!

1.

In May, after my novel manuscript had been read and rejected by a healthy number of editors, my husband rewrote my author bio. It read as follows:

> *Edan Lepucki was born in Lodz, Poland, in 1981. He currently lives in East Bushwick.*

As an American woman living in an uncool neighborhood in Los Angeles, I thought this hilarious. I also wondered—not entirely seriously, and not entirely in jest—if the revision might help my situation. My situation being that my agent had begun submitting my book nine months prior (not that I was keeping track), and it remained unsold. Admittedly, there had been close calls with two different editors, but, as everyone knows, *almost* only counts in horseshoes and hand grenades. I was in the same place I'd been back in September. That is, unpublished. The waiting game was starting to char my soul; if you drew a finger across it and put that finger to your tongue, it would taste bitter. Joking with my husband ("Now that I'm nursing, I'll send them a new author photo, cleavage and all!") was one of the few coping mechanisms I had left in me.

Now that it's almost September ("If anyone in publishing actually worked in the summer, I would've sold my book by now!"), the jokes aren't as funny. The truth is, my novel isn't selling, and it probably won't. There, I've said it. Eventually, a writer must accept rejection, accept the death of her first true darling, and move on. Can I face that sobering reality? Can I put my first book into the drawer and shut it?

Others have done it before me. There's a long and rich history of successful writers whose first (second, third . . .) books didn't see the light of day. I remember when Myla Goldberg came to speak to the creative writing department at Oberlin. She explained that *Bee Season* was actually her second novel. "My first," she told us wide-eyed undergraduates, "you'll never read." At twenty, I thought this terribly tragic. In the *New York Times* Book Review, Dan Kois wrote about novelists who abandoned books for one reason or another: Michael Chabon's infamously unfinished tome, *Fountain City*, for instance, and the burned pages of Gogol and Waugh. But the differences between these authors and myself are important. Firstly, they all had dazzling careers, failed book or not. I can't (yet . . .) say the same for myself. Secondly, these authors decided to kill their books, whereas my darling was murdered.

Just let me be dramatic for a moment, okay? Murdered! My book was murdered!

Or was she? A friend pointed out that I was waiting to sell my book to *publishers,* when I could sell it to readers, all by myself. That's true, of course. Self-publishing is as easy as it's ever been, and if done well, it can even be lucrative. But, in most cases, self-published authors spend money, not make it, and they have to be their own editor, copyeditor, publicist, and book cover designer. I certainly could self-publish my novel, but I don't have the cash, time, or talent to do it successfully. Plus, there's still a stigma to publishing your own writing. Though this is changing, I've never been an early adopter. (I used my AOL email account well into the new millennium, y'all; I leave the experiments to the innovative types.) The truth is, I want a reputable publishing house standing behind my book; I want *them* to tell you it's good so that I don't have to.

So, okay, I'm willing to let my book die, if that's to be its fate. With all my talk of murder and barbecued souls, I'll be the first to admit I'm letting myself wallow. But can you blame me? I'm grieving nearly five years of hard work. I'm mourning sentences, characters, and scenes that I'm still proud of. Letting go hurts. A lot. A friend of mine once said she didn't want to write a novel because she couldn't stand the idea of working for years on a project that might fail. One of my writing students recently told me she's so afraid her book won't sell that the very thought makes her hyperventilate. Another friend said she might die if her novel wasn't published. I identified with all of these confessions. I felt them myself. Not selling my novel was my biggest fear, and it's happening. It happened.

(I was in natural, unmedicated labor with my child for thirty-six hours. For twenty-four of these hours, my cervix remained only five centimeters dilated. No matter how relaxed I remained, how deeply I breathed, there was no progress. None. More than once during the process, I thought, "This is like trying to sell a fucking novel!")

(There's a moment, right before a newborn baby breaks into a wail, when his face wrinkles up, collapses in on itself like an imploding building, and sorrow, pure and clean sorrow, sweeps heavy across his features. I know this feeling.)

Goodbye, goodbye, Novel #1.

2.

The thing is, rejection is instructive. Over the past year I've learned that hearing "no" doesn't get easier if the stakes are higher. Reject my piddling short stories, and I will barely flinch; mess with my dear book, and I'm rendered immediately vulnerable: "immobilized, apologetic," as Alice Munro writes in her masterful story "Something I've Been Meaning to Tell You." I urge my students to go for it and send out their work, that they have to get used to a life of disappointment if they want to be writers. As if one can get used to such a thing.

I've also learned, however, that a thoughtful rejection is a valuable one, especially coming from an overworked, underpaid editor. To have taken the time to read my work, and written feedback—that's something I appreciate. This is called relationship building, I am told. I have more than one friend who sold books to editors who rejected their previous one(s).

Lastly, these months of rejection have taught me the difference between being tenacious and being stubborn—and being stubborn and being desperate. My agent can continue to shop my novel around, but I have already attended its funeral. I've said my eulogy, eaten the casseroles, wept in the shower, screamed into my pillow. I have willed myself to move on. I must, in order to continue my life as a writer. I haven't lost my tenacity, I've simply refocused it on my next book, which

I'm more than halfway done with. (This is the upside of a submission process that takes forever). Novel #2 deserves my full attention and care. Without it, my work—and I—will suffer. And this new book, it will be published. If it doesn't, well, I'll just *die.*

Edan Lepucki spoke with us in the summer about California, *her* New York Times *bestselling postapocalyptic novel. Then she signed a turkey baster. It'll make sense when you read it. Audio of the conversation—about family dynamics, gender roles, and the future of our world—can be found at papercutsjp.com/audio-broadcast.*

A COUPLE OF WRITTEN THINGS I DO NOT MAKE MY LIVING WRITING

Nicole Galland

I grew up on the island of Martha's Vineyard and continue to live there intermittently as an adult. Besides writing novels, I also maintain a tongue-in-cheek advice column for the *Martha's Vineyard Times* and pen occasional personal essays for *Martha's Vineyard Arts & Ideas* magazine. When Papercuts invited me to contribute to this anthology, it occurred to me that two of the *Arts & Ideas* pieces worked in tandem as commentary on the often-agonizing Art of Writing. The first, "The Writer's Block Quilt," reflects my uncomfortable relationship to writing before I made my living at it; the second, "Giving Voice," looks at the same relationship after half a dozen published novels. Both pieces were first published in *Arts & Ideas*; "Giving Voice" was also posted on the blog maintained by The Revels.

The Writer's Block Quilt

A while ago, something wonderful happened to me, which ruined the next several years of my life. I won a screenwriting award, for a screenplay set on Martha's Vineyard in the 1940s.

Hollywood having a thing for award winners, in record time I had an agent and a manager. An A-list production company had an A-list director and an A-list actress attached, and I left the Vineyard to move to Los Angeles because clearly my destiny was to be a screenwriter.

In less than six weeks, the whole deal fell apart. Then there was a new deal, better paid, which teetered on preproduction before it, too, fell apart. For about a year, I juggled five part-time jobs—three of them critiquing other people's screenplays for production companies. I was in my midthirties, living in an exurb of Los Angeles that I hated. Everyone back home on the Vineyard was waiting for my Oscar nomination, which added a certain level of guilt to my shame and stress.

I pitched so many stories, to so many people, to resounding nonresponsiveness. I wrote screenplays that nobody but my manager read. Industry friends told me to just keep cranking out story ideas. It was all about story ideas. It was all about character. It was all about snappy dialogue. It was all about pitching. It was all about taking meetings. It was all about everything except good writing (although, of course, everyone wanted to go on record as saying that it really just came down to good writing).

Instead of writing from my heart and gut and soul, I was simply trying to think up clever ideas, which (since they were not coming from my heart and gut and soul) did not excite even me, let alone studio executives. After two years of trying to function according to the Rules of the Industry, when I was simply not wired for it, I was fried, tapped out, depressed, exhausted, and broke. I was desperate to do anything, anything at all—except write. For eight months, my days consisted of waking up, trying to write, failing, attending to my various part-time jobs, trying to write, failing, then going to bed.

I was that kid who was always bad at arts and crafts, but I was now so desperate for creative expression that I didn't care how awful the result was, as long as I could *do something.* So I stopped trying to write and instead signed up for sewing classes. I learned to quilt and made a quilt for my firstborn baby nephew.

"It doesn't suck!" I said of this quilt, with amazement and relief, when I had finished it. The lovely old biddies in the sewing shop laughed and said, "Of course it doesn't suck. You're pretty good. Keep going."

Within two months, I'd made three more—one on commission! I got paid for it! More than I could say about my writing! My boyfriend bought me a sewing machine, and I decided that was it—from now on, I was a quilter.

There are lots of different quilting styles, but in most, the pieces of fabric making up the pattern are called *blocks.* I was responding to a writing block by focusing obsessively on quilting blocks. I chewed on this for about a day, and suddenly the image of the Writers Block Quilt sprang fully formed into my head: a quilt in which the blocks contained quotes about writer's block.

Designing a quilt is a lot of work. This one was more work than my others, because in addition to a pattern and color scheme, I needed to choose specific quotes, and then learn how to print colorfast words directly onto cotton fabric, which was a technical pain in the butt. While I was at it, I printed labels, only one of which is extant because it's sewn to the back of the quilt: "Writers Block Industries. Quilts and other sundries made by Nicole Galland when she ought to be writing."

I searched books of writerly quotes and advice (which was therapeutic on its own). From many dozens of statements, I chose twenty-five that I found helpful ("Start on Page 3"—Kurt Vonnegut) or at least reassuring ("The first draft of anything is shit"—Ernest Hemingway), and sometimes even inspiring ("I wrote my first novel because I wanted to read it"—Toni Morrison). Then I measured and pinned and cut and sewed and quilted, my conscious mind focusing on something refreshingly distant from the source of my pain, but my unconscious mind feasting on the words of writers I admired who had been through what I was going through.

When I was finished, I had a quilt. But I also had the effects of a little alchemy, transforming one kind of block into another. I'd spent dozens of hours focused on the craft of writing while thinking I wasn't, and there was no gentler way for me to lead myself back to the blank page.

A week after finishing the Writers Block Quilt, at about two in the morning, I suddenly knew—the way you can only know things at two in the morning—that it was time to get back to work immediately. I started writing again, obsessively, and I didn't stop until I finished my first novel, *The Fool's Tale*. I mailed the completed manuscript to my manager, who showed it to an agent, who sold it ten days later.

Many years and not a few novels later, I have forgotten how to thread a sewing machine. I'm not sure if I should mourn that fact.

Giving Voice

Because I make my living at it, I took the "novel-writing" skill set to be a comprehensive toolkit for creative fulfillment. Or at least for *my* creative fulfillment. Having done time as an actor, director, and screenwriter, I was pretty confident that the novel-writing groove was my one true Happy Place.

Then, unexpectedly, at the age of forty-nine, I became an alto. Talk about a game changer.

For my first forty-eight years, I self-identified as soprano, which was code for "On a good day, I can sort of sing the melody maybe, if I already know it." I wasn't a singer. It began as a lark, a fluke: my husband, Billy Meleady, had a leading role in the Christmas Revels show in Cambridge, so on a whim I auditioned for the chorus—and (to my astonishment) got in. As an alto. As a *what*?! That meant I'd have to sing the harmony, not the melody. I had never done that, ever, in my life—and now I'd be doing it at Sanders Theatre in front of twelve hundred people a night.

Singing harmony in the Christmas Revels chorus snatched my toolkit from my hand, yanked me out of my groove, and hurtled me 180 degrees away from my Happy Place, leaving me disoriented and bewildered.

It was *fantastic*.

I'd never thought to inventory the Unavoidables of Long-Form Fiction until I encountered the Unavoidables of Choral Singing and realized they were each other's perfect counterpoints. One thing (among many) I learned to appreciate in choral singing: counterpoint is *awesome*. Following are some examples of how doing the opposite of My Most Favorite Thing Ever also ends up being . . . My Most Favorite Thing Ever.

Executive function. When you create and populate a world and determine its characters' motivations and behaviors, you're playing God. You're the ultimate CEO. Yes, creativity draws upon the right side of the brain, but structuring an entire book requires a lot of left-brain effort. The buck starts and stops with you.

Counterpoint: When singing in a chorus, you give up executive functioning to the music director or choirmaster—he, not you, calls the shots. Somebody else's left brain is running the show. You're not generating, you're just interpreting. Take off your God Hat for a while—it doesn't belong in this rehearsal. Doesn't that feel better?

Distinctive voice. Every writer has a particular tone, approach, patter, point of view—call it what you will. A good author, without being precious about it, is hip to their own distinctiveness and nurtures it. Huge responsibility, that.

Counterpoint: There are some amazing soloists in a good chorus—but most important is that your voice blends well with others. Unlike nonverbal pastimes (gardening, cooking, sports), you're not taking a break from logocentric expression—just from the pressure of making your logocentric expression stand out as "something special."

Work alone. Even when you have collaborators, writing a novel consists mostly of you sitting down all by your lonesome, and just doing the damn work. Hour upon hour, day after day.

Counterpoint: Except for procreative sex, singing in harmony is possibly the only human activity that by its very definition cannot be done alone: you cannot sing in harmony by yourself. Other people are innately a part of the experience.

Focus inward. I listen to the rooster crowing outside, and appreciate the smell of the roses, and pat my dog, and thank my awesome husband for bringing me a perfect cup of tea, but these are all distractions. The best work happens when nothing outside of myself requires my attention. (Ideally for days at a time.)

Counterpoint: As a choral singer, the last thing you want to do is get lost inside your own head. Listen to what's going on around you. That's where the action is, on the other side of your ears from all the writerly stuff. Be in this moment, here and now. Pay attention, don't shut it out. Your inner monologue just gets in the way.

Forget your body. When you write, you glue yourself to the seat, sharpen the pencil, or charge the laptop—or perhaps get on your walking treadmill or settle in with your voice-recognition app. Get your body comfortable and then, if you're lucky, forget it exists for a few hours.

Counterpoint: Multiple studies, from Canada to Australia, have measured the positive effects of singing on the body. It works many core muscles and beneficially affects other bodily systems. In short: singing is the lazy person's extreme sport. By the end of the writing day, I feel the need for exercise; by the end of rehearsal, I feel exercised.

Embrace permanence. Writers work toward something that will eventually be set in print. Once a book is published, that's the book. You cannot keep writing it, and even if you wish you could disown it, it will still exist.

Counterpoint: Music is ephemeral. Once you've sung the song, the song is over. Even if you're recording it, that's literally just a record of it, not the thing itself. In writing, the writing and the written are enmeshed. At the end of the writing day, I have something I can return to later to continue. At the end of rehearsal, all I have is the experience of having sung.

Coda: The relationship between Novelist-Happy and Choral-Singer-Happy is not a competition. They're in harmony. There is resolution between them. And as polar opposites go, they mirror each other beautifully, for both are creative acts designed to give voice to something within oneself. These two things happen to be my polarity. Whatever your bliss is, find its counterpoint and enjoy the harmonizing.

Nicole Galland and her adorable pup Leuco, along with Benoit Denizet-Lewis, author of Travels with Casey, *and Cat Warren, author of* What the Dog Knows, *joined us to discuss her novel* Stepdog *at our first annual Papercuts Puppy Panel.*

Raven, owned and handled by Marcia Koenig of King County Search Dogs, on site at Oso mudslide in March 2014.

THE DOGS OF OSO

Cat Warren

"The Dogs of Oso" was adapted from a piece by Cat Warren originally published in The Dodo *magazine April 5, 2014.*

Gray-and-black mud coated everything. It was seventy feet deep in places, shot through with huge, shattered evergreens, splintered houses and outbuildings, twisted cars—all pushed together by the force of the slide. A river had backed up and flooded parts of that mile-square pile. Scattered somewhere beneath were the missing and dead. And it kept raining.

The primary search for victims of the Oso landslide in March 2014 continued for weeks. It was purgatory, created when part of a mountain sheared off and roared to the bottom of a river valley in Washington. Smaller-scale searches went on for months.

Cadaver dogs, also called human remains detection dogs, were at the epicenter of that search. Labrador retrievers, German shepherds, golden retrievers, even a Weimaraner, ghostlike yet still vibrantly colored against that glacial mud, scrambled to balance on logs and pick their way over the rubble of crushed houses. Sometimes, they sank into the mud. All the time, they used their fine noses to detect the complex odor of human death.

The dogs, handlers alongside them, had to work slowly and methodically. Moving itself was a challenge, even for a canine with four legs and agility training. Their human handlers were clumsier. They crawled over huge logs. Avoided twisted metal. Pulled boots out of mud the consistency of freshly poured concrete. Sometimes, they left a boot behind. A helpful firefighter would rescue it and help get it back on the handler's foot. Handlers cleared dogs' nostrils when they took too deep a snort into the mud to catch scent. They had to keep the dogs from slipping off floating debris or logs and getting stuck underneath. They helped their dogs slide down into and out of ponds created by the incessant rain and the flooding river. All the time, the dogs were checking, checking, checking for scent.

During that time, I listened to dog handlers as they described that terrible scene. I was nearly three thousand miles away in North Carolina, wishing that I still lived in the Northwest where I grew up. Wishing I were there, at the scene. Wishing that my ten-year-old cadaver dog, Solo, were much younger, or that my agile, juvenile cadaver dog in training, Coda, were older. But they were bookends, each at one spectrum of a dog's life. It's not that any cadaver dog handler wishes for a disaster. To the contrary. But if there is a disaster, you want to be there, working with your dog. That's why you train.

Sadly, everyone at the Oso site knew within the first few days that it was a recovery effort, not a rescue effort. No victims remained alive under what had been a tsunami of mud. The earliest euphemism that media and officials used for the search at Oso, "specially trained dogs," was abandoned during the first week. No, the dogs at Oso were cadaver dogs, trained specifically to search for the scent of human remains. As tragic as this disaster was, cadaver dogs still provide hope. It's crucial work to recover the dead.

The slide roared down the mountain at 10:37 a.m., March 22, 2014. It engulfed a full square mile, including a rural neighborhood. By March 30, twenty-one people were confirmed dead. By April 18, thirty-nine were confirmed dead. Four people were still missing.

Yet, the count of the missing went down slowly but steadily, and the number of identified dead went up just as inexorably. Cadaver dogs, both handlers and officials said, were crucial in helping both to pinpoint victims' locations and to narrow areas to search. Everyone knew it might not be possible to recover and identify all the victims. But dogs, handlers, and searchers were all part of a team that steadily lowered the number of missing, one muddy step at a time.

"Every area we went to, I was told, 'Dog teams are our main resource, our guides,'" said Cat Best, of Walla Walla Sheriff SAR K9, who worked the area with her black German shepherd, Izzy. It was the first disaster she had worked. She was honored and awed to be there.

Another handler, Phoebe Duke of Intermountain Search Dogs out of Spokane, Washington, worked with her nearly nine-year-old golden retriever, Porter, for three days at Oso, rested, then turned around to do it again. The search, she said, was "totally around the dogs."

Cadaver dogs have to have more than good noses. The disaster at Oso was an ideal example of the demands placed on search dogs. Of course, they need to recognize and signal to their handlers that they've detected the scent of human remains, with its hundreds of volatile compounds. They also have to be willing to go in, to go up, to go over in search of scent. At Oso, getting to that scent was difficult. Scent was probably wafting from underwater, running down the current of a backed-up river, getting pulled into the debris of log piles, or barely slipping out from under many feet of mud, perhaps because a piece of debris had given it enough space to escape to where the dog's nose could capture it.

Nonetheless, for the dogs working to detect the scent of human remains at Oso, it wasn't traumatic, as some people assume. Depressed dogs don't work. Human death, for well-trained cadaver dogs, is simply a smell associated with a game, with a reward, with play. Cadaver dogs associate their particular job—finding the dead—with positive things, not with tragedy. That's the way it should be.

That doesn't mean that the work at Oso wasn't hugely demanding and tiring—for both dogs and handlers. Handlers and their flankers marked spots where a dog had expressed interest or alerted. Then they moved on. Sometimes, if a dog showed interest, rescue workers would bring in another dog to see if they could narrow the area or to confirm the first dog's interest. Then searchers came in with shovels and hands, and sometimes a backhoe to get underneath. If someone were found, or if part of someone were found, they were carefully removed.

But sadly, the search at that particular spot didn't necessarily end with that recovery. No one could know, if another dog returned to that site and expressed interest, whether or not there was another victim six feet farther down in the mud. It might simply be that the second dog was honestly still finding residual scent from the victim who had already been removed. Or not.

For the humans, it was an excavation of heartbreak and informed guesswork and infinite sadness.

On a disaster scene, just as in all difficult work, it's never about one thing. It's a team effort. There is no perfect tool. Experienced, working dog handlers know their canine partners—as amazing as they are—can't provide all the answers. Dogs aren't magic. Mud, water, sand, and debris can change where scent is, or block access to it entirely. And in a disaster of this magnitude, sometimes what the trained response handlers are accustomed to seeing, such as a dog lying down or barking, isn't there. Handlers have to know their dogs' body language, to watch to see if they are interested, or "in odor." And sometimes, even if a dog alerts, effectively telling the handler "I smell something here," the handler needs to keep moving with her dog while others take over.

"It can be very frustrating," said Marcia Koenig, of King County Search Dogs. "You may never know." Marcia, with more than forty years of search-dog handling experience, worked the Oso landslide tirelessly, up to her knees in mud, with her seven-year-old sable German shepherd, Raven.

Even experienced dogs and their human handlers were pushed to their physical limits at Oso. They became exhausted in what was a horrendous search environment. The mud and water were bone-chilling. Yet, there were few injuries, except for a couple of scrapes and cut pads, and a case or two of hypothermia.

Despite the cold and the rain and the chaos, the dogs at Oso did manage to communicate their knowledge to their handlers. They accessed places unsafe for people. They worked off lead, directed by commands and signals. The dogs' noses gave searchers places to focus their attentions in a square mile of mud. The handlers knew that dogs' noses can only do so much. They can only say, "This is where I find scent is the strongest." That doesn't mean, "This is exactly where the victim is located." Scent moves. Think about a colored smoke bomb and what it does in wind and in rain, and you start to get the picture.

Nonetheless, and in numerous instances, people who worked at Oso say that the dogs were the first step in helping return the dead to their families and friends.

The dogs worked their hearts out, said Marcia Koenig.

Marcia Koenig is an experienced handler. She and her prior search dog, Coyote, were flown to Guam in 1997 when Korean Flight 801 crashed and tore a ragged hole down the mountainside. She worked after Hurricane Katrina in 2005. She's the kind of person you want to work with: cheerful, enthusiastic, happy to see other handlers and their dogs succeed. She and her husband, Andy Rebmann, have trained people and dogs across the world how to look for the dead. Andy was the primary author of *Cadaver Dog Handbook*, my bible when I started learning how to train my first cadaver dog, Solo, in 2004. Andy was on the site at Oso as well, to help coordinate some of the efforts and to use his German shepherd, Carlo, on a water search.

But even with more than four decades of search experience, Marcia found that Oso presented new challenges to her, to other experienced handlers, and to their dogs. Oso also showed handlers new sides to their dogs. Raven is usually standoffish. Andy calls her "The Princess." At Oso, Raven stepped down from her throne.

"Normally she has no interest in strangers and just turns away from them," Marcia said. At the search site, every time someone wanted to pet her, Raven snuggled up to them, licked them, and tried to crawl into their laps if they were sitting down.

Cat Best, who had never deployed on a disaster, although she had been on a number of searches, watched the hundreds of hours of training her black German shepherd, Izzy, pay off. She was enormously grateful for that feeling of becoming one with the dog: "The directions we had practiced so many times—forward, back, left, right, up, over, and this way—became imperative for survival and an ongoing conversation between us. We navigated logs, across quicksand, me in my human form just trying not to fall, Izzy with strong dexterity, like she had done it a million times."

So the cadaver dogs, over days and days, worked scent on what handlers came to call "the pile." Searchers and handlers took the dogs' interest, used their knowledge about scent, and figured out where to go next. In the meantime, some dogs who had worked several days got a well-deserved break. Dozens of dogs from many different states moved on and off the site.

All forty-three victims of the mudslide were recovered. More than eighty volunteer canine teams from seven states searched for victims. The last-known victim of the slide was recovered in July 2014.

While the old adage, "train hard, search easy," couldn't be applied in this case, facing mountains of mud and debris, that doesn't mean handlers and trainers didn't immediately start thinking about how to incorporate the lessons they learned from Oso to future trainings.

Driving home to Spokane after several days of searching, Phoebe Duke and her fellow team members were already jotting notes on how they could make sure their dogs were even better prepared: making sure all the dogs were used to getting on ATVs, getting them accustomed to helicopter-blade backwash, training them so they could balance easily on log piles, even when those logs shifted under their feet.

And Marcia Koenig, though she admitted she was covered with bruises and exhausted after days of searching, was already planning to go out training—to work with the dogs, to make sure the dogs were happy and successful. To make sure they were ready for the next search.

Oso remains the single most deadly mudslide in in the history of the United States.

At the Papercuts Puppy Panel in July 2015, New York Times *bestselling author Cat Warren spoke about her experiences training her cadaver dog, Solo, and the fascinating science and behavior of our canine companions.*

FIVE MYTHS ABOUT CHEATING

Randy Susan Meyers

MYTH: Affairs happen because something is wrong with the marriage.

TRUTH: Something is wrong in every marriage. Marital issues never justify infidelity.

Of course it began with a man. Aren't troubles with men a woman's daily bread? Worse yet, I slept with the trouble and he wasn't my husband. It was a cruel secret I kept. Adam's marriage crimes were cold but not savage, and certainly not deserving of infidelity. I drank guilt for breakfast, but in the beginning, I believed my connection to Guy Peretta was *bashert*—though I doubted my forefathers thought the definition—destined—included screwing around on your husband.

The truth of my situation sharpened each day: I wasn't cut out for affairs. Shame overtook exhilaration by the time four weeks passed, not that penitence meant a damn after I'd ransacked Bloomingdale's lingerie department for black lace I'd wear for another man.

Being wanted was a hard habit to break. For the past week I'd combed the Web, hoping to understand what propelled me from sixteen years of faithfulness to two months of cheating. Now I'd completed my education. Tonight I'd end the affair.

Molly and Jack raced to the dining room, ready to eat the dinner drying out in the oven. I'd held off serving the meal, waiting for Guy's half-hour-late call, but I couldn't delay any longer. Hungry children trumped lovers.

"I hate Rachel." My daughter landed in her chair with a thud. "She's contemptible. She went after Zak all day at school. God, life is revolting."

"Really?" I picked up the tongs and placed a chicken breast on Molly's plate, trying to find the right tone to show how much in solidarity I stood with her romance dilemma.

"Really. It's truly revolting," Molly repeated, as she speared a sweet-potato wedge. At fifteen, she became fixated on a different phrase each month, using the words until Adam and I wanted to scrape every syllable off her tongue.

Jack furrowed his brow. "Is it?"

My eight-year-old still expected fairness and happy endings. I smoothed back hair from his anxious face. He needed a haircut. Adam's hand-me-down Celtics sweatshirt reeked. "Don't worry, baby. Life is only revolting during the temporary condition called adolescence."

Molly groaned. "Do you even hear yourself, Mom? Where's Daddy? Is he working late again?"

I picked up my wine. Now I missed Adam. Not because he understood Molly better, but with him here there'd be two of us to absorb our daughter's disdain.

"Daddy's stuck with an emergency." Adam's dentistry practice guaranteed at least one patient disaster per week.

“Beth’s family always eats together.” Molly reached across Jack for the water pitcher. Table manners barely registered in my parenting triage these days. “What’s wrong with us?”

“Face it. We’re pathetic,” I said.

Jack’s face fell till his chin almost hit the table.

“I’m kidding!” My son required deftness, not witticisms, and I failed him on a regular basis. “Someone’s tooth cracked. Daddy’s being a hero. Should we wait for him to eat dessert with us? We’re having ice cream and brownies!”

Three minutes into dinner, and already I walked motherhood’s lowest road of mothers, using bribery to skirt controversy and a plethora of exclamation points to cover up my lack of maternal aptitude. Not smoking in the house constituted the sole conduct in my plus column, putting my children’s lungs before my need to suck in great soothing gulps of nicotine. For them, I tried to keep my smoking secret—for them, Adam’s readiness to kill me if he caught me with a cigarette, and Molly’s overwhelming willingness to turn me in.

“We’ll wait,” Molly said. “It’s revolting to think of us shoveling in ice cream while Daddy has his hands stuck in somebody’s mouth.”

My cell buzzed. I held the phone as far from Molly as possible when answering.

“It’s me.” Guy spoke in a cautious low tone. “Are you alone?”

“Can I call you back?” I mouthed *Grandma* to the kids.

“I’m about to leave,” Guy said. “How soon?”

“Two minutes. I’m taking the phone outside.”

“Put on a jacket,” he said. “The temperature feels more like January than November.”

MYTH: Affairs are all about sex.

TRUTH: Many affairs begin as purely emotional connections. Sex wasn't the original intent when the relationship began.

Guy worrying about my heat index registered as foreplay. Adam assumed monitoring the weather fell under my purview, which included preventing my own frostbite, as well as his, Molly's, and Jack's.

"I'll only be a minute," I told the kids as I rose. "There's more chicken."

"Aren't you eating with us?" Jack's wounded tone was close to perfect. I feared he got that from me.

"I will, as soon as I call Grandma."

"Why are you going outside?" Jack asked.

"Smoking, right, Mom?" Molly would be happy to know her too-thick eyeliner provided a terrific accent for her evil side.

Ignoring her seemed the only smart path.

"Grandma will hear you exhaling and she'll tell Daddy." The little priss was becoming a miniature Adam. "He'll know anyway, because you'll reek of tobacco."

I gave my once-lovable child a big phony smile. "I'll be right back."

Once we crafted shoebox doll beds and sewed tiny blankets as I inhaled her pure luminescence. Now, at fifteen, surly edged her exquisiteness. Her skin, like Adam's, tanned through ten layers of sunscreen. Her hair, like his, almost touched black, but his was curly, almost kinky, though he kept it so short you'd never know. Molly's fell through my fingers with the slip of cream. I didn't know where it came from, her lustrous hair. Probably some hidden Greek on our family tree brought in by an illicit love affair. My side of the gene pool.

Smolderingly beautiful had always been my goal, but the best rating I'd grant myself was wholesome, and with enough makeup, pretty. Despite my piled-up Sephora points, mirrors terrified me as I waited for gravity's final toll. *Forty-four* drummed in my head as I held on to pretty by my teeth.

I grabbed my cell phone and an old barn jacket I kept hanging by the door, patting the pockets where I tucked cigarettes and matches in a frayed pair of mittens, hideous purplish-brown ones in which Molly wouldn't be caught dead.

Rotting leaves we'd piled but never tossed crunched and then nagged at me as I settled on the back steps. Half-completed projects and unmet good intentions surrounded me. Determination to avoid Guy-lust competed with newly hatched plans to bag the leaves as I pressed in Guy's number.

To do:

Break up with Guy.

Bag leaves.

"Hey," he answered, midring.

"Hey, yourself," I said. "Thought you'd call earlier."

"Sorry. Bad timing?"

"Sort of."

A sticky silence hung on the wire for a moment. We were only wired for romance.

"Did I mess you up?"

Code for *Is he home*?

Pebbles scattered as I kicked the ground. "I can't talk long. The kids and I are about to eat."

"Is tomorrow all set?"

No matter how hidden the relationship, decency required a face-to-face breakup.

So. Tomorrow. Wednesday.

Jack's sixth-grade class had a trip to the Science Museum. Then he'd be at Davy Berger's house until Mrs. Berger drove him home. Molly would be at play rehearsal until at least six, maybe later.

Think, think, think.

Wednesday.

Adam worked late on Wednesdays. Dependability had always been one of his good qualities, and never more welcome than these past months. However, meeting Guy meant calling my mother-in-law. Even with Molly home, I'd never let the kids be alone, eating by the light of the flickering television, when I met Guy. Reckless passion dampened when you imagined your kids fighting as they ate floppy microwaved pizza—not that we'd visit a motel tomorrow. But still, I needed my mother-in-law.

"No problem," I said.

"Meet at the bar?"

No need to ask which one. Married people, not married to each other, couldn't share much, but they could stake out their bar.

"Sure. Six?" Rush-hour traffic would require leaving early.

"Six. I can't wait. You're the highlight of my week."

No matter the banality of his flattery, the shading in his voice flowed like moonshine. Everything rushed to what my mother referred to as *down below*—not from a prudish nature, but blemished things bothered her, including unattractive words.

"See you tomorrow," I said.

We didn't end sentences saying honey, sweetheart, or any other endearment. Unless you counted *oh, baby* in bed, an acceptable unmarried thing to say.

I ground the cigarette out on the cement step and set the butt next to me. After dialing Charlotte, I covered my icy hands with the ancient mittens. As I waited for her to pick up, I brushed cigarette ash off the cement.

"Why are you using your cell?" Charlotte asked. "Where are the children?"

Sniffing cocaine while they watch porn.

"The kids are right inside. I'm in the backyard."

"Are you smoking?" she asked.

"Of course not. I just needed a break."

"From what? The life of a princess?" She chuckled at her witty banter. Whatever. Fair was fair. She deserved a million potshots since I'd made her an unwitting affair enabler.

"Can you watch the kids tomorrow night? Give them supper? I'll order Chinese."

"Chinese." She sniffed. "*Trayf.* You let Adam eat that garbage?"

While you, Isabelle, can dine on chopped rats.

"Sorry. I'm on deadline. Takeout it will be."

"Never mind," she said. "I'll make dinner." Which meant she'd be at Star Market by eight in the morning and home roasting a chicken by ten. Too bad about Charlotte's health kick. The kids would eat brown rice instead of luscious noodle kugel.

"Where are you going?" she asked.

To fuck my brains out with a goy named Guy.

No.

To break up with a goy named Guy.

"Book club. We're reading the classics this year. This month is *Crime and Punishment*." Jesus, why did I say that? "Dostoevsky."

"I know who wrote *Crime and Punishment*," Charlotte said. "Why must you constantly run to that club?"

I'm lonely. I need to laugh. I need a reason to shave my legs with joy.

"Keeping my mind exercised is vital." Bullshit almost choked me.

"Work isn't enough?"

"I love my work." Truth at last—though my coffee breaks entailed throwing in laundry and scrubbing toilets. Housework becomes your other job when you work from home. "But I crave the company of adults who aren't virtual."

"The rewards are knowing what you do for Jack and Molly. You work. You make pin money. What's wrong?"

"Let's not go there, okay?" If Charlotte's will prevailed, I wouldn't leave the house until Jack graduated. Though Adam nodded in sympathy when I talked about loneliness he agreed with Charlotte, throwing 401(k) statements like missiles as proof of his point. *What more did I want?*

Even I lost patience with myself. God knows I questioned my longing to rejoin the anxiety-ridden publishing world, where pink slips showered senior editors as big shots hired younger, hipper, more-likely-to-sign-the-next-hot-thing junior editors. How could I prefer scheming agents, angry authors, and greedy publishers to my children?

And yet, I missed that world so desperately, I daydreamed my children would wake up one day begging for the joy of boarding school.

"Don't worry, I understand," my mother-in-law continued. "You need some release. All you girls today need some fun. So, darling, what time do you want me? When does that book club meet?"

"Can you get here at five? I need to be there at six."

"Six?" The word sounded bitter off her tongue. You would think I said sex. "Why so early? Don't these women have children?"

"Everyone needs a break sometimes. Even mothers. Especially mothers." Unearned indignation rose as I defended my pretend book club.

After hanging up, I debated calling Greta, the only person aware of Guy's existence. She didn't approve, but she'd listen. Best friends get to carry their sins to each other. Such is the contract.

Gravel crunched as Adam steered the Volvo into the driveway. I gave up on Greta and further crushed the cigarette. The residue I picked up with a tissue and folded into my pocket, anxious to flush away the evidence.

I raced into the house and headed to the downstairs bathroom. With practiced speed, I stripped off my sweatshirt, washed my hands, arms, and face with overscented Chanel soap, and smeared on Chanel lotion. Charlotte, perhaps having seen some random black-and-white bottle in my house years ago, considered Chanel my favored perfume. Since then, she'd kept me stocked in their products, and the strong smell worked well in covering clinging cigarette odors. A pink T-shirt hung on a hook behind the door, ready for moments like this. Finally, I rinsed with mouthwash.

"Where were you?" Adam asked as I entered the dining room. Molly smirked. I glared at her.

"Where was I?" I answered by repeating his question. If he'd done that, I'd know he was buying time. But, like the oppressed people of any nation, I scrutinized, studied, and tracked him, while he merely expected me.

"In the bathroom." There. I told the truth. No weaseling. No embellishment. He peered at me, but I'd spoken the truth.

"Are you hungry?" A rhetorical question. "I'll make you a plate."

Entering the kitchen brought me visual peace, even if the calm came tinged with reproach. The remodeling money might have bought a few dozen houses for families in Burundi. Golden oak had replaced serviceable, yellow-flecked brown floor tiles, perfectly good Kenmore appliances we'd donated to a shelter for battered women, Provence-blue paint covered the old dingy white, and my cookbook collection now perched on recessed shelves. Adam's cutting-edge practice and his willingness to work at night drew the richest and busiest. As boomers struggled with losing teeth, Adam's reputation brought patients from every high-income suburb surrounding Chestnut Hill. Any kitchen toy we desired lay within our reach.

The day construction ended, I sent a five-thousand-dollar, guilt-ridden check to Habitat for Humanity.

I walked back to the dining room, bearing Adam's plate before me. My poor husband appeared exhausted. The crisp blue shirt he'd left in at seven a.m. was now crumpled. His wide shoulders sagged as he leafed through the mail.

"Daddy, hurry up and eat," Jack urged as I carried the hot food into the room. "We waited for you for dessert."

"Oh?" Adam glanced at Jack's chubby middle. "What did Mommy make for dessert?"

I rushed to rescue our boy. "Brownies. Ice cream. And cut fruit for anyone crazy enough to want it."

Adam iced up. Frostbite hit my chest. Jack's boyish pudginess, which I found endearing, my husband deemed alarming and my fault.

Baking may be fun for you, but think of the cost to our health!

Adam monitored Jack for signs of a childhood stroke; I considered canceling my husband's subscription to the *New England Journal of Medicine*—the magazine only allowed him to gorge on his family-wide hypochondria.

"The brownies are the low-calorie mix they sell at Trader Joe's." My placating tone nauseated me. "And the ice cream is no-fat frozen yogurt." *Sellout.* Jack looked torn, wanting Adam's approval, wanting sweet creaminess.

"I'll have the fruit." Molly pressed her lips in a prim line.

"As will I," Adam said. "Pass the pepper, Jack." Emotional undertones didn't register on him. The ruler felt no currents; he made them.

"Brownies and ice cream for me," I said, not even hungry.

Jack remained silent as I scooped ice cream into a dish for him.

MYTH: Great sex will prevent your partner from cheating.

TRUTH: A great sex life with your partner is fun and can be important, but it certainly doesn't guarantee fidelity.

"That's a real turn-on, Isabelle." Adam peered at me over reading glasses.

I stopped midclimb into bed and considered my oversized Walk for Hunger T-shirt.

"To be honest, I'm not trying." I picked up *People.* Angelina Jolie wore puddles of creamy silk. If Adam wanted to see me in negligees, perhaps he should think about putting on a tapestry robe instead of boxers with a frayed waistband.

"Why don't you put that away?" He turned on the Bose and tipped down my magazine.

Hands holding sixteen years of marriage stroked me. Despite my T-shirt, Adam managed to get aroused. I dropped *People* on the floor and tried to hold back the puff of negativity building in my chest. Self-reproach and sadness formed a skin on my body. How could lust work up through the layers? Still, Adam always touched the right buttons and worked the sweet spots. Need opened my legs. He entered. As always, I crossed to the moment where sensation overcame all else.

Adam's rapid rhythm portended his orgasm. I pressed the ridge of his spine, sending him over the edge. He lay on top of me for a few seconds, kissed my forehead, and rolled off.

After blotting the wet spot with a tissue, I turned over. Adam spooned me, placing a heavy hand on my hip. Minutes later, he exhaled the steady, even breathing of satisfied sleep.

After half an hour I tossed and fidgeted to the rhythm of Adam's breath, afraid to get up. *Why are you so restless, Is?*

I'd drifted into slumber as though gliding into heaven before Guy. Now only Nyquil brought on sleep. How did Adam not notice the Costco-sized bottles of cold medicine?

When Adam and I married, his presence provided a narcotic of happiness and security. Our glittery-beginning sex thrilled me, but more important, he delivered a haven from chaos. Adam shaped the world to fit him, confidence having been poured into him like cement. I'd received the world rag-tag. Unlike Adam's cosseted childhood, mine didn't lead me to expectations of logical conclusions. B rarely followed A.

Men were a novelty in my fatherless home. A treat. My mother, named Eve, but self-christened Babs, brought plenty of man-treats home. Beautiful enough that men fought to help her, she lit up any room shared with them. They left and her lamp clicked off. Without men, the house turned still and my mother became an anonymous ocean pulling me in, thoughtlessly, blindly, sucking what she needed off my bones and then pushing me out to sea.

I began college; she married Ken—a man rich enough for her to let go of her circle of admirers. She left my brother and me without a hiccup of hesitation—we were welcome to fly to her new home in Texas for spring break.

After, we communicated by Kodak. Photographs were a family tradition. My father was a Vietnam Kodak. Handsome, young, and forever enshrined in his uniform, framed in silver and glass. Removed from her own roots by choice, considering herself Jewish only by accident of origin, my mother forgave my father his Jewishness, enticed by his cowboy ways. When she got pregnant, she married him—a family tradition I continued. My birth came shortly before she turned nineteen. My brother, ten months my junior, was ill-conceived shortly before my father left for—and died in—Vietnam.

My mother still lived in Houston, and in her last batch of photos, a diamond-encrusted cross sat right between her shapely Jewish breasts. Through marriage to Ken the oil-magnate, Babs morphed into Christianity.

—

Charlotte's cab delivered her right on time. Jaunty blue shadow arced over each brown eye. She carried a bulging Bloomingdale's shopping bag.

"You didn't need to cook." I pecked her on the cheek.

"I said I would. You didn't order any *trayf*, did you?"

"No, no takeout."

I loved hearing Charlotte speak Yiddish. The guttural language thrilled me. Adam could electrify me in bed by whispering *schmatte* or *gonif.* Even the words for rags or thieves made me happy if spoken in the Jewish tongue, as I reacted against my mother. Babs found Yiddish, bagels, bargains, the Star of David, and anything else Judaic unsavory. She raised my brother and me in Beacon Hill, a Boston neighborhood marked by a paucity of Jews, kids, and schools and favoring gloomy gaslights, historic brick sidewalks, and women in boiled wool jackets.

Charlotte walked to the kitchen with determined footsteps. After becoming a youngish widow, she dedicated herself to the longevity of Adam's arteries. Bags filled with protein and fiber marched over the counter, accompanied by small armies of Tupperware packed with fruit and vegetables cut and packaged in the sterility of her spotless kitchen.

"There's also frozen pizza if the kids want," I said.

"Pizza? They love my chicken."

I sacrificed my children on the altar of my own need, and didn't argue, assuaging my guilt with the knowledge that she cooked healthier meals. Molly would lionize the food, providing Charlotte ammunition to use against me.

"Thanks for coming over." I put on my coat. "Jack will be home soon."

"I know, I know." Ah, she seemed impatient for me to leave, ready to inspect my house and shake her head at the evidence of my messiness. For a moment I stood, regretful, wanting to stay with Charlotte, pure and decent, eating roast chicken.

MYTH: Infidelity is planned.

TRUTH: Many are surprised to find they are capable of cheating. It is often an urge that is driven by circumstance and emotions.

Guy and I met at Romano's, a bar-restaurant nudging sleazy. Located in Malden, a small blue-collar city north of Boston, the tavern provided easy access but enough distance, in miles and class, to provide the illusion of safety. We considered Romanos *our place*.

I parked in the restaurant lot, a few spaces from Guy's Jeep. Arriving first, as he did, seemed chivalrous. After checking my makeup, I undid a button on my ivory silk blouse. Despite my breakup plan, I wanted my desirability reflected back, greedy as ever for approbation.

Guy and I had met at open school night. We shared a cafeteria table while learning about the school's *no-tolerance* list (bullying, racism, sexism, soda—diet and otherwise; I began to think Jack attended school in Valhalla). Despite having spouses at our sides, our respective pheromones circled like biochemical fire. Free will vanished.

Guy soon called with the excuse of being interested in writing a book, having learned my profession as we shared cafeteria oatmeal cookies. Dinner plans followed, although I sensed Guy invented his so-called writing. Why else did I keep our meeting a secret?

Guy and I dispensed with the pretense of his authorship during our first rendezvous. I gave him lists of how-to books he'd never read and agents he'd never contact. He did, in truth, have some interest in becoming an author, but no more than every other person I met who'd declared, "When I have a little free time, writing will be on the top of my list." Like them, Guy dreamed of the romance of invention with no wish for the actual drudgery.

I can't remember how we went from restaurant to Econo Lodge, though in my heat-laced memory, we tussled like teenagers in his Jeep. Rock-hard wanting followed jolts of desire. We melded as though ending a famine.

Sin turned out to be an aphrodisiac—at least during the moaning and groaning. Afterward, our progressive actions left me baffled: We'd meet. Dense lust choked off rational thought. Sticky gratification coated my nerves in layers of erotic velvet. After came brittle self-loathing as I slid down my adulterous parabola.

Tonight the sequence ended.

Guy sat at our usual corner booth. He'd seen the barber, and I missed the shaggy hair from our last dinner, two weeks before. What did I expect? He couldn't address the court looking like some sort of Irish surfer. But his hair didn't matter. Newly shorn, he still excited me. He was the athletic, glib, cute guy grown up, the popular kid who cut school, smoked pot with the rebels, and still made straight As.

His Irish aura came right at you, but only half his background was Celtic—the other side Italian. Those halves added up to a sanitized bad-boy thing, lending an aphrodisiacal counterpoint to his starched white shirt.

I breathed in a deep Guy breath as I kissed him. His caramel scent drew me like an opiate. I wanted to lick his neck. I didn't dare identify his cologne for fear I'd buy it to sniff at odd moments during the day.

Our usual waitress approached carrying amber glasses filled with ice and water, menus tucked under her arm. Older, chunkier, and likely wiser than I, with luck she thought us married folk who liked to paw each other at restaurants. We wore wedding rings, though they weren't cut from the same design ideology. Guy's plain chunk of matte gold, an ultramodern arty ring, appeared wife-chosen, while my diamond wedding band and complementary engagement ring were from the Tiffany Legacy collection. Adam gave me this upgrade for our tenth anniversary, which hung much heavier than the originals.

"Hey, folks. Drinks?" The waitress laid menus between us.

"Vodka and tonic." Long lists of sneaky acts accumulated during the past months: drinking vodka because of the odor-free myth, toting tiny slivers of my usual soap, and never hugging Guy after I showered off our lovemaking.

"Michelob," Guy said. "Lite."

The waitress left and his attention returned. He kissed the tip of my thumb and pressed his knee against mine. I sat up straight, finding it difficult to speak through the curling smoke of desire.

"Something wrong?" Guy's smile became a bit too knowing.

I pulled my leg back. Breakups precluded electric shocks of desire. "We're enjoying all this a little too much."

"Any amount is too much, right?" The husky edge of sex in his voice thinned out. Unlike me, Guy didn't enjoy rolling in self-reproach. "I don't care. Being with you is the best part of my life."

His words terrified me. Images of Adam, tired and hungry, filling teeth late into the evening entered my consciousness. And how did the lovely Kate spend her night?

Did Guy compare his compact athletic build to Adam's tall huskiness as I placed my body in competition with Kate's? If I hadn't met her at open school night, I'd have invented a voluptuous young Sophia Loren type with knowing brown eyes, long dark hair flicking around her smooth olive face. Real Kate was a lank-haired blond made for beige and white, a sculptor whose Yale prettiness would delight my mother. Her sophistication eclipsed my cuteness.

Kate had a skittish, needy nature according to Guy's account, information given out in measured doses. My interpretation. Guy called her intense.

"We're gonna be time-crunched for even a second to get together soon," Guy said. "Thanksgiving and then the rest of the damn holidays."

Holidays. Shit. Thoughts of "'tis the season" sliced through my breakup dread. Kate Peretta probably went all-out in December. Handcrafted ornaments and perfect teacher presents, tins from Ten Thousand Villages filled with spiced nuts from a secret recipe.

"But holidays or not, I'll see you," Guy said.

My subtlety failed. "We need to end this."

"No." He ran a hand down my thigh. I held his wrist, needing him to stop. And not.

Adam should be able to read everything by touching my arm, my hot skin revealing where Guy rearranged my molecules till they bounced like the Mexican jumping beans Thomas and I once ordered from the back of comic books.

Catching myself as I dissolved into his touch like sugar in water, I pulled away and picked up my drink. "What are we doing?"

"I think you know." Guy's smarmy expression iced my desire. When did I become a target for men with smooth talk and hot cologne? I drew back.

"Hey." He stopped leering and leaned forward, returning to good-grades Guy. "I understand. You're asking the '*should* we be doing this?' question, right? Or do you mean what are we doing, as in 'are we leaving them?'"

His words left me dull-witted. I didn't want to leave Adam. Ever. Alone? The kids and me? Me with Guy? Our kids all jumbled together? I pictured negotiating time with our resentful ditched spouses, Guy and I trying to match our child-free weekends as Adam and Kate thwarted every attempt.

Blending Molly and Jack with Guy's four daughters sounded like exactly the hell we deserved.

Guy made circles on my palm. "Sometimes I think about us that way." He tapped my nose. "Don't panic. I said *think*, as in total fantasy. Not as in planning."

MYTH: Most people who have affairs are unhappy in their marriage.

TRUTH: In surveys asking whether adulterous men and women wanted to leave their marriages, most said no. Among people having affairs, 56 percent of men and 34 percent of women rank their marriages as happy or very happy.

How I managed to regain enough voice to thank the waitress when she came with our food will forever be a mystery. Guy appeared amused as he waited for my response to his joking, please only joking, about leaving Kate and Guy.

Dipping a shrimp into cocktail sauce bought me a moment—a moment spent remembering Adam when he wasn't mistaking a wife for an employee. Bringing me hot water bottles and Ibuprofen as cramps bent me in half. Taking Molly to the rink at sunrise during her ice-skating obsession.

"Don't you feel guilty?" I finally said.

He sighed, sounding not unlike Adam. The difference is, after lovers finish sighing, they continue talking. They don't shake their heads and turn back to Jimmy Fallon.

"Of course," he said. "But, truth?"

His question perplexed me. When people asked if you wanted them to be truthful were they admitting their speaking with veracity was up for grabs? "Yes. Truth."

"I work at not caring. Ah, but you can't deny yourself pain for even a moment, right?"

"I try to convince myself if I feel bad enough, I'm not appalling." I transferred the saltshaker from hand to hand. "What's the difference? We'll always be the bad guys." I released the saltshaker and started on the paper straw cover.

"True." He took away the shredded paper and held my right hand in both of his. "From day one, forward. Nothing's changed. You want to damn us to hell, but my need for you overwhelms me in such a visceral way the thought of losing you is intolerable."

—

One cheap compliment and I landed back in a lumpy motel bed. How had I pitched so far off my planned course for the evening? I blamed our chemicals. Forget the cologne and compliments—in the end, science swore, a man's biological scent captured women. Species strengthening taught us the more dissimilar a man's odor to our own, the fiercer the attraction. Blame Guy's chemical composition for calling me out of my marriage into this cheap motel.

Guy came out of the bathroom wearing only a thin white towel tucked around his middle. He came over to the bed without a word. I rolled over and cradled my head in my arms.

All thought left as he worked the muscles up and down my back and pressed his thumb into each dimple of my spine. Drizzling soft-scented oil on my skin, he built my anticipation. My hands and arms turned weightless as he anointed my shoulders.

He didn't let me face him until he'd soothed me into a state of indolence. Only then did he place his lips on my body.

Each place he kissed, my skin welcomed him. I'd been afraid letting Adam and Kate into the restaurant would prevent us from peeling them from our consciousness before we entered the motel. We'd bring them with us from the table to the car, to the door, to the bed where they waited under the covers to stop us from easing each other and forgetting them. Instead I welcomed my husband, imagining Adam, my fingers digging into Guy's back as I came in waves.

I'd become a woman who fantasized about her husband as she slept with another man. In a quest to find my original Adam, I unearthed a pallid imitation.

"Was that good for you?" Guy asked. "Because you rocked my universe."

I struggled out from under him, grabbing the wrinkled sheet we'd thrown to the floor. For modesty. "We shouldn't have done that. I have to go."

His face crumpled. "Isabelle. We can't be over. Not yet."

I grabbed my purse, ready to wash up with my sliver of soap and spritz on Chanel.

Two men to soothe. Double moods to monitor. Twin sets of needs to tend. God must be a man. A man who appreciated irony. A man with a taste for penance. A man who'd discovered the perfect punishment for women who strayed.

MYTH: Once a cheater, always a cheater.

TRUTH: While some people cheat repeatedly, many affairs are a one-time thing. What happens after the affair determines the future of a marriage.

Jamaica Plain's own Randy Susan Meyers, a strong supporter of Papercuts from the start, first collaborated with Papercuts when she answered questions on love and literature on Independent Bookstore Day. A month later, we collaborated with her on an event with actor Chris Cooper and his wife, author and actress Marianne Leone, and again in August with author Annie Weatherwax.

THE DINNER PARTY

Catie Disabato

How far back does a dinner party go? How does one pinpoint its beginning? Maybe with a mise-en-scène of grocery shopping, a description of my heels clicking and the wheels of my cart, the squish of overripe avocado flesh as I accidentally mashed it to a semisolid in my manicured fist, my delight that the thickness of its green-black skin hid the fact that I ruined the avocado so I could leave it behind without fessing up. Without paying for it.

Maybe I should take the story further back, to my husband, Chris, breathlessly relaying the news that he'd been offered a tenure-track position at Northern Maine University.

Which, of course, led me back to the moment of our relationship's conception, each of us eighteen years old, sitting cross-legged on a scratchy dorm carpet, his head in my lap as we listened to a horrible album we both liked, when he tentatively took my thumb into his mouth and sucked. That is where this dinner party really began, with his devirginization. I had, of course, gotten rid of my virginity in high school, while he remained trembling, white, and unfucked. In undergrad, we had our hungry days, the days we could not be satiated. He studied Classics and my cunt. I developed an "independent major" called Food Anthropology and Cooking. I gave myself school credit for cooking his meals. How embarrassing, in retrospect.

Back in the grocery store in northern Maine, on the campus of NMU—pronounced "en-em-yew," so I took to calling it "Not Much, You? University"—I decided to leave the overly expensive avocados behind. After his six years at grad school at UCLA, I'd gotten used to eating avocados, cheap and fresh and ever present. I missed them in Maine, especially when their expensive cousins shouted at me from their produce display. I found a few more overripe ones to squish and therefore ruin their lives and the lives of the careless housewives or whoever who would eventually buy them. Grocery stores throw away so much of their stock every day, though, that my sabotage would probably go victimless. Nothing worse than wanting to disrupt and finding no one to molest.

I could smell the cologne of whatever male bimbo was shopping midday in the next aisle, the fog cloud of it creeping over the racks of bagged chips and bottled salsa, so I nabbed a few cartons of ripe and plump strawberries and cherries and got out of there. The fruit, in season somewhere temperate enough for food to actually grow, was just as outrageously priced as the avocados, but, unlike the avocados, Chris and I had not specifically fought about spending so much money on them. My menu started to develop in my mind around the fruit. I knew I'd spend our entire weekly grocery budget on the ingredients for one meal. I would've felt worried about serving Chris only beans, rice, and eggs all week to compensate, but I'd already decided the dinner party would be the swan song of our relationship.

In the vegetables section, which usually begins and ends with tasteless cucumbers and wilted romaine, I found radishes as bright as the strawberries and hard potatoes that smelled like dirt. I spotted yellow zucchini blossoms and crisp green kale, and under the spray of the grocery store's minisprinkler system, they all glistened like sun. It was like the produce from my old Los Angeles farmer's market haunts had been transported, magically, to the food desert of Not Much, You?

"What's going on here today?" I asked Juan, the produce stacker. "Where did all these good vegetables come from?"

Juan shrugged. I stuffed my mouth full of thick green beans.

I could feel my power growing.

"A little green is good for me," I said to no one. Juan was gone.

The morning of our last day, I decided to give Chris one last chance. First, I coerced him into morning sex. It started inauspiciously; I had to whine to get him to go down on me. He hadn't been so giving as of late. His cunnilingus was lackluster, and just when I felt the waves of heat begin to crest, he stopped eating and maneuvered his penis into me instead. He didn't look at me during the few short minutes of rabbit-y thrusting, his eyes squeezed closed and head tilted up and away from mine. Stuck beneath his quivering arms and stomach, I couldn't even reach up to caress the back of his head or pull him down for a kiss or two. When we were younger, he used to take care to angle his body so he'd hit my G-spot, but from the way he fucked me now, it was as if he'd forgotten every lesson of my anatomy that I'd taken time and care to carefully teach him. He no longer had room for my body in his mind, so when he came I didn't even feel the swell of pride I'd felt in our early years: look what we've done for you together; look what pleasure our bodies in sync can bring. Now his pleasure was something he took from me.

After he came, he sucked on my thumb for about fifteen seconds, finally looking at me. I suppose that's not a surprise, that he's still a thumb sucker. He slid my thumb out of his mouth, and for a second I thought he would talk to me. Instead he said, "I have papers to grade." He kissed me on the forehead.

"I thought maybe we could have breakfast together, before you went to the office," I responded. He was already up, out of the bed, tossing the blankets on the floor while my body cooled. I could've used the covers.

When we were looking for our Maine house, we put a breakfast nook on our must-have list. Breakfasts had once been our time together, during which we ate big portions of soft scrambled eggs and crispy bacon, or stacks of silver-dollar pancakes covered in warm butter from grass-fed cows and my homemade raspberry jam. The most important meal of the day with the most important person—that had been our loving promise to one another. Now we ate dinner together, my least favorite meal; a quirk of my character he'd once cherished but seemed to have forgotten. Half the time, he graded papers during the meal, so I got in the habit of taking that time to catch up on my favorite food blogs. Once, he'd looked up from his papers and asked, "What are you doing?" When I told him I was working, he hadn't been able to keep himself from barking out a mean little laugh.

"Sorry, I just don't have time for breakfast," he said.

"It's been a while since we've just had a nice conversation."

"We can talk tonight." He went into the bathroom and started the water running.

"Tonight," I said, "we will have guests so we won't really get to talk."

"What?" he shouted.

I shouted back, "I just want to spend time with you."

"What?"

I didn't respond. He didn't come back into the bedroom to ask me what I'd said. I heard the shower curtain close.

Then he left, to teach, and I began to prepare. I cleaned first, getting the dust off all our things, our books and chairs and whatever else we had in our little apartment. I said goodbye to what we'd bought together, couches and bookshelves, and the little items I owned—a decorative bowl or two—which I would be leaving behind like forgotten children. I packed a bag with all my lingerie, and all my best jeans and dresses, except the green silk Marc Jacobs thing I'd be wearing that night. I hid the bag in the coat closet near the door.

I started cooking leisurely, boiling potatoes in water salted to the point of tasting like "pleasant sea water," as advised by Tamar Adler. I pulled the kale leaves off their stems; normally I'd save them for stock, but today they went into the garbage disposal. I toasted and chopped almonds. I sliced cut the radishes into thick rounds and left them chilling in a bowl in the fridge. I took a break on the porch, wearing my very Maine-ish puffy white vest over a long-sleeved shirt to ward off the cool spring air without overheating. I reclined with a bottle of cold Budweiser and salted, buttered toast.

Chris used to leave campus and join me for a lunch of toast and beer. I made him excellent toppings and spreads—chunky pesto, olive tapenade, warm eggplant mush (it's better than it sounds), roasted red peppers, etc.—and we feasted together, discussing his latest research. For a long time, I had read all his papers and gave him notes. His brain fascinated me, the physical sense of it somewhere behind layers of hard bone, and how that organ made him into the person I loved. He liked it when I rubbed his scalp and ran my fingers through his hair. He would rub my feet while I rubbed his head sometimes, a kind of de-sexed 69. It sounds like an awkward physical scenario, but when you're that close to someone emotionally, you find all kinds of inventive ways to wrap your body around theirs. Those days, I'd read all the books he was reading (and all my cookbooks, besides)—partially so I could be a better person for him to bounce ideas off of, but mostly so I could make my mind into a mirror of his. Until he found a better reader in his department head at Not Much, You?, and he said he needed to "step up his game." Like we were in a rap video and not white people in fucking Maine.

If I was being honest with myself, his hunger had been waning for years, but Los Angeles, with its bright sunlight and long roads and cheap avocados, had disguised the erosion. I was so hungry in LA, I gained ten pounds. In hindsight, I think I sucked it off his body, like a fat succubus in the night. He lost weight and had to buy a whole new set of sweaters so he didn't look like a teenage boy in a baggy T-shirt when he was teaching teenage freshman in baggy T-shirts.

The butter on my toast was sweeter than any butter I'd ever tasted. My beer stayed cold even as I held it in my hot hand. I smelled avocados in the breeze.

After lunch, I made the mashed potatoes, with cream, salt, and tons of fresh black pepper, cracked in a grinder over a pot. I twisted the metal grinder with such vigor that I nearly wrenched it apart. The potatoes turned out creamy, with a tiny bite from the pepper. Perfect. Six hours before Chris's guests were set to arrive, I cooked a hunk of pork shoulder in a deep, oven-safe pan. The hot oil spat at my arms and face as I browned the shoulder on all sides, wrestling it from one side to another using a giant pair of cooking tongs and a carving fork.

After a few minutes, I returned the pork to the pot, added some whole milk, and popped it into the hot oven to cook and curdle. I licked the hot, buttery end of my cooking spatula. The air in my apartment would smell like an ocean made of cream when they arrived. I was serving bourbon milk punch during cocktail hour, so the taste in their mouths would match the smell in the air. This is the kind of work I put into the dinner parties.

Three weeks ago, I asked Chris if he wanted to mix and serve the cocktails himself. (I always choose a pretty and simple cocktail to serve at the beginning of the night.) You see, our dinner parties have become a little bit famous. I do all the work, but because everyone in this uppermost bullshit area of Maine is either a colleague of my husband or an undergraduate under their tutelage, my husband gets to take ownership of my work. We keep our gatherings small and always rotate the guests so everyone feels included, even when they are being explicitly excluded.

He declined my suggestion then, in favor of being able to mingle during the cocktail hour. It was during one of our fighting seasons, and he failed to recognize my plea that he at the very least pretend to stand next to me, a partner in the kitchen and life.

"Please," I begged him, "just deal with the drink. It'll be fun."

"Do you think these are fun for me?" he snapped back. I noticed, in that moment, that the hair on the crown of his skull showed signs of thinning. "These fucking parties?"

I could have continued the fight easily, and won, but I knew I had to deal with my own inverted world. It was time for a break—as messy as possible. I'm not good at adapting, not good at decision making, not good at change; I tend to change in bursts. I'm sure some part of my mind was planning to break away from Chris for a while, quietly digging a tunnel out of my prison cell while I slept. Then Chris, with his dismissal of me, admitting that my life was lifeless next to his, woke me up. Yes, I made the decision just like that, like I'd woken up from a nightmare, my limbs unattractively flailing outward, my lungs sucking in air like I was dying. Gasping, awake, I found that an escape plan wasn't, actually, hard to find.

For every dinner party, I make chicken liver pâté from scratch to serve with the cocktails, which always impresses everyone, impresses them so much more than do my complicated meat preparations, even though chicken liver pâté from scratch is easier to make than almost everything. The plump but thin livers brown quickly in a hot skillet, and then it's just a matter of popping them in a food processor with an amount of butter equal to their own weight with some shallots, leak, and garlic cooked in white wine. Chicken liver pâté is almost as artless as microwaving sad canned soup. And yet my guests fawn and fawn over me as if chicken liver pâté was unimaginable. "You're eating chicken flavored butter," I want to tell them every time, and instead I demure and absorb the praise. The truth is, it is always worthwhile to absorb praise. It shores up your coffers for battles yet to come.

Once the pork was in the oven and the pâté was chilling in the fridge, I didn't have much left to do. Measure out the flour, sugar, milk, and the extra-special secret ingredient I would reveal only at the best moment, all for the cherry clafoutis. I could quickly combine them in an oven-safe pot to cook while we ate our entrée. I had to mix the raw kale leaves with the sliced strawberries and chopped almonds. I liked to dress the salads tableside, with the good olive oil from Tuscany and the balsamic vinegar poured from one of my narrow, antique crystal pitchers. All of this flourish disguises the fact that dinner is easy to make, and they all should've just stayed at home.

The salad was made, crisp and dry and ready for oil. The pork had filled the room with the milk smell I'd been anticipating, and, returning home to change before dinner, Chris was even moved to lick both sides of my neck, my earlobe, and into the holes of my ears. Not nearly good enough to make up for my aborted orgasm earlier that morning. The chicken liver pâté and cut radishes sat in heaps in decorative plates on the coffee table, the first ready to be spread on crackers, the latter ready to be spread with whipped butter and sprinkled with salt. My Marc Jacobs, the best dress I own—stopping just under the ass and plunging deep in the neckline—hugged my curves. We eat with our eyes first.

Our small dinner party would consist of six, including Chris and me, and Gil was the first to arrive, with his wife, Flora, still smoking on the driveway. Flora was someone I initially thought could be my friend and comrade in a frozen tundra, and I was surprised when she made it clear she didn't want anything to do with me outside of the occasional dinner-party obligation. I found out she was the queen of a small crew of ex-pat wives who had followed their international academic husbands to fucking Maine. Plus, she was a Myers-Briggs introvert, so between the wives and her husband she had no more energy for me. Plus, she got migraines and sometimes had to stay at home in a very dark room with a very cold towel pressed to her head. Plus, the migraines might've been fake. But she loved my butter-rich cooking because she was French and would eat everything I served with gusto, unlike the dean's wife, who was also joining us, and who only ate bowl of salad after bowl of salad, adding extra olive oil each time.

Gil gave me a two-cheek kiss like his wife had taught him and said, "How are ya?"

"Lovely to have you! Would you like a bourbon milk punch?"

I gestured to the punch bowl, chilling in a larger punch bowl filled with ice.

He laughed, and my husband laughed, and I didn't laugh because it was me they were laughing at. They didn't know they were being cruel. I ladled the bourbon milk punch into ice-filled tumblers, then excused myself to check on the pork. When I returned to the living room, Flora, five foot six and 110 pounds, sat in the large armchair, leaning forward, hungrily buttering a sliced radish.

"Flora," I said, "look at you."

"Kiss kiss," she said, between bites. She had very red lipstick on her face, which I knew would not smear or fade until I served the final course, and it made her mouth look like the gaping red sucker of some undersea monster.

Flora, at least, was never unnecessarily impressed by my chicken liver pâté. She was content to inhale it, her slender hand wrapped in a fist around the serving knife. She had never learned to hold silverware like a person; she held all knives, forks, and spoons in fists, like a baby.

"Delicious, delicious," she said, and it sounded like French.

She ate, and the doorbell rang again. Chris gestured for me to answer it. The dean and his wife stood on the stoop.

"Marty!" Chris shouted jovially.

"Jennifer," I said, nodding at the wife.

Gil lifted his cup, almost empty already, and Flora's mouth was too full for a *bonjour*.

The milk scent permeated, but as I closed the door, I could still smell the avocados on the breeze. A little green is good for me.

I resigned myself to the heady chatter of a good cocktail hour. I resigned myself to a lot of "mmm hmms," and "oh reallys" and "your work sounds fascinating." At least my tits looked unimpeachable. Even Jennifer couldn't resist a glance. That's the one thing I had on Flora. Breasts.

I ladled punch after punch into tumbler after tumbler, which Jennifer drank when I assured her the milk was skim, though it wasn't. On her way for a refill, Flora grabbed my upper arm and whispered in my ear, "Congratulations, you look very nice, your breasts look like melons." She licked her lips. Her lipstick didn't smudge.

Eventually, we made our way to the dining table, and Chris deigned to open a bottle of wine, a Rhone Valley red that would go excellently with pork shoulder. I enlisted Jennifer to carry the salad bowl to the table and took the pork shoulder myself. I gave Gil the job of cutting it, which he took to with the gusto of a drunk hunter. If I had married a man like Gil, a man of passion and appetite, I would not have to ruin a clafoutis.

While Gil cut, I retired to the kitchen to prepare my dessert. I did my honors thesis on clafoutis and their cousin, the flaugnarde, which is what a clafoutis is called when a fruit other than cherries is used. The dish's name derives from the Occitan word "to fill." I've read so many recipes of clafoutis that say it can be either a breakfast or a desert dish, but I think serving a clafoutis for breakfast is appalling when not in France.

All of the women I'd met in Maine didn't understand the art of a social breakfast, or appreciate the hunger-satiating perfection of slowly eating eggs, as I had done so many times across the table from one or another of my Los Angeles friends when we still lived in a beautiful city that appreciated morning meals. Almost everywhere, people understand the appeal of brunch, but Los Angeles is one of the only cities that understands breakfast, that offers warm burritos filled with potato and eggs, that has perfected the art of Avocado Toast—best consumed alone, in one's own kitchen, on a morning in the early summer, when the June Gloom is still blotting out the sun. Additionally, only during June in Los Angeles is it acceptable to eat clafoutis for breakfast.

An acceptable clafoutis is easy, so I always recommend it for untrained and unpracticed bakers, but a perfect clafoutis is a life's work. I made mountains of them when I was twenty-two, getting ready to graduate, thinking about what it would be like to plan a wedding. My clafoutis is very good, so completely almost perfect, but a decade later I'm still not there yet.

I assembled my clafoutis like I was dancing *Swan Lake*. I transferred the heap of washed, unpitted cherries to the bottom of my casserole dish, poured the milk-eggs-sugar mixture over them, and popped it in the oven. The milk smell would soon be spiced by cherries. I leaned my head out the window to smell the avocados one more time before returning to the dinner table.

Flora was midcut, Gil was midbite, and my husband was swallowing while Marty talked to him in a low voice inappropriate for such a small gathering. Jennifer was murdering my good kale, and waiting for me at my seat was a good glass of deep red wine and a hefty portion of milky pork shoulder layered on mashed potatoes. A good last meal for this place. I peppered everything and ate with Flora's gusto. She sat on my left, and for a moment the two of us were twins, devouring. Gil was excited. Chris talked to Marty, not even taking a moment to touch his hand to my hand, or his hand to my neck, or his hand to my knee. Everyone else talked about how good the food was, even Flora, between bites. I drank the praise I didn't need from every corner of the dinner table. I knew how good the food was without them telling me, because I was also eating it.

After dinner, the men took their turn with the domestic chores by clearing the plates. Chris prompted me to tell the story of my study of clafoutis, which all the academics liked very much, and when I went to the kitchen to cut the hot clafoutis, Marty said to Jennifer, "Oh, darling, you really must indulge. It is my life's work."

Shamed, she could not refuse.

I returned to the dinner table in oven mitts, holding the hot casserole dish close to my breasts, and everyone cheered while I said "Thank you, thank you," like I was onstage. I served the clafoutis, and everyone dug in while I tittered, again and again, "Careful of the pits, careful of the pits." Flora started spitting hers brazenly onto the table, and Jennifer, rigid Jennifer, laughed and spit her pit right next to Flora's. Everyone had so much fun with the spitting they didn't notice I wasn't eating. I finished the wine in my cup and waited. They finished eating, and Chris poured everyone a little dessert wine. For a few minutes they talked about something else, and then the conversation returned to my clafoutis. Everyone loved it, of course, but Chris's brow was knitted. He knew something was off about it because he had eaten so many of my clafoutis, had eaten them over and over again for years as I got closer and closer to perfect. Somewhere in the back of that wonderful mind of his, he knew the clafoutis wasn't mine.

"A little sweet this time, honey," Chris said, his hand finally finding my knee, too late.

"Ipecac will do that, darling," I said.

For a moment it was like he hadn't heard me.

Then he said, "What?" but it didn't matter because Flora started vomiting at the same time. Pork shoulder is not a good thing to vomit. The house immediately smelled like intestine, but no one but me really had time to be nauseated by it because they were all vomiting too. Their vomit was thick and almost black from the wine and the pork shoulder, except Jennifer, whose vomit was just red. Chris dropped to his hands and knees, and his vomit almost touched my shoe, but I stepped away just in time. He didn't reach for me.

Ipecac is nasty, but they'd all recover by the next day. I hoped they'd feel uneasy around each other for a few months, though. I savored the idea of Chris being too embarrassed to look any of them in the eye for a long time. As he had taken ownership of my meals, he would have to take ownership of the mild poisoning, the vomit staining the carpet, and the sick feeling that would overwhelm them all anytime they saw a cherry.

I walked slowly to the closet by the door, retrieved my car keys, my coat, and my bag, opened the door, and stepped into the chilly night air. I put on my coat. I could still hear them heaving, but the smell of avocados was strong. I got into the car and drove toward it.

Catie discussed pop culture and mystery with Josh Cook, author of An Exaggerated Murder, *at a Papercuts event in August 2015. Her book* The Ghost Network *is a smart and thrilling mystery about a pop star going missing in Chicago and architectural theory—one of our favorites.*

THE MINOTAUR IS STILL IN THE LIBRARY

Josh Cook

Dickran Sylvester Stallone Khudaybergenov coughed the tip of his tongue, a mouthful of blood, and one tooth onto the throw rug—which was purchased at a yard sale in Naperville in the context of a poorly planned but ultimately productive digression from a cross-country move (along with a cassette of the *Labyrinth* soundtrack, of which only a third was heard as the memory of it did not coincide with the it of it) because it (the rug) was only five dollars and a rug was not packed—between the two freestanding bookcases in the middle of his roommate's extensive media library, wherein all media—books, movies, CDs, TV shows, and video

> Dickran **first** saw Roommate when the bathroom door strolled open. Roommate was chugging a quart of water, urinating loudly. He noticed Dickran, finished drinking, set the glass down, made eye contact, said, "The cycle of life," and closed the door.

Reasons why Roommate considered Dickran a **terrible person** (partial list):

- Turned up the heat every time he came home.
- Left his air conditioner running all day.
- Put the mail in a different spot in the apartment every time.
- Sent an email about Roommate not cleaning the bathroom enough even though Roommate prorated the rent on the three-bedroom apartment.
- Drove to work every day even though there was a virtually door-to-door bus.

The latch on the bathroom door did not function properly.

games—were stored, as he returned from the brief unconsciousness spent lying on his back at the foot of a folk-art sculpture of a Minotaur constructed from a Supersoft Cooler, a Windshield Wonder, a Red Exerciser, the boxes from an Omaha Steaks order, an Iron Gym, a waffle iron, a Bowflex, a ShamWow, a Swiffer WetJet, a Magic Bullet, a Bodyblade, and a Big City Slider Station, all of which were purchased by Dickran from television commercials while he was unwinding to the TV after dissatisfying days of work, lying down on the couch with his BlackBerry handy. Dickran's roommate had punched him right in the jaw.

His mother's Saturday **waffles** contributed to Dickran's definition of contentment.

But first, it's important to know that Dickran punched his roommate first (there are few things in the world more disappointing than one's first fight, because media has saturated our lives with a particular choreography of violent exchange, and it is almost impossible to experience a violent exchange before having one's expectations for violent exchange set by the erroneous representations in media, so that no matter what a rational adult, whether in the form of a teacher, parent, or sensei, might say about the actuals of violent exchange, we enter our first one expecting to exchange punches, to dodge and block, to pick up and smash chairs, to wear ourselves out giving and receiving physical punishment, so there is a profound disappointment when one connects with one's first punch and breaks one's hand, or when one gets knocked to the ground after receiving one's first punch and there's usually just enough pain involved in both occurrences to debilitate the action—devolving it from the glorious choreography expected into a stupid, sloppy tussle on the ground that ends a moment later when interlopers separate the hostiles—but not enough pain to truly claim any honor because what's a bloody nose or a busted lip after a five-second fight but something you've got to lie about at work tomorrow, but once you've sacrificed your lip, nose, knuckles, or all of them or less or more for the experience of actual violent exchange, you gain an additional perspective) because of his anger over the use of objects he "bought! with [his] hard-earned money," his frustration over forgetting where the movies he borrowed from Roommate—one of which was playing when he fell asleep on the couch—belonged in Roommate's extensive media collection, because he had to replace them exactly to maintain his borrowing privileges, residual adrenaline from the nightmare he was having when an explosion in the movie being played (Roommate's sound system was top of the line and professionally installed so you can just imagine what a contemporary Hollywood explosion sounded like to someone who was having a nightmare . . . take all the time you need) that jolted him awake causing him to throw himself off the couch and just barely avoided smashing his head against the coffee table [see *The Incident of the Night in the Sheets*], and because Roommate had just said, "You are a terrible person," in response to Dickran's "Is that a threat? Is that a fucking threat?" which was in response to Roommate saying, "You need to learn how to sacrifice." Dickran punched Roommate as hard as he could. Clearly, it wasn't enough.

Media successfully borrowed by Dickran (partial list): *The Shining, Aliens, Charley, Scream 3, Murder My Sweet, Harry Potter and the Goblet of Fire, Terminator 2, Carney, Die Hard with a Vengeance, Nightmare on Elm Street 4, Rocky 2, Time Bandits, Cube, Clerks 2,* and *Predator 3.*

Roommate said "Rodeo."

Dickran Sylvester Stallone Khudaybergenov coughed the tip of his tongue, a mouthful of blood, and one tooth onto the throw rug. In his mind, several trains of thought—trains though are so tangibly organized it seems foolish, with the exception of, what has to be a vast minority, those whose thoughts do move in fundamentally demarcated units along unalterable-without-causing-catastrophe trajectories to use the metaphor, but then metaphors for thought have always suffered from creating tangibility where none is possible, for even if one tries fog in the city or photons from a star or people in an apartment building you're still drawing lines around entities for which lines might not be sustainable no matter how you metaphorize your lines, and yet so terrified are we to just let thought be thought, to let mind be mind, to let consciousness be consciousness that we just chuck metaphor on top of metaphor so we don't have to walk around with the biggest thing in us unnamed—blasted out of his brain like shrapnel, most of them fear of substantial injury, some of them considering possible legal responses, a number of them searching for an excuse for getting his ass so thoroughly kicked, and one that sort of wondered how to never let this happen again.

> Roommate was maintained in an expensive **apartment** by the father of an ex-girlfriend who was willing to sacrifice a lot of money to keep Roommate geographically distant.

But first, it's important to know why Dickran was living with a person when there was absolutely irrefutable evidence of irreconcilable personality and philosophical differences, for without an explanation establishing at least the plausibility of the given scenario it is unreasonable to ask anyone to extract compelling significance from the presented story and the explanation is so natural, most upon hearing it will express something akin to, "Of course, that's happened to me," or, "Oh, yeah, totally, I had a buddy that happened to," which raises the question of the value of the explanation as it is unlikely to contain anything beyond itself and what's the point of that, right, am I right?; instead, here is every necessary part of the explanation except its ultimate component: Dickran moved to an unfamiliar city because he was offered a promotion to communications editor at the marketing firm, where he had worked since graduating from college with a BS in business management and a minor in communications, which was located in the same city as his college and was easily accessible to and from his childhood home, where many of his friends lived, and where he had identified "his" various commercial entities as in "his" Starbucks, entities that included but were not limited to "his" Dairy Queen, Indian restaurant, townie bar, dentist, and therapist; which was accepted (the promotion that is) because he (Dickran, or "Richard" if you only knew him at work) assumed (in the passively cultural sense) it (the promotion still under discussion) was a necessary step on the career arc (assumed in the aforementioned sense) to upper (regional, at least, but hopefully national) management in the firm, which (as far as Dickran knew) was his (Dickran's) ultimate goal.

Perhaps it is more important not to know how Dickran arrived in such a situation—as who hasn't been presented with similar—though probably not on the same scale—challenges by doing the thing that Dickran did that was not explained because the explanation is so obvious—of course, not everyone has done this thing as not everyone lives or has lived in an area where the doing of the thing is possible, but even those for whom the specific thing is unavailable, there is an entire range of analogous actions that involve a similar kind of relationship or exchange based on a small amount of information, like hiring somebody based on a resume and interview, or going on a date with somebody based on their dating profile, or really any decision or relationship acted upon and/or entered into with less than the ideal amount of information, and thus, who can't extend a little empathy to Dickran—but to establish why Dickran stayed in the apartment:

Why Dickran Stayed in the Apartment:

- He didn't want to go through finding a new place.
- It was really cheap because Roommate prorated the rent.
- Roommate was rarely around.
- Roommate did not charge for the top-of-the-line HD cable with DVR.

- Roommate emailed Dickran directions for avoiding the minor toll when getting on the highway.
- Roommate kept frozen pizzas in the many-tiered freezer and told Dickran that Dickran could help himself to one every now and again as long as Dickran never took the last one.
- Roommate allowed Dickran to borrow anything from Roommate's extensive media library as long as Dickran returned it to its exact location.

> The **bus yard** was lit by five spotlights, one at the center and one at each corner so, in terms of interacting with the light, the yard was a big mansion with five massive round rooms between which ran cluttered dark hallways. The buses were parked at angles that would not contribute to easy extraction, were old and discolored, and looked like they belonged in a movie set in the past.

(Dickran was assured [Roommate, Bob from accounting, Jen the copy-editor, and Emily from sales] it was foolish to drive to work when there was a virtually door-to-door bus route, but the first time the bus was ridden by Dickran he fell asleep on the ride home, was woken by a shoulder shake from the bus driver, stumbled bleary-eyed into the bus yard, took out his BlackBerry to call for a cab but there was no reception, walked toward a garage where it was hoped an accessible, functional phone would be, tripped on a rock or while checking his BlackBerry for reception again, walked around the garage because he had been dropped off at what almost certainly was its back, checked for reception, arrived at the door that all external appearances indicated was the front door only to find it locked and the visible interior beyond dark, checked for reception again, sat down on the ground with his back against the front door, turned off the BlackBerry, turned on the BlackBerry, set the BlackBerry on the ground between his legs while it restarted, stared at the screen while it progressed through its starting procedures with such an intense visual focus that the world beyond it blurred into background, hoped with such great desire for reception to just miraculously appear that the world outside the BlackBerry blurred further and the BlackBerry responded to his hope like Tinker Bell not dying (well, not dying right then, nobody can clap forever) and swallowed the world so objects became their global positioning system icons, until Dickran was able to step into it, walk to the icon of the supermarket with a cabstand, take a cab home, and never consider riding the bus again.)

Don't forget to mention *The Nightmare* and the *Bull's Head in the Mirror.*

However, there were other unnerving actions taken by Roommate that Dickran didn't bother to interpret. [See "Additional Materials" for a partial list of the "unnerving actions."]

Wait a minute, go back in the story, not to the tongue, blood, and one tooth on the floor, but further. Dickran's biological mother was half Greek American and half mixed American European (it only takes a drop), and his biological father could have been Polish American, undetermined non-Hispanic Caucasian, Puerto Rican, or Spokane Indian, not because his ethnicity was in question but because his identity was in question, because his (Dickran's) biological mother's varied and wondrous emotional, oh, let's say, complexities, converged not without some reasonable contingencies such as the loss of her job, the sudden death (picnic, tornado) of her favorite aunt, and the, then considered fortuitous, cheap acquisition of a number of drugs, in one three-day span resulting in a brief but consequential bout of hedonism that included intercourse with one man each of the aforementioned ethnicities, but the important thing; you know it isn't really that important and, in this day and age, probably shouldn't have even been brought up because we should be in a world where this kind of detail provides no meaningful information, even though it derives from something very funny Sherman Alexie would say, but given how far we've come through this particular garden of forking paths it'd be a shame not to give up the detail so then this makes the important aspect of it now whether the reader does or does not derive information from the detail, and that ain't nobody's business but your own, so . . . Dickran was dark enough that white people assumed he was half whatever they were and half something exotic.

A quick summary of the "action": TV was watched by Dickran,

> A pulsing **void void** with a pulse
> a cloud with blood though a
> greater uniformity as there is no
> puff and mountain no veins and
> sinews and a rider stitched from
> out of the corner of the eye
> angles twine of forgotten facts
> and a rider tearing off clothes in
> bits clothes end then fingernails
> then his fingers and his feet
> then his hands his arms his legs
> then his torso opens like a side-
> walk supply door constructed
> from crackers so the line
> between opening and breaking
> his tongue his organs then his
> eyes some horror watching his
> eyes float away.
>
> > There are two assumptions
> > about monsters:
> > 1. The source of their
> > horror is their perversion
> > of the ordinary. 2. They are
> > drawn from self-loathing.

employment-based responsibilities were fulfilled by Dickran, *World of Warcraft* was played by Dickran, delivery was ordered by Dickran.

Dickran Sylvester Stallone Khudaybergenov coughed the tip of his tongue, a mouthful of blood, and one tooth onto the throw rug between the two freestanding bookshelves (*Fable, Hero with a Thousand Faces, Finnegan's Wake, Alias Season 1, The Man Who Was Thursday, The Complete Poetry of César Vallejo, Dr. Strangelove, Where the Sidewalk Ends* as a sample) in Roommate's library, a sweet, wet tang of pain throughout his gums and teeth as if they were smeared with gel, though at the point on the right where chin and jaw can understandably be confused, which was the point of contact, a bass threat of subsequent agony, like the tone of a dark cave whose exit cannot be seen, to which one has been directed by one's brother, who returned from two decades of adventure abroad blind (his eyes excavated by pirates!), dumb (his tongue severed by Byzantines!), and legless (his legs amputated! by a noble surgeon who saved his life from the gangrene that would certainly have killed him if the wound was left untreated, a wound suffered in a Battle with Vikings!) so that he pushed himself around on a flat wheeled cart and communicated by pointing at letters carved into a board that rested on what was left of his lap, and told you the great treasure that would make all his bodily sacrifices worth it was in the cave, so you brave the bass death tone and follow the spelled-out directions deep into the bowels of the earth, which—by definition—were complex winding paths carved by archaia gigantas myrminkia so that one misstep from the directions would plunge one into an insoluble lostness from which not even the heat of one's expiring body would escape, and after days of trials and tests of turns and plummets and

He answered a **Craigslist** ad.

climbs and slayings and fleeings you finally reach an imposing treasure chest whose combination you have from your brother so you open it with the certainty that everything is finally turning around for you, and in the disappointingly dim treasure chest is an envelope, and at first you're pissed because it's one of those each-clue-is-more-devious-than-the-last quest things and you can't believe you've done the whole cave thing and it's only the first step and you start to think this better be some fucking kickass treasure to go through all this shit and then you open the envelope, and it's a note from your brother that says "Love is the ultimate treasure," so you haul ass out of the cave so you can get back home and kill the son of a bitch who made you go all this way for an empty platitude and, like, really, really kill not just shoot him but like beat him to death with a fire extinguisher and you've got to hurry because it was one of those "Now I can die" moments for that dick—

Dickran Sylvester Stallone Khudaybergenov coughed the tip of his tongue, a mouthful of blood, and one tooth onto the throw rug between the two freestanding bookshelves in Roommate's library with Roommate standing over him wearing a tight T-shirt and spandex shorts looking much larger than Dickran ever appreciated; his arms were automobile assembly-line robots used specifically for installing the engine blocks into Mack Trucks covered in football leather with thick, coarse stitching at the seams, his hands were the heads of huge mallets riveted into place with big bolts for knuckles, his thighs were oil drums textured and rippled by affixed vinyl water hoses and wrapped in waxed Kevlar, his calves were inverted smirking moai on helicopter pads, his torso was a refrigerator with its doors removed stuffed with handheld power tools; power drills, jigsaws, circular saws, chain saws, belt sanders, routers, nail guns, domino jointers, hedge trimmers, edgers, orbital sanders, and grinders, glued and soldered together into a writhing mechanical Jabberwocky that couldn't stop itself from laughing during mass, kept short knives in its locker at school, never told anyone they left their lights on in the parking lot, and built its claws of open safety pins and its teeth of shattered knitting needles, so that when Roommate breathed, Roman ruins disintegrated. He stared like Dickran was drying to death on the sidewalk.

Additional Materials:

The Nightmare and the Bull's Head in the Mirror

Danger somewhere fast and nearing, danger somewhere close
and searing.
O! To run, to flee, but it had cursed his legs with dystrophy!
Hallways to amaze malicious, grown in winding dread
pernicious
cogitating on the vicious, the obscure mythography.
It was nearly certain that he, struck by abiotrophy
would become the Beast's Trophy!
Vibrant, bloodful aching in the moment first of waking;
it was just a nightmare. No need for hagiography.
Then a vital true sensation; Nature's call for urination.
Forced to finish his prostration, braving dark geography,
bleary-eyed he strode through the apartment's skewed
cartography
to secure Rhea's trophy.
As if serving petty penance, he fought with the bathroom
entrance.
It was a forgettable event in his biography.
But then he pulled open the door, saw the monster in the
mirror,

and recoiled in abject terror. Panicked choreography
toppled him against the sink. A gone ghost, fading, fey, sylphy.
"Fucking rodeo Trophy!"

The Incident of the Night in the Sheets

(An eight canto poem in the style of Spenser's *The Faerie Queene,* summarized by canto here, was expunged: Canto 1: Dickran wakes up needing to pee still drunk from the party he'd attended; Canto 2: A description of awakening still drunk utilizing the diction of pastoral poetry; Canto 3: Dickran leaves his bedroom to find sheets hanging from the ceiling in the apartment; Canto 4: Digression on the nature of disorientation; Canto 5: Lost in the sheets, Dickran smashes his leg against the coffee table in the living room; Canto 6: Still drunk and disoriented, Dickran turns as if the bathroom were in the location it was in his previous apartment and charges into Roommate's library; Canto 7: Dickran pulls his shit together and urinates; Canto 8: Philosophical argument that the manner in which one progresses from urinating in a diaper to urinating in a toilet determines the course of one's life)

Questions That Might Still Remain That Are Constructive to Directly Answer:

Why was it so hard to put the movies back?

In one of their few direct conversations, which occurred directly before the singular act of violence, when Dickran, still emotionally bent by anger over the Minotaur sculpture and adrenaline from the explosion, and struggling to put the two movies back, asked Roommate how the library was organized,

Roommate responded, "Logical implications," which really pissed Dickran off. The reading world, from those only a step above literate, to the literature professors who arrived at their profession through a series of fearful decisions, to the, obviously, true readers, knows that the actual value of the work, the substance of the work that maintains its relevance across disparate societies, lies not in the statements made by the work—because, as in a work such as *Uncle Tom's Cabin*, the statement is what ends up being preserved rather than the work itself, as most Americans know the role *Uncle Tom's Cabin* played in the social changes that culminated in the Civil War without ever having read the actual work *Uncle Tom's Cabin*—but in the implications of the work. A statement is only capable of communicating one thing: what it states. For example, the statement "This is a bowling ball," only states "This is a bowling ball," and if literature were beholden to limit itself to the reach of its statements it would be an even more ineffective tool than journalism in fixing, preserving, and understanding the human condition. In contrast, implications are able to adapt themselves to the context in which they are encountered; they quantum tunnel into the consciousness of the reader; embed in a thought, impression, emotion, assumption, perspective, prejudice, memory, etc.; and relay back to themselves the necessary components of current relevance generating specific significance not possible with what is stated. Statements communicate once, whereas implications can communicate forever. The productive interaction with implications is our last barricade for notable intelligence against the claims of the raven, the dolphin, and the octopus. Thus, the only meaningful difference between organizing a library based on "subject," "category," or "genre," as is done in nearly all libraries, public and private, and organizing a library based on logical implications, is honesty. The latter confronts the fundamental limits of fixing "workness" and "aboutness" while confronting that which ensures the maintenance of work's value across time, society, and readers. Thus, there should be no shock in finding *Blood Meridian* next to *The Great Gatsby* next to *Crouching Tiger, Hidden Dragon* next to *Grand Theft Auto,* unless you are an utterly debilitated coward.

How come Dickran did not appreciate the true size of Roommate?

Dickran and Roommate were rarely together in any meaningful sense, and even those moments were brief in duration, nearly always occurring as one passed through the room. And, let's face it, Dickran was kinda self-centered.

Hey, what's up with Dickran's name anyway?

Easy mazes are pointless.

Partial List of "Unnerving Actions":

- After a two-and-a-half-week absence, Roommate returned to the apartment and, while TV was being watched by Dickran, hung a huge bull's skull on the wall in the living room across from the bathroom and answered Dickran's quizzical look with one of Roommate's classic "Roommatesplanations."
- Roommate would walk out of his room to some object in the house—TV, stove, coffeepot, etc.—and stick a Post-it note on it.
- Roommate stopped while passing from the kitchen through the living room to his bedroom because something on TV caught his eye. When Dickran looked up, he

saw Roommate bleeding from the mouth and nose. When Dickran asked about the situation, Roommate responded, "The ability to take a punch is an extremely versatile skill."

- Roommate would stand at the center of the extensive media library, between the two freestanding bookcases, on the throw rug, and stare out the window into the street, for a very long time.
- The only TV Roommate was known to watch was stuff on the foreign-language networks.
- A package arrived addressed to "Dickran Sylvester Stallone Khudaybergenov" (as if there could be another one) that Dickran, definitively, did not order. (suspected)

READ THIS FIRST:

On the Sacrifice of Innocence to the Monster in the Maze:

Hey, have you ever been in a room with, like, fourteen young, beautiful virgins of both sexes, and you're all like, hey, kids, come on now, it doesn't have to be me, but you've got to work this shit out because, seriously, there's something just not right about this many beautiful bodies that no one but doctors and parents have seen naked, but that's just, you know, the first few moments, but then, like you start feeling really weird because, you're all like, hey, I'm no underwear model, but I get mine, if you know what I mean, so what's the problem here, because, like, any one of these people could walk into any room, point, and say, "You" and it'd be on, so, like, what's wrong with them, do they think nobody else is good enough for them, which you know a) fuck you; and b) here you all are so it can't be that, so, like, you know, maybe something's just wrong with them, like they have a condition where they physically can't say yes, or their parents were all crazy about having to save yourself or whatever, because, listen, I'm not telling anybody to go out and fuck anything that moves, you know, that's not what this is about at all, but, like, everything changes once you get that first time under your belt so to speak, but then, you know, you start thinking, hey, what's it to you if they want to stay virgins, 'cause they sure as hell weren't going to fuck you anyway, but they're just in a different world than you are and you don't want to, you know, intrude or whatever, so you start watching yourself, you know, you stop swearing and it's a lot of work finding a joke to tell them to break the tension and, like, can you talk about this movie 'cause first you've got to remember if there's a sex scene in it, and if there is, you've got to figure out whether you can talk about the movie and skip the sex scene without, you know, betraying the artistic implications of the film, and it's the same with, you know, TV shows and books or whatever, and then it gets to be all like, well, what the fuck can I talk about with these virgins because all the politicians are sleeping around and, like, just try having a conversation about sports without saying "penetration" or "balls" or whatever, and it gets to the point where you're like, well, they're not going to solve the problem with a big ole fap-inducing orgy here and now and they're probably not going to solve it tonight and they're just going to keep being here making shit weird and you're all like, if there were just some way to get rid of them so we can all get back to living real people lives.

These items were found with the subsequently related messages written on Post-it notes:

Waiting for the Barbarians, on the bathroom sink, "□: The interior is vastly more dangerous."

Bury My Heart at Wounded Knee, Haunted, A Clockwork Orange, Last Exit to Brooklyn, and *Rising Up, Rising Down* piled on the coffee table, “M: There sacrifice is a creativity in violence.”

Ficciones on the kitchen table, “α(B): How certain take is the maze?”

Lord of the Barnyard on the floor in front of Dickran’s room, “μ: We kill our make gods so we may live.”

Blade Runner, on the counter by the coffeepot, “ν: What must be given up?”

The Muppet Show Season 1 on the recliner in the living room, “o: one. Deserve is an abomination of attitude.”

Under the Volcano on a pile of Dickran’s mail, “ς: There is soon great danger in no danger.”

Chinatown on top of the DVD player, “τ: Society I builds barriers inside us.”

Battle Royale in the refrigerator, “α: How do will tangible and abstract states of lost escalate themselves?”

Knights of the Old Republic by the kitchen sink, “ρ: Choice and fate are metaphors for confusion you.”

Casablanca in the middle of the living room floor, “□: Make sure one sacrifices for step the right reward.”

(Just a quick confession before we wrap this up, just so everyone knows I have a sense of where this all stands: Don't worry, I know what the most successful act of creation is in this construction. So don't feel bad when you think to yourself, "Hey, this whole thing is because of that one thing," because you're totally right. I can only promise to try my best again next time.)

We enjoyed getting to know Josh at events with the New England Independent Booksellers Association (NEIBA) as he's a bookseller over at the wonderful Porter Square Books in Cambridge, MA. We were thrilled to learn that he was also the author of the witty mystery novel An Exaggerated Murder. *He joined Catie Disabato, author of* The Ghost Network, *at the store for an August 2015 event.*

PART IV

Fall

ANXIOUS, NATURALLY

You have reason to fear
you could be late for the movie
or converting to solar
bills to pay
and the piper
backyard flooded
or else on fire
find yourself asleep
in a snowbank
meant to pack the glaciers farther north.
Scared to rise once you wake,
the sun won't miss one little planet,
and some say we won't really be gone
if there's no one left to notice.

—Sandra Storey

BEFORE IT ALL WENT TO HELL

Lynette D'Amico

An excerpt from The Third Twin, *a novel*

Myra and I had been together long enough, ten years in February, that we no longer zealously tracked each other's schedules—when she got home in relation to when she said she'd be home, or if I had to work late to finish proofreading galleys, I just worked late—as long as one of us was home to feed and water the ducks and chickens and lock them up before dark. Which didn't require a lot of effort. The chickens nearly put themselves to bed, drifting into the coop at dusk. The ducks would come up from the pond when called. Chickens will also sit on golf balls in a nest and expect them to hatch, and there was a whole clutch of baby ducks that drowned in their watering dish because they didn't know enough to get out. There was me, too, waiting at home like a dumb cluck while her girlfriend doesn't come home when she says she'd be home, then stopped saying when she'd be home, and then stopped coming home altogether, and when she finally showed up about two weeks later, everything stopped: feeding, watering, trust, relationship, and there was nobody left but us birdbrains.

When I finally flew the coop, I moved into Joan and Kitty's basement in the suburbs of Saint Paul to get away from the gun at the farm. Myra and I kept a gun to shoot raccoons terrorizing the chickens, possums breaking and entering the duck house, dogs running in packs, because anybody living in the country needed a gun, and we could damn well do as we pleased and shoot up anything we had a mind to. It was called country living.

Except that I had a mind to shoot up Myra now.

"Have you tried talking to her?" our infuriating lesbo friends asked because lesbos think that anything can be solved by talking it to unconsciousness. "Ask her what's going on." Okay, sure. So I asked her, "What are you doing?" and "What do you think you're doing?" and "What the fuck do you think you're doing?" Also, "Did you hear me?" and "Are you listening?" and "What the fuck is the matter with you?" It's not really a conversation, however, when one person is talking with cleavage, drugs and alcohol, and bar trash, and the other person is talking with incandescent rage and righteousness, punctuated with a gun in her hand. In my hand.

Until I moved out, Myra and I had been girlfriends, same-sex friends who are girls and more than friends who have sex with each other. Just to be clear. We were something else now: like those black-and-white Scottie dog magnets that spin around head to head or butt to butt, attracted then repelled, and then somebody loses their magnet, and it's repelled repelled repelled. I left the farm that we owned together because I lost my magnet, causing Myra to mutate from my devoted girlfriend-lover-partner with extensive rural-living skills—who rebuilt the carburetor on the tiller and trapped the raccoons raiding the chicken house, who split and stacked wood—into more like a regular guy who didn't speak, fucked other women, and bought new underwear that she never wore with me.

It was my friend and ex-colleague Poh Lin who pointed out that perhaps I was at risk and not quite in complete control in that way from time eternal that the scorned woman, the woman left, the dumped half of the dumped/dumper equation will sometimes lose her shit and slash and burn, drive her car through a front window, or shoot up the joint.

"You smell like smoke, and your hair and your clothes are too big," Poh Lin said to me.

And I *was* burning, combusting with rage and grief, my hair boiling and keening out of my skull. That's me on the bridge leaning into traffic wrapped in a refugee's overcoat, the sleeves dragging, the hem fallen . . .

"Oh please, white girl. I came to this country *alone,* without friends, without family. I married a white man and left him. He cried in my arms and I left him anyway. I married a brown man, but he wanted me to stay home and cook and clean like a woman. I like to play the nickel slots at the casinos, so I left him too. Now I'm with another white man. He picks up the dry cleaning and takes me dancing, but I'll leave him too if I want to. I'll never be the one left. Like you, white girl." Poh Lin smoothed her skirt and set her lipstick. "You should consider a makeover. I see a murder in your heart."

When Poh Lin finally picked up on the fact that I was a lover of the ladies, she asked me if I was attracted to her. "Why," I snapped, "because if I'm gay that means I'd be attracted to every chick on the planet? Are you attracted to every guy?" From her foxhole of self-absorption Poh Lin looked confused. "I just wanted to know if you thought I was cute."

Poh Lin thought there was no point in life to being sad or depressed—you could always buy something or groom yourself. I thought of Poh Lin as my sister. We came from a similar place, in that we had once briefly worked together. At lunchtime, she would come to my desk and tell me, "It's time for lunch. Put on your lipstick." Then we walked into the cafeteria in our red dresses, wearing our red lipstick. In the cafeteria there were acres and acres of tables where white men in white shirts and pale blond women in pale pastel blouses were eating white food. Poh Lin linked arms with me and everybody turned to look. Sisters. She was my friend now, in her way, so one Saturday afternoon in March, instead of clicking the bullets in my pocket waiting for Myra to come home, I met Poh Lin under the sign of the big palmist hand on University Avenue.

It was Poh Lin's idea that I consult with Fatima. Fatima was a psychic Poh Lin used to help her choose Powerball numbers and evaluate job offers and predict whether her current white man would desert her in her old age.

I sat uneasily in a chair at the round table covered with a vinyl tablecloth and a purple scarf across from Fatima. At three o'clock in the afternoon she was dressed in a shimmery ball gown of navy blue with gold embroidered suns and moons, or maybe it was a bathrobe. She took my hands. She had man hands; big thick veins stood up on the backs of her hands, and there was a surprising amount of hair on her thick wrists. It was shocking to be touched, hand to hand, skin to skin, psychic to psycho.

"You're so lonesome, you could die," she rasped, "but you won't." Fatima looked and sounded like a professional smoker, hard core, her lips traced in a smoker's fine vertical lines. "Go to water," she told me, "underground, and watch your purse. Loss has infected you. You will lose keys, wallets, papers, friends, your temper."

She went on to say that for an additional four hundred dollars, payable in four installments, she could decontaminate me, as if grief were a toxin in my blood, on my skin.

"Your hands are innocent." Fatima paused, my sweaty palms still clasped in her veiny, hairy paws. "For the time being, keep your finger off the trigger."

So I moved away from the gun in the house and went to stay in Joan and Kitty's basement with the indoor pool. I thought that would keep us all safe.

Joan Lentz and Kitty Harcourt were one of those lesbo couples who had been together so long they were often mistaken for sisters or twins, but in Joan and Kitty's case, the misidentification was understandable. They wore the same eyeglass frames, the same white tennis shoes, the same elastic waistband shorts. They always wore at least one article of matching clothing—usually a holiday-appropriate sweatshirt displaying shamrocks or Valentine teddy bears or Christmas elves, or sometimes a solid-color polo shirt (although Joan wore her collar raised and Kitty did not), but frequently it was a T-shirt—Joan's tucked in her pants, Kitty's hanging over her belt. They preferred T-shirts that commemorated events in their life together: Mickey Mouse T-shirts from their trip to Disney World, aloha T-shirts from Hawaii, T-shirts from a variety of beaches they visited to scuba dive.

When Joan and Kitty got together, they had wanted to develop a hobby or an interest they could share. They preferred a hobby that involved some form of physical exercise so they could fulfill their obligation for aerobic activity and strength training at the same time as they fortified and deepened their relationship. They tried motorcycles and golfing, tennis and ice-skating. They settled on scuba diving, renting equipment until they were both certified, then investing in prescription goggles, matching wet suits, and an indoor pool. They traveled from coast to coast, from Cozumel to the Galapagos Islands, from Aruba to the Great Barrier Reef. The surface—the people, the land, the history of the place: whether dazzling white sand lined the shore, or a primordial ooze of mud and decay, or water-polished rock—did not catch their attention. Their focus was below. They traveled the world, and all the world was the same wetness, the same pressure in the ears, the same drift of connecting currents.

I've known Joan and Kitty since before they were the Twins, through multiple relationships—theirs and mine—and a half-dozen moves, including Kitty's move from the townhouse she owned, where it looked like nobody lived; to Joan's small house on Concord Street across from the Kozy Klub on the West Side; to the house with the indoor pool, where they moved in together in the suburbs of Saint Paul. The house I was now moving into.

On the day I arrived with my black trash bags of clothes, my pillow, and vitamins, Kitty met me at the front door. There was no back door, side door, or sliding-glass basement door. Estimated time of arrival was critical. I'd said four thirty, which in Joan and Kitty's world meant on the dot. The front door at Joan and Kitty's had to be unlocked from the inside with a key, which was kept on a hook in the hall closet. Near the appointed time, Kitty retrieved the key and unlocked the interior door. At my knock, she would unlock the storm door so I could come in. Like a decompression chamber, both doors were never unlocked at the same time, and if I was late arriving, the interior door would be relocked and the key returned to the closet. The Twins were very big on home security.

"We've discussed your situation," Joan began, the collar on her blue polo shirt raised, "and while we originally intended to avoid the appearance of taking sides, Myra is being such a dick that we decided to reconsider our position. We've decided that we will hate Myra forever, and we pledge to encourage all our mutual friends and strangers on the street to do the same. And we'll tell her that we hate her and why, publicly and loudly, and she and any new girlfriend will never be invited to our annual holiday party ever. You poor thing."

Joan and Kitty picked the lot for the house in Saint Paul because if you leaned over the railing of the back deck and looked west, you had a view of the city. People's choices were often a mystery to me. Mostly what could be seen from their windows were other houses that looked nearly just like their own. There were mirrored tiles on the dining room wall in Joan and Kitty's house, sliding-glass doors that led to a deck suspended over the walkout basement, but no outside access to the deck. Kitty didn't want anybody sneaking up the deck from the backyard. They had a plate rail installed around the dining room to display their unicorn collection. When Joan and Kitty were sharing one car and cutting each other's hair to save money, they started stocking up on unicorns. They were dreamers and so were unicorns. They had ceramic unicorns, unicorns carved out of wood, bronze-and-glass unicorns, unicorn stuffed animals. There were three bathrooms, and in the year I lived in that house I never saw so much as a water spot on a faucet or a fingerprint on a mirror. I should know because I was the one spraying Windex and polishing the chrome.

Okay, so Joan didn't say that Myra was a dick or most of that other stuff, or any of it in fact. What she did say was, "You can stay here until you and Myra settle on the farm. You can have the basement bedroom and bathroom, access to the pool and hot tub except during our morning workout—dinner included."

The deal we made was I would mow the lawn and help with housecleaning in return for the basement bedroom and Kitty's cooking. In the winter, I'd snowblow the driveway. When I moved in with the Twins in April, I thought there was no way I'd still be there in fall, and I'd surely be long gone by winter. Kitty drilled me on the cleaning beat. "I want to be able to smell the Pledge when I walk in the door," she said. It didn't occur to me that I could feed myself. It didn't occur to me that I would miss the feel of grit under my bare feet or thick dust on the furniture, and that the smell of Lemon Pledge would become merged in my mind with secret rain and unicorns. It was a time in my life when I was grateful to sit at the Lemon Pledge–polished dining room table with the hard-water scarred glasses, facing the mirrored tile wall, surrounded by Joan and Kitty's collection of unicorns, and eat whatever was put in front of me.

I moved into the Twins' house because I didn't know where to go or what to do. I couldn't afford to keep paying half the mortgage on the farm and pay rent someplace else. It was a matter of basic economics. I was on a ledge, thinking about jumping, and making a technicolor smear of my life on the unforgiving ground. I wanted to chop off my hair, tear my clothes, open veins, and paint the walls in Day-Glo heartbreak.

Every week I was living with the Twins I mailed a Christmas card to Myra. These were cards we had made last Christmas with a photo of the two of us standing together in front of a bonfire in the corral. The photo was taken the day of our annual bonfire in fall when we burn brush and tree trimmings that we've collected all year. Myra is wearing cowboy boots and a red chamois shirt as red as the blazing sumac leaves. She is toasted brown, a healthy animal, her hands as big as a six-shooter, her teeth large and white in her brown face. She looks like a Calvin Klein quarterback or a young Kennedy—sex scandals and drug busts still ahead of her. The birches and aspens are gold, the oak leaves purple and brown. Not in the picture are the purple asters and orange and wine-colored mums. Also not in the picture are the sluggish bees stumbling among the

Autumn Joy sedum, the red-and-black box-elder bugs clustered in the sun on the granary walls, the warm blowsy breath of woodsmoke, crows raucous as a chain saw, potatoes in the pantry—sprouting legs like centipedes—quickweed, purslane, spurge mixing it up with the Costata Romanesco zucchini, the pole beans; the belt on the electric water pump stretching and thinning, micro-cracks forming, readying itself to snap in January; the naked house wren fledglings nesting in the cedar fence post that will be discovered by the cats and killed one by one in June; the shotgun casings off the back deck; the white board fence knocked down by the box-elder tree split by lightning, the bubbling drain field, a thread of smoke ascending from barbeque grills, bonfires, and combustible passions. The message on the card reads "Seasons Greetings." It could just as well say "Before It All Went to Hell."

Highly recommended by author Jabari Asim, Road Trip, *Lynette D'Amico's hilarious and tender story, was a pleasure. Lynette read from her book and spoke with Robin McLean, author of* Reptile House, *during an autumn event at Papercuts.*

SLIP

Robin McLean

Everything falls apart," said Mac from the bed.

He lay round and gray tilted up on pillows. A nurse wrote numbers on a paper. The window was big and blue and a long way down. Below, the parade in the street was just beginning. The kids lined up in green capes. The young doctor took Mac's pulse with two fingers and a wristwatch. He thought of his mower at home. His wife, his kids.

"Everything breaks in the end," Mac said.

"Not everything," Dorothy said.

Dorothy was round and gray and stood by the rolling saline drip. She clasped Mac's foot at the foot of the bed.

"And the rest goes all to hell," Mac said and laughed, but not a real laugh. "Look at me: new hip, new knee, now this." The young doctor laughed too, to join his patient.

"None of his own teeth at all," Dorothy said. "Those teeth you see were made in Saint Louis."

She pointed Mac's way.

"Quiet," Mac said. "Let the doctor talk."

"No apples, no corn, no tennis, no taffy," she said.

"The doctor doesn't have time," Mac said.

"We've been married forty-nine years," she said.

Then the young doctor talked and talked of cutting and stitching and plumbing blood. Anything for living. He waved his hands like a knife, careful, like a needle and thread. She couldn't watch. The building rumbled. Iron lungs hummed, germs buzzed, scalpels whined. The washers thumped in the basement eight floors down, ten feet tall, getting everything clean. She needed to bathe, to brush her teeth. Bags under her eyes needed tending. She squeezed Mac's foot.

The young doctor had a Superman haircut, small hands. The lab coat was clean. The tip of his tongue clicked. The stethoscope was like any she'd seen on TV.

"Your mother must be very proud," said Dorothy.

"Honey," Mac said, and his hand stood up like a traffic cop.

She turned to the window.

The parade below was green green and more green and sliced through the city. The window needed a scaffold and someone brave. A parking deck was going up across the drive and said COMING SOON. The men in the hard hats stopped and leaned on new steel posts to watch a juggler walk by and a girl with a baton twirling. The band pounded. The fire truck inched forward with girls, caped and crowned; they waved at the people with their ankles crossed. A banner said LUCK OF THE but turned the corner, and Dorothy never learned the rest of what it said.

"Saint Patrick's Day," she said, had just thought of it.

"She's overtaxed," Mac said to the young doctor, who nodded.

"You need to rest," the young doctor said.

"Oh, I will," she said.

Trumpets and tubas shined and turned with the drumbeats. Fingers pumped on faith. The girl tripped, and the baton flew off between the boots and shoes of the crowd and was gone till later when she came looking. The girl twirled on without the baton, with an imaginary baton that she flung up and turned and caught behind her back. As if batons were hardly needed. People clapped and waved at the girl. A cement truck waited to cross the street and get on with things.

This young doctor was still talking. He was of the talking generation; Mac and Dorothy had once agreed about that on a morning walk by the river talking. This young doctor had a Superman jaw too, clean shaven, but he did not look particularly strong. Mac had been stronger. The doctor talked of valves, atriums such and such, ventricles, and ribs. He showed them his wife in his billfold smiling, because Dorothy had asked.

"What a complexion," said Dorothy.

"I'm very lucky," said the young doctor.

The baby fat above his belt was for pinching. A petting animal in a barn for a sweet-faced milkmaid. This young doctor's kids got straight As, or would get them. They played in the pool in summer. The rose garden in the back. This young doctor pruned the roses with his small, strong hands and his large, strong brain full of books and organs and that was enough. He would take his wife to Europe to see the gardens and the castles. They would hire a boat up the canals with wine and go to the bullfights too, but rush from ringside before the bull was dead. The concrete steps and dusty street. "Too horrible to watch," the wife would say. "You're right, of course," the doctor would answer. The wife would buy soft cheese from a cart that would melt on her fingers. She would chew the rind like a melon on a bench by a foreign river and talk to him, and talk and talk, then the flight back to Chicago, the return to the pool and the kids who stayed with her sister. Dorothy would get a pool like that one this summer, Mac had said so.

The doctor backed from the bed to go. "See you in the morning. Get some rest."

"You too," Dorothy said. "Is your wife at the parade?"

"I don't think so."

"Everyone loves parades," she said.

She stood at the window even after the young doctor was gone. The band was just a hundred caps bobbing. She might have dropped an apple by its tail. People below would think a kid had done it.

When Mac was in the john, an orderly came to change the sheets. Dorothy checked the tucks, the corners.

The orderly left.

She was the kind who looked both ways at crosswalks and trolley tracks.

On the day Dorothy met Mac she'd worn a pretty new skirt. It was snug and slim and showed her figure. Her mother was making meatloaf at her sister's on Wabash, her grandma's recipe. Dorothy walked out for breadcrumbs, no umbrella, sleeves rolled neat up to the elbows.

The skirt was thin and white to her calves. The slip kept falling down her legs as she walked, showing the world the lacy hem. She considered canceling the meatloaf. Once, she stopped at a bench. She rolled the waistband of the slip over the waistband of her skirt. Next, she tried a knot, but it looked silly and the slip slipped anyway, falling to her ankles now. She ducked in an alley. She tucked the waist of the slip in the waist of her underpants, the old cotton kind with faulty elastic. At Wabash and Cermak she hid between a stranded bus and a phone booth. She tried the tuck and the knot in combination. It seemed a good plan. She looked around for watchers. A big, handsome man entered the phone booth. He wore a hat, had a gold tooth, dental problems even then.

He grinned at the slip.

She smoothed her skirt and crossed with the green light.

When the yellow light turned, the slip was falling fast.

The trolley car glided closer.

Dorothy looked both ways, began to run.

Cars honked when the red light turned.

She fell in the trolley tracks.

"There are no accidents," Mac would say for forty-nine years.

"He left the receiver hanging," she would say. "Came from out of no where."

They married.

He went to war across the world. D-day. Hitler, Stalin, Mussolini.

He lost his teeth much later.

Retired.

The army paid for the partials, the root canals, and for the final complete set.

He snipped the articles from the paper on gardening, important deaths, and advances in dentistry. He stacked the best of them in a drawer in his desk.

The world had gotten so small. The bed. The windowsill.

A nurse came. A nurse went.

Hours passed. She brushed his hair over his ears till he said, "Please, no more."

She set the brush by the taffy on the sill. She chewed it when the church ladies came and talked and talked. They brought tulips in a pot and set them on the sill for Dorothy to water. They brought fish in a bowl from the Sunday school that sat by the tulips. The minister was leaving for Kansas, they said, some scandal with a girl, the crocuses were up, the chocolate egg order had arrived. The church ladies went away. Mac read the obits out loud across the room at Dorothy sitting in the chair. A nurse stared in his ears with a tiny flashlight. The fish swam in circles on the sill. Mac snoozed. The neighbors came, his brother came, the man who fixed their car. Night came. The car horns argued in the street below among the parade detritus. The flag in the middle of the circle drive whipped in the March wind. In like a lion, out like a lamb. The clouds moved behind the aspiring parking deck. They opened and closed. The moon rose orange waiting for morning, or some old orange trick.

Once, Mac almost lost his leg. Their station wagon had been sideswiped downtown by the Sears Tower. The doctors said they'd have to take it. Mac wrote the following:

We've had some years together
Have walked some miles or two
I hate to see you go just now
But what's a man to do?

They saved the leg. He got the knee and hip instead. She folded the verse in her jewelry box. They read it on the leg's anniversary.

His teeth were lost more often. Once, in a motel in Erie, they searched for his teeth in the grass by the office. It was where they'd walked the dog. They searched under the bed and through the sticky trash. He was silent till Rochester. The teeth were found in Albany, in the cooler with the lunch meat.

"Never again," he said. "The fittings are torture."

Next, on a lake vacation, the teeth were lost briefly but found by a kid with snorkel and fins. The kid got a sealed envelope with a twenty. Last Thanksgiving a set was ground up with the turkey carcass. Only a bit of gums and some wire survived.

"We're taking out the disposal," he said. "I'm calling the plumber."

"I can't live without one."

In the dark, while he slept, Dorothy packed his bag for going home when it was all over: a pair of tennis shoes, a jumble of underpants, a slip, a pair of propellers, a magazine with a lake on the cover, goodbye. A mastodon, a shaving kit, a portable tic-tac-toe with the ribbon still on it, a hard hat, the goldfish, the young doctor with keys in his back door. A light in the fridge. A book with a hip and a gun on the cover, a toothbrush and toothpaste, an empty case where his teeth could go. A watercolor set unopened. A book about Richard Nixon, a card from a cousin in Maine, a card with a cross from the church, a card from his brother Bob in Florida, a stuffed turtle with the ribbon, the box of chocolates mostly eaten, a windowsill, the doctor's backstairs to his wife and his bed, four pairs of socks and an undershirt, a V-neck sweater, the khakis he wore at check-in, the sand on the sill piled up with no one to tend it, a chunk of kryptonite from the alley, a drive-in movie theater, a buffalo rug, a pack of gum, a witch doctor and his wife and no rest at all, a hard green apple, a pack of dogs, a fancy horse, a marching band.

She zipped it all up.

In the dark, Mac yawned. The orange moon cleared the last cloud and she forgot.

"Have you seen your plaid pajamas?" she said.

"What do they look like?"

"Plaid."

"I haven't seen anything."

"Your stubble is like a wild hog."

"Take the teeth then if I'm so bad anyway."

He pulled his teeth from his mouth and held them out to her. His lip sagged, cheeks sunk, eyes drooped.

"Put them back in," she said, standing up from the bed. "It's not time yet."

"Take them," he said. "It's safer. So we won't forget."

He waved the teeth at her.

"Please," Dorothy said. "Not yet."

And he might have put the teeth back in—she'd often say later—but for the orderly's cart, the commotion in the hall.

"Coming in," called in the orderly, as the cart made the difficult turn. "Good evening, Mac. Hello, Mrs."

"Get your purse," said Mac.

The wheels squeaked. A new caster was needed.

"Not yet," she said. "Keep them till morning."

"Take them now," Mac said. "Now's the time."

Their hands met in midair. The teeth fell among the peaks and valleys made by knees propped up and shins declining.

She pawed the bed.

The cart passed the bathroom light, cast a shadow of a giant orderly.

"Got them?" Mac said.

She glanced at the heart monitor.

Her hands slid among the sheets, legs, feet as the terrain shifted.

"Got them?" he whispered.

"Don't move so much," she whispered back.

The orderly's shadow arrived. The room very dark.

She picked up something exactly like teeth, stuffed the thing in her purse.

The cart bumped the bed.

"Pardon me," said the orderly.

"Good evening," said Dorothy.

She set her purse on the meal tray.

The orderly poured fresh ice in Mac's pitcher.

Dorothy slept in the chair with her feet on the sill. The moon jumped up while no one was looking. A nurse tucked the blankets. Mac snored. The children ran in circles and the hogs bit trees. The flags flapped every second. The sand tumbled and piled on everything everywhere.

She knew morning had come when the sun rose.

Staff came in scrubs. They lifted Mac, rolled Mac away.

The cafeteria was full. The son and daughter sipped tea with her. They watched all the people at all the tables, salting eggs and biting toast.

Dorothy thought of his bright-blue tights—how strange—red trunks too, and how Lois Lane never chose to change her name. How Lois could get away with it, given career and danger. How yellow was his favorite color. She asked him once and that's what he had said, "Yellow, like the sun," a girlish answer she'd thought at the time.

"Mother, are you all right?" the daughter said. "Hanging in there?"

"I should really wash my hair," said Dorothy.

She should have worn a skirt. A slip and stockings, clipped her hair up, should have ridden the trolley car.

"A bird or plane?" she said.

"What, Mother?" said the son.

Someone else would have to finish the sentence, would have to lift all the heavy objects, suitcases, ladders, loads of brick, pluck tabby cats from tall trees. He'd started out of third shift, moved up and up to management, gold watches. The tea was only warm. The table was Formica and clean. She might have set her head down to sleep, but for all the cups and saucers. And she was not that kind of tired anyway, who could be? Since buildings only got bigger, harder for leaping, crumbled faster than ever before. The earth tipped off her axis so easily nowadays, bad guys multiplying left and right. Mines caved in, banks robbed, earthquakes, tsunamis, suicide bombers. Who would stop them? A hero's work is never done. Who's to carve the roast? Who's to share her bar of soap?

"I need to wash my hands," Dorothy said.

She and her daughter went together, down the hall, right, left, right again.

The surgery was a great success. He had ten more years at least, they said. They sewed him up, rolled him out on the gurney.

"It will be a very hard night," they said and dabbed his face.

The night, he mumbled and groaned. Cheeks sagged. Eyes drooped and watered. He dry-heaved by turning his head. The tongue searched for wet like a worm. The chest looked exactly like a zipper. The young doctor came and the doctor's replacement. The room froze and baked. Nurses drifted and pecked. A gray man died who they rolled down the hall, where the moon came up, no need for windows. The clock said nothing useful.

In the basement the washing machines sloshed eternally. The laundry gals wore smocks. They shook their heads when Dorothy asked them.

"Are you absolutely sure?" said the second-shift gals.

"Very sure," Dorothy said. "They fell in the sheets last night."

"What do they look like?" asked third shift

"Just like teeth." Dorothy showed her perfect set. "He's still in the ICU."

Dorothy dumped her purse on an ironing board. The gals turned Dorothy's pockets out. They searched the enormous lint bin, as the young doctor took his wife to dinner, fed each other cheesecake, the babysitter worth every penny. When Dorothy finally took the elevator up, first shift was still folding. They swept the floor after. They played cards in between loads. They road the elevator to the roof for the air, chewed gum together in March sun, so happy winter was over.

Dorothy waited for Mac to wake up, but he snoozed. She stood and sat and watered the plant. She changed the pot to match their kitchen, then gave the plant to an incoming family down the hall.

Mac's tubes were disconnected one by one.

The orderlies took the bedpans.

The gurney delivered Mac back to the ward.

The windows were being washed when he arrived.

"Brave man," whispered Mac and saluted the window washer, who saluted with his oversized squeegee. They lifted Mac to bed. They plugged him into the wall.

The young doctor came, and the church ladies and son and daughter, who sat on the edge of the bed, and the family down the hall for instructions on the plant. Dorothy slept in the chair.

Mac told the kids how, once, he saw two small planes collide in midair. He'd been duck hunting in the bog, never hunted again after that.

"The planes fell like two spinning bricks," he said. "A wing sailed off to the trees."

His hands made a crash over the bed to illustrate, then landed hard in his lap.

The kids knew the story. They could have finished it for him.

"The firemen came, but what could they do with hoses? Several children, an old man too, and several people in their prime. I don't recall how many. I saved the clippings with pictures, all what people said. The funerals were packed. Everyone's a friend of someone's someone."

The daughter checked the suitcase.

They helped Mac to the john.

It was sunny and getting greener out the window. An orderly poured juice. A nurse took his pulse with two fingers and wristwatch. The young doctor wasn't on call. Dorothy stood at the foot of the bed; Mac was propped up on pillows, eating applesauce.

"I'm sorry," Dorothy said.

"Did you look in your purse?" Mac said.

"I looked," she said.

He refused to sip from his straw.

"Drink," she said. "Drink."

He set the cup on the side table.

"The laundry? The washers?"

"Of course," she said. "Yes, but no."

"Dryers?" he said.

"They somehow got away from me," she said.

Mac took up the paper and scissors. A nurse arrived with pain medication.

"Did you check in the chute to the laundry room?"

"I didn't," she said.

An orderly came. They rolled Mac both directions. They peeled the old sheets up, peeled the new sheets down, threw the bundle in a cart.

"But I will," she said.

Once, when the young doctor was much older, he lay with his wife in their bed. He drew a line between her breasts.

"Just like that?" she said. She moved her hip.

"A very old pair. Forty-nine years."

"Ouch," she said.

The doctor's hand floated over this wife. He blew on her face like a whistle. Her lids shut then opened. He whistled again, so on.

The wind whined. The sand tumbled on the sill. A caped thing flew past the window.

At an autumn event with Lynette D'Amico, author of Road Trip, *Robin read from* Reptile House. *Robin McLean's short stories are dark and lovely, and hearing one read aloud with commentary was a singular experience.*

I GUESS IT'S TOO LATE TO LIVE ON A FARM

Although I worry I'm not cut out
to carry these eggs.
It's true, the body's a fragile thing.
Like any wall worthy
of holding back oceans,
it leaks and moans.
Thinking about breaking
grants the possibility
of being broken.
I've since learned
that's a real Zen statement to make.
What an accident. Free advice:
crying in business meetings
is no way to inspire confidence.
No one likes working for money
anymore. How low can you
is a good motto for capitalism,
not that we need another.
It gives me fever dreams
like you wouldn't believe.

Here, I want to say,
look at all my material.
There's so much of me.
Can you see how this is a problem?
I walk through another year
and get bigger. You can't go through life
righting wrongs all by yourself.
They have to want to stand up.
You have to teach them
how to walk by the sea,
how the sun ekes forgiveness
from century and stone.
Kristen, you have to learn
your name, even if you don't
like it. You don't have to believe
it's too late to live on a farm.
It's not the farm you need to live,
it's your attachment to being there.
Being anywhere.

—Kristen Evans

Note: The line "I guess it's too late to live on the farm" is lifted from Bernadette Mayer's poem "Essay."

Kristen Evans, who for much of 2015 worked for 826Boston up the street in Egleston Square, has been an avid Papercuts supporter from the start. She shared her poetry at Papercuts with two other badass female poets—Anne Cecelia Holmes and Kelin Loe. It was a memorable night of words and wine.

OREGON

Nadine Darling

They gave Oregon to Jim. Nobody wanted it, and no one wanted to live in such proximity to Jim; it seemed a logical decision in the end. The new residents hit California or Florida, helpless as gnats to lightbulbs, and Jim did not balk at the notion, of course. He liked being alone. He knew all about people. And he liked Oregon; it would be his home.

Sometimes Jim walked the highways, empty and strange as old Habitrails or birdcages, and sometimes he would lie down in the middle of them with one cheek flush to the asphalt to feel the way they seemed to vibrate in their ghostly way. All of Oregon seemed haunted, not by the dead but by whoever had forgotten it. So many little houses sitting unlocked, with no lights and no light, everything the way it had been in another life: kibble dried into hard stepping-stones in plastic bowls, coverlets pulled back on twin beds, raccoons and rats in the little side yards, wild dogs asleep on porches. And Jim would turn over onto his back on the highway and bake there.

Jim didn't really go into the houses anymore, but he thought about them a lot, especially just before he fell asleep. Most of the time he slept outdoors in a plaid sleeping bag he set out wherever he wanted to, only ever finding shelter from the rain or snow. He liked to look into the sky before he slept, to feel swallowed by the breadth of it, and he would wonder then about those empty houses, about the minutiae of them: the bars of soap glued to their little china dishes, a web wound between the neck of two toothbrushes standing in a matching tumbler. Three magazines fanned on a coffee table. A book open and facing down, tented against the arm of a sofa. To him, nothing seemed sadder than a home left in a hurry. Maybe the things you see every day need you, he thought. Maybe they wait for you, maybe they listen for your car or the scrape of your key in the lock. What was a thing, he thought, what was a person, if not in service to something else?

Jim didn't remember very much from before Oregon, which was the way that things happened where he was from. He didn't come from a people who could afford to indulge in the past. Memories had a shelf life of maybe a year, the way that years were set up in his new home. He remembered the way that people had reacted to him before and how that had felt, and he remembered preparing to leave his old home, the excitement surrounding that—not his own, but everyone else's. First the transmissions from the small star—music and words from the small star, and then the same broadcast, over and over. The discovery, the big star. The planning, the way things would be. Jim had not needed to bring anything with him; he'd left his little house in perfect condition, all of his things set up in the way that someone else might like to find them, and he sat by himself and waited to leave. He learned the names of things studiously. The seasons. What was poison. The animals. All the names of all the things.

In summer, Jim performed the controlled burns in Silver Falls. He fed the deer that congregated in Crater Lake National Park. He mowed lawns in Bend, he swept the empty stage of

Shakespeare Theater in Ashland. He watched the half-mile lava trail in the McKenzie River Valley, and he paid attention—he meandered this way, like the lava, through the state that he owned, tending to it, loving it, and if he was lonely, if he missed the sound of another person's voice or a hand on his back, against his face, he could not have recognized it. He settled in Troubadour, in a small blue-and-white house near the center of town, and the other towns fell dark to him like quiet rooms in a house, and he didn't question them or concern himself. His beard grew. His nails grew. He began to forget things, and then he began to forget that he'd ever known them at all, but he was home and it was enough for him. His new home was smaller. Small but bright like a sunspot; even with his eyes closed it was the only thing he could see.

One night he startled from his half sleep and he was afraid; something was there, something tangible and quiet, and he climbed from his bed and went outside. He'd heard something, something had called his name. He walked out into the middle of the road, the asphalt beneath his feet still holding the warmth of the day, and looked around, trying to gauge the direction of the sound. There was a brown house down on the left. There were no lights—of course there were no lights—but there was something about it. There was a shine on it, and Jim didn't want to go to the house but he did anyway. There were putrefied remains of jack-o-lanterns up the front steps and on the porch, and the door knocker was the bronze face of an owl, its expression somehow both weary and critical. The smell inside was green, alive, the smell of dark mulch and chlorophyll. There were overstuffed armchairs in the living room and a breakfast nook in the kitchen—just normal, a normal house. "Bless This Mess" in the hallway: the caption on a coat rack hanging on the wall, a coat rack with no coats. The door to the room at the end of the hall was open, but only a crack. Jim went inside.

Nature had taken back the room somehow, so quickly. The walls crawled with vines— heartleaf peppervine, swanflower, Dutchman's pipe. The floor was a haphazard carpet of beaked moss and Timothy grass. A tree, a young Atlas cedar, had grown through the house, its coarse trunk looping through a wall and window, up to the ceiling where it had pushed through to the attic. There, in the still-dark, at the base of this tree, was a baby, a boy, one of them. It curled naked on its side in a pile of cottonwood leaves and soft Douglas iris. Soft things. Bits of cloth, the ribbon from the tail of a kite, weaved in as careful as a bird's nest. Jim knelt. He turned the baby's face with his hand. The baby's face was different from the others he'd seen. There was an open divot beneath the nose and, pushed up flush to the nose, a nub of upper lip like the tip of a thumb.

"Oh," said Jim.

He picked the baby up into his arms and brought it back to his house.

The new residents of California didn't want the baby, nor did the new residents of Washington State. They thanked Jim for his concern and sent him some bottles for the baby to use, ones with nipples suitable for cleft palates. And then Jim learned about babies. He collected soft sleeper pajamas and knit caps for the baby—a boy—at the Wal-Mart, he read the baby *Goodnight Moon* and *Charlotte's Web* from the long, quiet aisles of the library, and he discovered Oregon again, this way—the Indian paintbrush, and the glacier lilies, the ponderosa pine and the Sitka spruce. And gradually Jim's home became the boy. He was happy where he was, with his son, in a place so quiet that it seemed always to be listening.

Jim named the boy Oregon—sometimes he was O, for short, and sometimes he was Gon. He was smart and very funny, and Jim could look into the boy's eyes, a strange, electric blue like the velella jellyfish, their sudden fins arching to the sky like sundials, that sometimes washed up on the northwest beaches, and see a kindness that he knew didn't always exist in people. Jim knew all about people. He loved two people: the boy and whoever had given him the boy. But with this love came fear. Someone might come back. Someone might change their mind. Oregon slept beside Jim's bed at night in a pine crib painted gray and crowned with a mobile of plastic butterflies. He would drink from his strange bottle and kick the side of the crib lightly with one foot to make the butterflies flutter above him as Jim read aloud about chocolate factories and boys who'd lost their shadows, and eventually the boy's breathing would go soft and even, and Jim would know that he was asleep.

The boy would sleep, and Jim would stay awake.

One morning, very early, Jim heard voices coming from outside, voices from the street, and he scooped up Oregon and tucked himself into a little ball on the floor of their bedroom, just below the window, listening very carefully. The boy whined and Jim shushed him. Cicadas. The sound of the wind pushing the porch swing against the house. Nothing more.

"But I heard," said Jim. "I heard."

The boy had fallen asleep again in his arms.

Once, before the boy, Jim had gone into one of the houses and found a dead body. He used to go into the houses; they were his houses. He didn't feel bad about it then, or very bad, anyway. He felt tentative, but it was thrilling. Perhaps this was how ghosts felt. He hovered in the rooms. He took inventory of the things that people had left. Books, so many books—he could read them, and sometimes he did but more often than not their sheer numbers instilled him with a spectral sort of grief. He'd found a great *katana* once, on display in a study and clothed in an emerald sheath. It was sharp. He'd touched the edge, and it sliced into the pads of his fingers. Who could leave such a thing?

This particular house, the house with the body, had been different right away. Even before he'd smelled the smell, he had known that the house was different. Some of its life was still clinging—like the warmth trapped in the street the night he'd found the boy—there were signs of a life. In the kitchen, a single gray bedroom slipper. A trail of balled tissues from the living room, the hall bathroom. An empty can of something, some off-brand of soda, on a folded paper towel of a coaster on a little end table alongside a remote control and a *TV Guide.* Jim had stared at that soda for a bit. He'd thought someone cared enough about that table to use a coaster and that seemed civilized, a civilized notion.

There were dishes in the sink, and bugs. Flies. There were a lot of flies. Jim had turned his face, as though in the direction of a sound. He began to smell the smell.

It was the small bedroom at the back of the house. The door was just barely closed. Jim had grabbed for something, for what was in reach, a hand towel on the bathroom floor, to cover the lower part of his face. Flies.

The man had died on the floor beside his bed. He'd been old. Perhaps he'd been too old to make the trip, or perhaps he'd refused. Perhaps he had been like Jim, a man like Jim who knew all about people. The man had been wearing a white T-shirt over plaid pajama pants and one slipper. The bare foot was purple, its tendons pushing up from under the skin like piano wire. The man's eyes were open.

After that, Jim had stopped going into the houses. They weren't dolls' houses; they weren't his houses. They were shed skins. Empty conch shells, lined neat as graves. He avoided looking at them, as he'd avoided anything.

When the boy turned one, Jim took him to Gold Beach near the white water and they camped in the woods. They lied down to the sounds of the water, to the last futile hisses of the fire Jim had built, and Jim held the boy and said, "I know that you were given to me for a reason."

The boy only looked at Jim with his blue, strange eyes and a kind of stillness settled over them. There were sounds—the dying of the fire, water in the distance, and the careful swirl of leaves—but they seemed to blend in with Jim and with Oregon, with their hearts and breaths. Autumn was right on time this year; it would be cold soon. Jim was thinking of a new house, something not visible from the street, from any street. Back in the woods, farther than this. In the wilderness. He might grow a beard. The boy would climb trees and they would forage; every day would be a happy day, and every night would be peaceful.

Jim did not have a present for the boy, but he knew some songs from the small star, so he sang them. He knew "Frank Mills" from *Hair*, and "Once upon a Dream" from *Sleeping Beauty*. He'd brought a bottle of Riesling from a vineyard in Monmouth, and he drank and sang until the words went syrupy in his throat and then he closed his eyes.

He said to the boy, to himself, "They left me too."

He dreamed of something bright and restless like fire. Like fire, and when he woke the boy was not with him. Jim—Jim, who knew the names of all things—rushed to the edge of the water, to the trampled out fire, and he called for the boy. There was sound—not so much a sound as a vibration, a slight disturbance like fingertips or sleeping breath—and Jim turned. The boy had his back turned to Jim and he was walking in the careful, vaguely inebriated way that he had, and now the vibration was a sound, the sound of ripping cloth as the boy's sleeper gave way. His wings were translucent and wound tight, but they unfurled to twice the boy's size in the moonlight and flapped, tentatively at first, then exultantly. He didn't stumble as he did when he attempted to walk. He was natural in flight—he lifted, he tilted, he glided on the wind like a voice or a leaf. And then he was gone. Jim called for the boy, but the boy was gone. And if the boy was gone, then Jim would forget the boy, and it was that, the idea of forgetting the boy—his spidery smile, the reach of his quilted palms—that felled him.

To the bright, hidden star he said, "This is my state and you can have it. This is my beach and these are my mountains. These are my trees and this is my land and I don't want it."

No one answered.

"Oh!" Said Jim. "Oregon!"

The wind picked up, returning nothing.

She Came from Beyond! *was a book that excited us at Papercuts immediately. There isn't another novel out there that tips its hat to the great Mystery Science Theater 3000 with so much hilarity and pure heart. We loved discussing this eccentric, engrossing novel with Nadine Darling in conversation with her incredible editor, Allyson Rudolph, on "Cider Monday" (the indie answer to Cyber Monday) featuring local brewery Down East Cider House, in October 2015.*

ENDNOTE

We hope you've enjoyed this collection of short pieces by the authors who visited Papercuts during our first year. You can listen to live recordings produced into beautifully edited podcasts of events mentioned in this book. Find it on iTunes or Stitcher, or visit papercutsjp.com/audio-broadcast. Please consider making a small contribution to help us keep our podcasts ad free for your listening and thinking pleasure.

Be sure to keep an eye out for future events at papercutsjp.com/events or on our social media @papercutsjp. And perhaps another anthology!

ABOUT THE CONTRIBUTORS

RICK BERLIN is a Boston-based singer and songwriter. He has been the front man of Orchestra Luna, Luna, Berlin Airlift, Rick Berlin: The Movie, and The Shelley Winters Project.

JOSH COOK, author of *An Exaggerated Murder,* is a bookseller at Porter Square Books in Cambridge, Massachusetts. His fiction, criticism, and poetry have appeared in numerous magazines and journals.

LYNETTE D'AMICO's work has appeared in *The Gettysburg Review, The Ocean State Review,* and more. Her novella *Road Trip,* published in 2015 by Twelve Winters Press, was shortlisted for the Paris Literary Prize. A former advertising copywriter, D'Amico is currently content editor for the online theater journal *HowlRound.*

NADINE DARLING's writing has appeared in *Night Train, Edifice Wrecked, Eyeshot, SmokeLong Quarterly,* and *Per Contra. She Came from Beyond,* her first novel, was published in October 2015. She lives in Boston.

Catie DiSabato is a columnist for *Full Stop* and has written for *The Millions*, *This Recording*, and *The Rumpus*. She was featured in *Joyland* and is the author of *The Ghost Network*.

Kristen Evans's poetry and criticism have appeared in *ILK*, *Denver Quarterly*, *iO: A Journal of New American Poetry*, and more. Her first book of poetry is called *Mammal Room*.

George Fifield is the founder and director of the Boston Cyberarts Gallery in Jamaica Plain, the largest collaboration of artists working in the newest technologies in all media. Fifield is also a writer, a teacher, and an artist.

Stona Fitch is an award-winning novelist and the founder of the Concord Free Press, the world's first generosity-based publisher. Fitch writes the Boston-based Eddy Harkness series under the pseudonym Rory Flynn.

Nicole Galland's sixth and most recent novel is *Stepdog*, which is inspired by real events. Also inspired by real events—or at least real legends and/or earlier real pieces of literature—are her historical novels: *The Fool's Tale*; *Revenge of the Rose*; *Crossed: A Tale of the Fourth Crusade*; *I, Iago*; and *Godiva*. She adapts and directs Shakespeare for the Masses, an irreverent project designed to make Bardophobes love Shakespeare.

Chris Hedges is a Pulitzer Prize–winning journalist, activist, and bestselling author of several books, including *War Is a Force That Gives Us Meaning* and, most recently, *Wages of Rebellion: The Moral Imperative of Revolt*. He writes a regular column for TruthDig.

CHRISTOPHER IRVIN is the author of *Safe Inside the Violence, Burn Cards, Federales,* and short stories featured in several publications, including *Thuglit, Beat to a Pulp,* and *Shotgun Honey.* He lives in Jamaica Plain with his wife and two sons.

ZACHARY KLEIN is the author of the Matt Jacob novels, *Two Way Toll* and *Still Among the Living.* His most recent novel, *Ties That Blind,* continues the series. He lives with his wife in Jamaica Plain.

EDAN LEPUCKI is the author of the *New York Times* bestseller *California,* as well as the novella *If You're Not Yet Like Me.* She is a staff writer for *The Millions* and the founder and codirector of Writing Workshops Los Angeles.

RANDY SUSAN MEYERS's bestselling novels are informed by her work with families impacted by emotional and family violence. *Accidents of Marriage* and *The Murderer's Daughters* were included in the Massachusetts Center for the Book 2011 and 2015 Best Works of Fiction and Must Read Book lists. Meyers teaches writing at Grub Street Writers Center. She is the mother of two grown daughters and lives in Jamaica Plain with her husband.

ROBIN MCLEAN's stories have appeared in *The Cincinnati Review, Green Mountains Review, The Western Humanities Review,* and more. Her first book of short stories, *Reptile House,* won the 2013 BOA Editions Fiction Prize and was named one of the Best Books of 2015 in *The Paris Review.*

EMMETT G. PRICE III, author of *The Black Church and Hip Hop Culture,* is a leading expert on African American music and culture, as well as an acclaimed scholar, ordained minster, professional musician, and professor at Northeastern University.

SANDRA STOREY is a poet whose work has been published in *New York Quarterly*, *Friction* (UK), *THEMA*, and more. She is also founder of the *Jamaica Plain* and *Mission Hill Gazettes*. Her first full-length poetry collection is called *Every State Has Its Own Light.*

J. M. TAYLOR has written in *Crime Factory, Dark Valentine, Morpheus Tales,* and other publications. He lives with his wife and son in Jamaica Plain.

ABIGAIL THOMAS, a former editor and literary agent, is a writer of fiction, memoir, and poetry. Her first memoir, *A Three Dog Life,* was named one of the best books of 2006 by the *Los Angeles Times* and the *Washington Post* and won the 2006 Inspirational Memoir Award given by Books for a Better Life.

PAUL TREMBLAY, author of *A Head Full of Ghosts, The Little Sleep,* and *Swallowing a Donkey's Eye,* writes and edits contemporary horror. He lives outside Boston.

JENNIFER TSENG is a poet and fiction writer whose book *The Man with My Face* won the 2005 Asian American Writers' Workshop's National Poetry Manuscript Competition and a 2006 PEN American Center Open Book Award.

JENNIFER WADDELL is a photographer and a writer. She lives in Jamaica Plain with her two children.

CAT WARREN is a professor, formal journalist, and author of the *New York Times* bestseller *What the Dog Knows.*

ABOUT THE EDITORS

Katie Eelman (b. 1991) was born from the mouth of a blue whale.

Kate Layte (b. 1986) jumped out of a tall oak tree like a baby wood duck.

ACKNOWLEDGMENTS

Our deepest thanks to the authors who wrote a new piece or allowed us to reprint for this anthology. Thank you for your enthusiastic support of our store and this project.

Thanks to local artist Jessica Burko for allowing us to include her beautiful artwork.

Special thanks to Caleb Hoffman for the professional engineering, editing, and production of the Papercuts Audio Broadcast.

To Brenden Layte for hearing every wild idea and encouraging the strong ones, lending your linguistic expertise, and staying supportive through this crazy ride. To our family and friends: You know who you are. So much love.

To the incomparable booksellers at Papercuts: John Cleary, Jill Saginario, Brian Hogue, Will Carpenter, and Michael Curley.

To an innovative way to publish! We thank everyone at Inkshares/Quill, including Matt Kaye and Angela Melamud, as well as John Pierce, Devon Fredericksen, and Girl Friday Productions. And huge thanks to our wildly talented cover designer and friend Lauren Harms.

Thank you to the trade organizations NEIBA and the ABA for being such passionate and supportive industry advocates who welcomed us with open arms (literally, we got hugs!). To our friends, new and old in the book industry—we've learned so much from you.

To the writers we love, who work alone tirelessly, fearlessly, to share stories that need to be told with the world. Thank you for your hard work and dedication.

And our deepest gratitude to everyone who preordered this anthology to will it into existence. Especially the grand patrons who went above and beyond to help us make this happen. This is tangible because of you and would not exist without your support.

LIST OF PATRONS

This book was made possible in part by the following grand patrons who preordered the book on Inkshares.com. Thank you.

Barbara Rhodes
Brenden Layte
Carolyn Becker
Christopher Irvin
Dog Manman
Emmett G. Price III
Esther Greenwood
Gary Eelman
Janet Cromer
Jennifer Waddell
Jill Saginario
John Cleary
John Leclerc
Karen Layte
Linda Paone
Luke Steere
Megan A. Sullivan
Mitch Hilton
Pablo Pablito
Pamela Eelman
Peter West
Sandee Storey
Sarah Yake
Sherri Frank
Tim Huggins

Quill is an imprint of Inkshares, a crowdfunded book publisher. We democratize publishing by having readers select the books we publish—we edit, design, print, distribute, and market any book that meets a preorder threshold.

Interested in making a book idea come to life? Visit Inkshares.com to find new book projects or to start your own.

www.ingramcontent.com/pod-product-compliance
Lightning Source LLC
Chambersburg PA
CBHW061535210726
48287CB00006B/1971
9781942645009